W9-ACC-532

The Moon Looked Down

Books by Dorothy Garlock

After the Parade
Almost Eden
Annie Lash
Dreamkeepers
Dream River
The Edge of Town
Forever Victoria
A Gentle Giving
Glorious Dawn
High on a Hill
Homeplace
Hope's Highway
Larkspur
Leaving Whiskey Bend
The Listening Sky
Lonesome River
Love and Cherish
Loveseekers
Midnight Blue
More than Memory
Mother Road
Nightrose
On Tall Pine Lake
A Place Called Rainwater
Promisegivers
Restless Wind
Ribbon in the Sky
River Rising
River of Tomorrow
The Searching Hearts
Sins of Summer
Song of the Road
Sweetwater
Tenderness
This Loving Land
Train from Marietta
Wayward Wind
A Week from Sunday
Wild Sweet Wilderness
Will You Still Be Mine?
Wind of Promise
Wishmakers
With Heart
With Hope
With Song
Yesteryear

DOROTHY GARLOCK

The Moon Looked Down

Doubleday Large Print
Home Library Edition

GRAND CENTRAL
PUBLISHING

NEW YORK BOSTON

This Large Print Edition, prepared especially for Doubleday Large Print Home Library, contains the complete, unabridged text of the original Publisher's Edition.

Grand Central Publishing
Hachette Book Group
237 Park Avenue
New York, NY 10017

Printed in the United States of America

Grand Central Publishing is a division of Hachette Book Group, Inc.
The Grand Central Publishing name and logo is a trademark of Hachette Book Group, Inc.

ISBN 978-1-61523-237-6

This book is lovingly dedicated to Marion

THE MOON LOOKS DOWN

I climb alone to my secret place
And gaze from my rocky perch
To commune with the moon.

I ask that circling silvery stone the
Questions that perplex me so.
Can the moon on high tell me why . . .

Why dark souls aflame with hate
Ignite the fires that terrify me,
Why those whom once I trusted
Plot to harm the ones I love.

I look with hope into the night
And the moon looks down.
How absurd! It says not a word.

—F.S.I.

The Moon Looked Down

Prologue

Victory, Illinois—June 1942

FIRE! FIRE!"

Sophie Heller woke suddenly from a dream in which she had been picking wild daisies and entered into a nightmare of confusion and fear. Karl, seven years her junior at thirteen, stood beside her bed in his nightshirt. Even in the darkened room, she could see that his face was anxious.

"What are you . . . ?" she muttered. "What's happening?"

"Get up, Sophie! You have to come quick! There's a fire!"

"Wait . . . wait a minute . . ."

"We don't have a minute!"

Before Sophie could protest further, Karl grabbed her arm and pulled her from the bed and toward the door. She had scarcely enough time to grab a shawl from her dresser and hurriedly wrap it about her shoulders before they were out of the room, across the narrow landing, and racing down the picture-lined stairs.

Struggling not to stumble on the stairs, Sophie caught a glimpse of her reflection in one of the glass panes. Looking back at her through wide, bluish green eyes was a young woman of twenty years. Her straight, shoulder-length black hair framed high cheekbones, a small nose, and full lips. The image quickly passed from view as she and Karl passed through the front door, crossed the enclosed porch, and burst out onto the front step, only to stop and stare in amazement and disbelief at what they saw.

"Oh, no!" Karl cried.

The large red barn their father had built shortly after the family's arrival in Victory was on fire!

Crimson flames poured from the barn's front doors and the broken windows on the building's sides, reaching toward the sky. Thick black smoke billowed upward and the air was filled with the smell of burning wood and hay. The quiet of the night was split by the sound of crackling flames and the occasional snap of wood as it surrendered to its fate and crashed to the ground below. Still, Sophie could only watch in amazement. Frightening though it was, the barn's destruction was also captivating, hypnotizing.

With effort, Sophie pulled her eyes from the barn and looked around for the rest of her family. Karl stood rooted beside her, the dancing flames mirrored in his wide eyes. A precocious boy who loved baseball, Karl was a help on the farm, essential to their father. Handsome, with a lanky frame and deep blue eyes, he would grow to be a fine man, Sophie was sure. At that moment, she was glad that he was next to her.

Standing closer to the barn, her parents clung to each other. Her father, Hermann, was a short, squat man whose lifetime as a farmer had given him muscular arms and heavily calloused hands. He ran desperate fingers through his thick black hair and his shoulders sagged deep with hopelessness.

Ever at his side, Maria, Sophie's mother, had both of her tiny hands wrapped around one of her husband's thick arms. She was a petite woman who, with her long, golden brown hair and thin waistline, looked far younger than her thirty-nine years. Now, reflecting the light of the fire, her eyes were wide with fright.

Sophie turned back toward the house. There, in one of the windows, she saw her grandmother, Gitta, peering out from behind the curtain of her room. Though Sophie could not see the older woman's face, she knew that she would be worried yet calm. Her father's mother, at eighty, found little left to surprise her in life.

A large crack split the night air. Sophie looked back just in time to see part of the barn's roof collapse in on itself, the wood crashing to the ground with a deafening roar. The flames paused only for a moment before growing even higher and hotter in intensity. There would be no chance to save the barn. Their closest neighbors were the Sanderses, but they lived a couple of miles to the north. Even if they had seen the fire, they would be far too late to help by the time they arrived.

"What happened?" Sophie asked her brother. "How did it start?"

"I don't know," Karl muttered, lost in the blaze.

"Was it lightning?"

"I don't . . . I don't know," he said again.

Sleeping peacefully in her daisy-filled dream, Sophie had not heard a storm, but that didn't mean that one hadn't occurred. Summer storms in Illinois could be unpredictable and violent, leaving much destruction in their wake. Her eyes scanned the sky but she couldn't see any cloud other than the one the fire was making. The moon looked back at her, a crescent three-quarters hidden, as if it were trying to shield itself from the chaos below. A crowd of stars filled the rest of the heavens, like gawkers at an accident.

If lightning had not struck, what caused the fire?

In answer to her unspoken question, the night was split by another loud crack, this one coming from the corner of the house. Sophie's heart froze at the sight that awaited her. Three men stood side by side, all of them wearing burlap sacks over their heads. Through the narrow eyeholes they had cut, she could see nothing but a blackness she knew matched their intentions. All of them wore rough clothing; overalls spattered with grease stains and shirts peppered with holes. The one in the middle loosely carried the rifle that had fired the startling shot.

"Goddamn Kraut bastards!" he spat.

In that instant, Sophie faced a horrendous truth. The men standing before her had set fire to the barn and they had intended to herd the family outside because they wanted to do them *more* harm.

"What is the meaning of this?" her father bellowed in his heavily accented English, his German origins coloring every word. "Are you responsible for this outrage?"

"Damn right we are," the man answered defiantly.

"Why . . . why would you do such a thing?"

"Don't ya dare play dumb with me, ya stupid Kraut! I'd bet ya thought we'd all just stand around with our fingers up our noses and not say a word, but ya was wrong!

Ain't no way we're gonna let no Germans just go on livin' here and not do nothin' about it! You're just waitin' to make your move. Just waitin' to wreck a train or poison the water!"

"What are you talking about? I'm an American citizen!"

"Ya ain't no American, you're a damn Nazi!"

The armed man's words cut through Sophie like a knife, though what he was saying couldn't have been further from the truth. The Heller family had emigrated from Germany in early 1933, the same year that Adolf Hitler had become the chancellor of the nation. While many had believed Hitler's promises, Hermann had seen only danger. Their exodus had been fraught with peril, their reasons for leaving many. Settling in Victory, Hermann Heller took great pride in considering himself to be as American as any of his neighbors.

"I'm not a Nazi!" he now protested.

"The hell ya ain't," countered the man standing just to the right of the one with the rifle. Smaller than his armed companion, he glanced nervously from Hermann to his ally as if he were searching for approval. The man to the left of the gunman remained silent and impassive. From the way they behaved it was obvious to Sophie that the one with the gun was in charge.

"Just another Kraut lie," the leader said.

With her heart pounding in her chest, Sophie closed her eyes tightly, as if by wishing hard enough the nightmare before her would just miraculously disappear. But when she opened them again, nothing had changed. Sweat glistened on her brow, not from the heat of the burning barn but from fear.

The fear of death!

"Sophie," Hermann said sternly. "I want you to take Karl and go in the house."

"I wouldn't do that if I were you, girlie," the gunman warned. Catching the light of the flickering flames, the gun's barrel rose upward and another shot rang out. The bullet smashed into the wooden planks of the front steps, launching a shower of splinters. Glancing down, Sophie saw that the shot had pierced the wood no more than a couple of inches from her foot. Her shawl fell from her shoulders, landing at her bare feet. Her mouth opened and closed with no sound. Beside her, her brother trembled with fright.

"Next one hits her," the gunman said coolly, as a thin tendril of smoke curled skyward from the end of the rifle.

"How dare you!" Hermann bellowed. "How dare you come here and do this to us, threatening my children! If you so much as touch them I will kill you! Only cowards would hide behind a mask!"

"Hermann . . ." Maria tried to restrain him, but her husband shook off her grasp.

"You best watch who you're callin' a coward," the gunman said as he moved the rifle so that it pointed toward Hermann. "Now, if you wanna keep on drawin' breath, what you're gonna do is take this here family of yours and get the hell out of Victory County. Go back to Germany and Hitler. We don't want your kind here."

Ominously, one side of the burning barn chose that moment to give way, and a cascade of wood crashed to the ground with such force that Sophie jumped in fright. The sound was so raw that it seemed as if the barn were in pain. Once the rubble had settled, she could see that all that remained of the building was part of one wall and the frame of the front doors.

"We are not leaving!" Hermann shouted defiantly.

"Then you'll die."

"Goddamn right, ya will!" the one to the left echoed.

Sophie looked hard at her father. She could sense the anger rising in his breast. He and his family had been hounded and threatened out of one home in the nation where he had been born, and now his new life in America was also in jeopardy. She had never seen him so angry. She also knew that he meant to act, and that made her blood run cold.

"Ya ain't got no other choice."

"You will not tell me what to do!"

Hermann Heller strode across his property toward the three men. With each step he gained determination, his heavy hands clenching and unclenching with a rage that threatened to consume him. The two men to either side of the gunman stepped backward; the sight of their prey pursuing them was unsettling. The gunman, however, stood his ground. For Sophie, time seemed to stand still.

Her father was going to die!

She cringed, waiting for the shot that would rip her father from her life, but still it didn't come. Instead, Hermann moved closer and closer to the men, his strong hands before him as if he meant to wring the life out of them before he even got them in his grasp.

Finally, when Hermann was only a couple of feet from them, the hooded leader stepped quickly forward and, with both hands and all the strength he could muster, swung the rifle's butt at his attacker. The hard wooden stock hit the side of Hermann's head with an audible crack. The farmer fell hard to the ground, his face striking the earth. With great effort, he struggled up to his hands and knees, his body quivering. In the light of the still raging fire, Sophie saw a wetness on the side of her father's face and knew that it was blood.

"Hermann!" Maria shouted as she fell sobbing onto her knees.

"Father," Sophie said, her voice little more than a whisper.

The armed man stepped behind Hermann, raised the rifle high above him, and drove the butt of the gun into the back of the wounded man's head. The blow knocked Hermann back to the ground, where he lay silent and unmoving.

"Stupid son of a bitch," the gunman snarled.

Watching her father being savagely beaten struck Sophie as worse than seeing him shot and killed. Death would have been final, but his suffering from the blows that had felled him continued. Unsure whether her father was dead or alive, she felt consumed by anger.

"Just shoot that Nazi bastard!" the smaller of the masked men shouted as he danced from one foot to the other in excitement. "What in the hell'd he think he was doin' chargin' after ya like that?"

"He weren't thinkin' at all."

Hot tears began to run down Sophie's cheeks and fall onto the coarse fabric of her nightshirt. She could hear her mother's sobbing mix with the gulping breaths Karl was taking to control his panic, but she couldn't bring herself to look at either of them . . . she couldn't look away from her father and the men who had done him harm!

Her parents had taught her to know the difference between right and wrong. If you were to see a wrong being done, and you had the ability to stop it, you had to act! To do otherwise was as great a sin as the wrong itself! As she stared at her father's motionless body, Sophie felt the full force of her parents' lesson.

She stepped off the porch.

The dew that covered the grass was cool against her feet but Sophie couldn't feel anything; even the heat of the roaring fire was beyond her. Her anger at the heinous acts of the three men propelled her forward.

"Sophie!" her mother shouted. "No!"

"Well, would ya lookee here?" The gunman chuckled.

As she approached, Sophie could see the man's hands tighten on the stock of the rifle and she began to brace herself for the blow she would certainly receive. There was nothing she could do to stop them, to hurt them like they had hurt her family, but she didn't care. Her father was defenseless, and he needed someone, *needed her*, to protect him.

She covered the distance quickly, falling hard to the ground next to her father. Running her hands across his back and up to his neck, she tried to give all the comfort she could. Faintly, she could see the rise and fall of his chest and thanked the stars that he was still alive. With a start, her hands found the wound on his scalp. When she held her hands up to her face, she could see the bright crimson blood. Tightly holding one of her father's rough hands, she turned her face to glare at the three hooded men.

"I won't let you hurt him again!" she shouted.

"Ain't nothin' ya can do about it!" the smaller man said with a laugh.

The leader stepped closer, raising the rifle until the barrel was pointed right at her head. Now that she was close enough to the man, she could see his eyes through the holes in the burlap bag; they danced wildly as they sized her up. Anger continued to rise inside her. No matter what was about to happen, she'd face it with her head held high!

"It's like I always say," the man said. "The only good Kraut is a dead one."

There wasn't even time to say a prayer before her whole world went black.

Chapter One

SOPHIE HELLER HURRIED down the busy street, oblivious to the hustle and bustle, the cars and trucks, the daily life of Victory. Her eyes passed from one sight to the next quickly, not alighting on anything or anyone for long as she kept moving ever forward. She could not, would not be late!

Above her, the summer sun pounded down mercilessly. Rain had been promised for days, but those promises had proven to be every bit as empty as the cloudless afternoon sky. This day was a scorcher if there ever was one! Red, white, and blue American flags hung limply from every storefront, stirred by only the slightest of breezes. Pushing one errant strand of hair from her eyes, Sophie wiped the back of her hand across her brow. Her simple blue blouse clung tightly to her skin, the fabric as wet as if it had just been pulled from the wash.

"Good afternoon, Sophie," a woman's voice called to her from somewhere near the bakery.

She gave no response save a nod before hurrying on, clutching her purse tightly to her chest, aware that whoever had spoken to her would find her behavior rude. Still, her concern was not great enough for her to stop. She had a task that would afford no wait, and, moments later, she finally reached her destination.

Ambrose Hardware sat in a long, thin brick building on a corner of Main Street, right next door to the grocer. With its wide display windows, crisp sign, and long awning, Robert Ambrose's business was as familiar a sight to the town's residents as Marge's Diner, McKenzie's Barber Shop, or the post office, and every bit as vital. Victory's lone hardware store served everyone from the town's most venerable families to the newest arrival.

Stepping into the welcome shade provided by the awning, Sophie looked through the large show window. Past the stenciled lettering on the glass, she could see hammers, saws, several buckets of paint, and a pair of shovels, but it was the centerpiece of the display that grabbed her attention, sending a chill racing across her skin, even on such a hot summer day.

Two large posters stood side by side on a pair of chairs, their bright headlines shouting a clear message to every passerby. The first showed a smiling man holding a treasury bond in one hand under the banner of:

WANTED—FIGHTING DOLLARS

MAKE EVERY PAY DAY BOND DAY

The second poster was far more sinister-looking than its companion. On it, the dark eyes of a German soldier looked out from under the brim of an iron helmet, his steely gaze clearly showing his harmful intentions. The poster read:

HE'S WATCHING YOU

Sophie had seen these posters and others like them in the windows of stores and homes across town, attached to lampposts and telephone poles, and even in the back window of a pickup truck. While she shared their sentiment as a proud American, she couldn't help but worry that the more sinister poster had it backward; she and her German family were the ones being watched!

Faintly, Sophie caught her own reflection looking back at her in the glass. She looked haggard, bone-tired from lack of sleep. She hadn't bothered to put on any makeup or do a thing with her hair. To do so had suddenly seemed so unimportant, so trivial! But she certainly looked a mess. Gingerly, she rubbed the swollen knot at her temple; the slightest touch was enough to send sharp ripples of pain racing across her head.

Now, even a week after the burning of her family's barn, the wound was still angry and tender. She hadn't so much as seen the blow coming! When the gunman brought the butt of his rifle down upon her skull, the brief flare of pain had not been as bad as the pounding headaches that had plagued her for days afterward. Thankfully, the wound was hidden in her hairline, far enough out of sight to keep anyone from asking any questions.

As she stood before the hardware store, Sophie knew that the physical pain she had suffered was nothing compared to the shame and hurt she still felt at the indignities that had been visited upon her family. These wounds were deeper and more difficult to heal. She wondered if their scars would ever truly vanish. Taking a deep breath, she pushed open the door.

Sophie entered Ambrose Hardware to the sound of small bells ringing above the door. The blistering heat of the summer day followed her inside as if it were a shawl wrapped around her shoulders. After the bright glare of outdoors, it took a moment for her eyes to adjust to the store's darkened interior.

The store was crowded with goods in every nook and cranny; pots and pans, spools of thread, wire and rope, buckets of paint, and tin pails full of nails. Small compartments ran the length of the nearer wall, rising from the worn wooden floor to the high tin ceiling, their treasures hidden behind the smoky dark glass of each drawer. The very air carried with it the scent of available goods—oils, soaps, and wood—all gently pushed by the ceiling fans that turned lazily above her head.

"Afternoon, Miss Heller."

Robert Ambrose stepped from the store's stockroom, wiping his hands upon the dark vest that covered his button-down shirt and matching tie. Though Sophie felt certain that the store owner was nearly as old as her father, he carried himself like a much younger man. He was betrayed only by the slightest of hints to his true age; the silver hairs that were sprinkled across his black mane, the round, wire-rimmed glasses that sat high upon his thin nose, and the deep wrinkles that spread from around his mouth when he smiled all spoke of a man in his early fifties. Of medium height and build, he had a reputation about town as a bit of a teetotaler; no tobacco stained his long fingers or teeth and he would never be found staggering from a tavern as the morning sun broke the horizon. Decent and hardworking, he had built his business with his own two hands.

"Good afternoon to you, Mr. Ambrose," she answered.

"Still blazing away?" He nodded toward the front door.

"I'm afraid so."

"I swear it's not fit for man or beast out there," he remarked. "It gets a mite lonely in here when folks aren't brave enough to venture outside on days like this. Between the war and this darn heat, I'm going to have a bear of a time this year!"

"Did you have enough time to go over my father's list?" Sophie asked, a bit too anxious to engage in talk of the weather. "I know you asked me to come back today, but if you need more time—"

"No, my dear, it's fine," Mr. Ambrose said as he slid a pencil out from behind one ear and consulted the list she had left with him earlier in the week. "I've managed to round up most of what your father was asking for, all except for the roofing pitch. That will have to be ordered from Springfield, but it shouldn't take more than a week at best."

"He's certainly grateful for all that you can do."

"Your father's been coming here from the first day you and yours set foot in town." The hardware store owner smiled. "Darn shame losing a building like that, but I'll do all I can to get him back on his feet."

"He'll be glad—"

"Gosh darn it all," the man suddenly blurted, snapping his fingers across the piece of paper with a crack. "I forgot all about those hammers! I best check and make sure I don't . . ." He mumbled to himself as he disappeared back into the inky darkness of the storeroom.

As much as it shamed her to admit it, Sophie was thankful that Mr. Ambrose had left her when he did; casual talk of what had happened on that fateful night made her skin crawl. Remembering the flames that had stretched toward the night sky, the sounds of the barn collapsing, the armed and hooded men, and the dark crimson of her father's blood as she cradled his head in her arms still made her tremble. She knew that she should go forward with her life, leave the past in the past, but she found it too hard.

Her father had no such trouble. The morning after their lives had been forever changed, Hermann Heller had been out picking through the still smoldering wreckage of the barn, his head swathed in thick cloth bandages. Within days, he'd written a list of things he would need to reconstruct what they had lost. He would harbor no talk of the police or of following the advice given to them by the hooded men to leave their home, to leave Victory behind. Whenever he was asked about that night, he became upset, his voice quickly rising in anger. Sophie could not understand her father's defiance; she could not stop asking the questions her father refused to give voice.

Who were the hooded men? Why had they committed such acts?

These questions haunted Sophie every bit as deeply as the events of that night. From the moment she woke every morning to the instant she fell asleep at night, she thought of the men who had hurt her family. She waited, fearful that they would return to make good on their horrific promise, but every night their failure to reappear made her all the more fearful. Her dreams had also been poisoned; gone were the visions of wildflowers, replaced by biting laughter and hungry flames.

Even in this store, Sophie's eyes sought out the hated men, straining to find them hiding behind the stacks of washpans or for sight of their reflections in the dark glass of the wall of compartments. To her, they potentially lurked behind every corner, across every street, and even within every nod, smile, or stare that came her way.

They could be anyone . . . anywhere.

Her thoughts were broken by the ringing of bells as the door to the store was opened and a pair of men entered, one of them nearly as large as one of Mr. Ambrose's display cases, the other as reed-thin as a broom. Sophie immediately recognized them and smiled brightly.

Charley Tatum was nearly as wide as he was tall, with a personality that was more than a match for his girth. A farmer who worked the land just south of Victory's limits, he was a familiar sight to the town's inhabitants. He was quick to laugh, and his voice boomed over every conversation he joined and filled the church with a deep baritone every Sunday morning. Dressed in dark overalls, he wiped his sweat-beaded brow and flushed red cheeks with a handkerchief before burying it deep in his pockets.

"Well, I do declare, Miss Sophie!" he bellowed, breaking into a toothy grin. "You get more lovely just about every time I see you! 'Fore long, the simple folks of this here town are gonna see you on one of them there movie posters!"

"My mother says it's not nice to tease," she chided him.

"Who's teasin'? Why, there ain't but nothin' any of them Hollywood beauties has got on you! Not that Betty Grable, Ginger Rogers, Marlene Dietrich, nor that Vivien Leigh neither!"

"My pa ain't lyin', that's for sure," Will Tatum offered in defense of his father's proclamation. Unlike his larger-than-life father, Will was timid and skinny, still boyish in many ways though he was nearly a man. His personality was just the opposite of Charley's, his voice almost a whisper spit in the face of a storm.

"Then you're *both* teasing me!"

"Am I going to have a problem with you

harassing my customers?" Mr. Ambrose kidded as he stepped from the storeroom. His eyes rose from her father's list just long enough for the businessman to give Sophie a knowing wink. "I'd hate to have to call the sheriff."

"I swear this might be the first time I ever heard of a woman complainin' about a man sayin' she was pretty," Charley cackled, slapping one wide hand upon his knee. Leaning back, he rested his weight against one of the long display cases. Sophie felt sure that she could hear the old wood groan with the load. "What is the world comin' to?"

To that, they all laughed heartily.

"I was mighty sorry to hear what happened to your barn," Charley offered in a more somber tone. "With a tipped-over lantern, it'll only take a few shakes of a sow's tail 'fore the whole thing is ablaze. That happens, ain't but nothin' you can do but stand back, watch, and pray for rain."

"And we sure ain't gettin' much of that," Will added.

"We should all be a mite extra careful this time of year," Robert said as he wiped his glasses on his apron. "As much as I appreciate the business, it's a shame to lose a building like that."

"An outright shame," Charley echoed.

Sophie nodded solemnly. The story that had been given, the *outright lie* that had been created, was that Hermann had accidentally tipped over a lantern when checking upon their animals. Before he could hope to contain it, the fire had raced out of control. The entire Heller family had agreed that this was the story they would tell, but Sophie still felt the shame of their untruth coloring her cheeks.

"I appreciate your kind words." She smiled at them. "But my father says that we shouldn't feel sorry about what happened. We just need to roll up our sleeves and get back to work making it all right again."

"That's the spirit!" Charley exclaimed. "Why, if I know Hermann, he'll have that barn back up so fast that you'll wonder if you imagined that pesky fire! It'll look better than new, what with a fresh coat of paint and all!"

"I wouldn't doubt that for a minute," Robert Ambrose agreed.

"And you make sure to tell Hermann that

if he needs any help gettin' that barn of his back together, he shouldn't hesitate to ask us," Charley offered, patting his son so heavily on his shoulder that the boy's knees sagged. "We ain't against hard work to help out a neighbor. Ain't that right, boy?"

"Darn right, Pa!" Will agreed.

"After all, an accident like that could have happened to anyone. 'There but for the grace of God' and all. I sure ain't the most graceful man alive," the large farmer chuckled, patting his ample stomach. "It could just have easy been me knocking over that lantern and you can bet a helping of my Martha's biscuits that I wouldn't have hesitated a second to ask for a touch of help."

While Sophie appreciated Charley Tatum's sentiment, that it could have been any of Victory's many farmers who had lost their barn, she knew that his words rang hollow. What had happened a week before would only have happened to them.

Because we came from Germany . . .

"Thank . . . thank you, Mr. Tatum," Sophie stammered, forcing a smile. "I'll make sure to tell my father of your offer."

"You do that." He nodded. "Anything at all, just let us know."

After making arrangements with Mr. Ambrose for her father and brother to pick up the supplies they would need to rebuild the barn and saying her good-byes to the Tatums, Sophie hurried from the hardware store and again stood under the awning. She gulped the hot air as waves of heat rose from the pavement. She knew that she should begin the long trek home but her feet would not move. A persistent, gnawing fear had grabbed her. Stomach-churning thoughts flashed across her head too worrisome to ignore.

Could Charley Tatum know anything about what had happened to their barn? Could Mr. Ambrose? Was it possible that they were involved? While Charley undoubtedly would have stood out like a sore thumb, would she have recognized Will if he had been one of the men? What if—

Struggling with the effort, Sophie put a stop to her panicked thoughts. Her breathing had started to come in fits and her heart pounded hard in her chest like a jackrabbit's. What was she thinking? The very idea of such things was sheer madness!

Would she wonder about everyone she knew? Would she look at friends differently? Was hurtful intent hiding behind every face or kind word, even those of the people she had known nearly all her life?

Chapter Two

ROBERT AMBROSE TURNED the key in the lock of his hardware store, tried the door to make sure it was secure, and stood back to look in his storefront window. How he liked the look of those posters! Both of the posters' colors had already started to fade in the sun's glare, but he swore that they, or ones like them, would remain in the window of Ambrose Hardware for the duration of the war. He would do his part, by God! Why, if he were a younger man, he'd have been the first in line to enlist the day after Pearl Harbor!

"Damn heat," he muttered under his breath.

Far enough along on its path through the sky to be past the awning's protection at four o'clock in the afternoon, the sun blazed down on him relentlessly. It had already been a hot summer with little rainfall. The grumblings of the farmers who frequented his store were getting louder by the day. August and September surely promised more of the same. Pulling a handkerchief from his pocket, Robert wiped the sweat from his brow. He didn't have time to dally in this heat.

A quick glance at his pocket watch showed that he had less than twenty minutes to get to the train station. It had been a hard decision to close the store early, but he supposed there wasn't much of a choice to be had. Cole would expect him to be there. Still, he hated the idea of losing a sale; he hadn't gotten where he had by ignoring customers! Robert knew it was the right thing to do . . . but he didn't have to like it.

It was hard to admit to himself, but this was a day he had been dreading ever since he'd received the telegram from Chicago. Even with all there was for him to be proud of in life, his successful business and Jason's accomplishments, he had always feared that this day would come. And, like the rising and falling of the sun above, it had.

With a sigh and a resignation that galled him, Robert set off for the station.

For better or worse . . . Cole was coming home.

"And then he punches him in the face!"

Cole Ambrose turned in his seat on the train and looked across the aisle. A young boy—he guessed him to be no older than seven—stood in the space between the seats and was wildly throwing punches into the air. His blond hair was as tousled as his clothing. A comic book was rolled up and clutched tightly in one small fist. Cole could just make out the words *Fight Comics.*

"That Japanese soldier tried to hit that lady but then Rip Carson grabbed him by the arm and tossed him over the edge of the cliff!" the boy continued, his voice high and animated. He'd been so impressed by the goings-on in the comic book that he'd been unable to contain his excitement, choosing instead to act it out. "He screamed the whole way down until he went splat!"

"That's nice, dear," his mother answered absently from behind her *Ladies' Home Journal*, her eyes never leaving the page.

"Take that, you dirty Jap!"

Pulling his attention from the phantom fight beside him, Cole looked over the rest of the railcar. The space was packed tightly with people, their bags piled high in the seats beside them, many spilling over onto the floor. Traffic to the Mississippi River was always high; boats led to the scores of ports that dotted the great waterway. The air inside the car was stiflingly hot, even for July, and several passengers were fanning themselves with newspapers or handkerchiefs. Few spoke, content to be lulled by the heat and the constant rocking of the train. Somewhere behind him, a baby cried a soft wail that was occasionally punctuated by an old man's cough.

Three seats ahead of him and on the opposite side of the aisle was a young man dressed in the khaki tan of the United States Army. The soldier's head lolled to one side as he tried to sleep through the miserable heat of the railcar. Cole guessed them to be of a similar age; he was twenty-four, but there was something about the man in uniform that seemed to be older, wiser, and even stronger. Had the experience of basic training changed him or was it the simple fact that he was willing to risk his life for the sake of his country?

At the last stop, an older woman had climbed aboard the train and handed the soldier a small bag full of fruit. As the young man dug into his pocket to find some money to pay her, she shook her head and gently touched his cheek before getting off the train.

Before even seeing combat, the soldier was a hero.

More than anything, Cole Ambrose wished that he could wear that uniform, could fight for the United States of America, and that someone, anyone, could look upon him as a hero. But that was impossible! Men like him weren't able to do those things. Coming to grips with that fact was proving to be difficult, hell, just about impossible. His impotence and frustration made him nearly sick with anger. Like nearly every other American man his age, Cole had wanted nothing more than to run to the nearest recruiting station after the Pearl Harbor attack . . . but he couldn't run *anywhere*! He tried as hard as he could to stop thinking about what could not be and instead focus on what lay ahead. His future would be different from that of the soldier, but that didn't mean it couldn't be fulfilling.

"On to Tokyo!" the little boy shouted.

Cole still felt a twinge of amazement that he was returning to Victory. After everything that had happened, after all of the difficulty and hardship, he had devoted all of himself to leaving. Escape had been his only ambition. With every fiber of his being, he had thrown himself into his schoolwork. He had excelled in English and history, but had found his true passion in mathematics. The numbers had literally danced before his eyes, the complex theories and equations easily giving up their secrets. He supposed that he had fallen in love with math because the field was based on order, an alluring thing to a young boy whose life had none. After high school, he had gone off to college in Chicago, where he had earned honors and the respect of his peers. He had been poised for greater things when a phone call had changed his life. Clarence Collins, his high school math instructor, was retiring after thirty years and Cole had been offered the job of replacing him. Without even a moment's hesitation, he had accepted the position. He'd spent the last month trying to figure out why.

Glancing out the window, Cole watched as the landscape slowly became more familiar. Tall grasses whipped by in a rush of greens, browns, and yellows. The ribbon of Sunner's Creek, its bed laid bare by the scorching summer heat, began to wind its way toward Victory. Cows congregated beneath the shade of a scattering of trees that dotted the river's edge. Off in the distance, next to a thick stand of elm, he could see the distinct shapes of the buildings on the Kent family farm. Someone, he was too far away to be sure who, was leading a horse toward a pair of open barn doors.

As the sights became more recognizable, a feeling of apprehension began to form in the pit of Cole's stomach. One particular sight in Victory would be familiar to him as his own face; the disapproving look of his father. When he'd phoned to tell him of the job and his decision to return, there had been a long moment of awkward silence from the other end of the line. That he would be staying with his father until he could find a place of his own only made matters worse. Every day in that house would be a reminder of what they both had lost. Much had changed since the last time they had lived under the same roof. What concerned Cole was that he knew just how much remained exactly the same.

Slowly, the train lost speed as it entered Victory. Fields and farms had given way to new homes and streets. Cars and trucks now replaced horses and wagons. The shrill whistle of the engine signaled the train's arrival, and it soon came to a stop at the small depot set back from the town's center. People began to stir from their seats, gather their belongings, and head for the doors.

"I'm gonna get me a machine gun!" the boy shouted as he bounded down the aisle, the comic book still clutched in his waving hand. "And then I'm gonna kill all them dirty Japs!"

"Ask your father," his mother absently answered as she followed along behind.

Cole waited until much of the initial commotion had died down before he slowly rose out of his own seat. He'd learned long ago that it was much easier to stay out of people's way. Grabbing his small suitcase, he slid out into the aisle and took a tentative step.

Born with a defect that was every bit as restricting as an ox's harness, Cole Ambrose had a left foot that was pointed downward and twisted inward at an unnatural angle. It was a condition that was commonly known as clubfoot, and from a very young age he had needed to wear special shoes. As he grew to adulthood, the condition had worsened, and it became hard for him to walk for any great length of time. The spot where his left foot struck the ground was often sore and painful as it was not equipped to sustain his full weight. He had to move slowly, his left hip pushing itself outward in a sweeping motion. It was very slow going. Patience was a virtue he still struggled to attain. Picking his way down the aisle, he used his right hand to balance himself on each seatback. His eyes scanned the floor for any loose bags or wayward shoes that might trip him up or otherwise unbalance him.

"Just keep going, Cole," he prodded himself.

Near the door, he glanced up to see the eyes of the soldier open and staring at him. The young man looked him up and down and, when their eyes met, Cole could see pity in the soldier's gaze. He felt the urge to stop, to try to explain himself, to say that he wished he could be fighting alongside him against the Nazis or hopping from island to island across the Pacific. He wanted to tell the soldier that he should save his pity and compassion, that his handicap didn't make him any less of a man, and that his look of condolence only made Cole feel worse. But in the end he walked on saying nothing.

Gingerly, he moved down the steps of the train car. An older man offered his hand and Cole took it, steadying himself on the platform and nodding his thanks. In front of him, people were hugging, shaking hands, and slapping each other on the back.

Would such a reunion be waiting for him?

"Are you waiting on any bags, sir?" a porter asked him, breaking his reverie.

"No, I'm not," he answered. "I only have this one."

Before leaving Chicago, he had packed all of his clothes, books, and other belongings into a large trunk he had had sent on ahead; it would have been next to impossible for him to move something so large and awkward on his own.

Looking first down one side of the platform and then the other, Cole could see no sign of his father. Had he forgotten or simply decided not to come? Had something happened to him or Jason that had kept them from meeting him? Finally, just as he was about to resign himself to a long wait, he peered into the gloom of the depot's interior and spotted his father leaning against the ticket counter.

Robert Ambrose looked much the same as the last time his son had seen him nearly six years earlier. His hair was a bit thinner and the lines on his face were more pronounced, but he was otherwise unchanged. Cole felt a brief spark at seeing his father but doubted that the feeling was returned; the older man's face was still an unsettling mix of unhappiness and indifference. His hands were thrust into his pockets and he remained unmoving in the shade.

Swallowing his pride, Cole walked toward the ticket counter. As he stepped awkwardly forward, his father looked down at his feet and scuffed the toe of his shoe against the ground. Had something caught his eye or was he just ashamed of the way his youngest son walked? Cole stopped in front of him and placed his suitcase down with a thud.

"Hello, Father."

"Hello," Robert said as he looked up into his son's eyes.

"I hope it wasn't too much trouble for you to—"

"It wasn't."

For several long and uncomfortable moments, both men stood and silently stared at each other. It struck Cole that each of them was appraising the other, searching for a sign of any change. There was little doubt that he no longer resembled the youth who had left Victory years earlier. While he still had the same sky-blue eyes, thin nose, and square jaw framed under a mop of blond hair, he had grown taller and his frame had filled out across his broad shoulders. With his button-down shirt's sleeves rolled to his elbows, his tie loosened around his neck, and a brown hat pushed back on his head, he now was a man . . . albeit one with a very noticeable handicap.

Still, neither man spoke; silence was the language they used. Before Cole had left for Chicago, many of their conversations had contained only harsh and hurtful words and they had simply begun to say nothing at all. Now, they communicated with their eyes. Unlike the soldier on the train, no pity shone in his father's eyes, only unease and disdain.

"I suppose I could have picked a cooler day to come home," Cole offered.

"Could have."

"Did Jason have—"

"Are you ready to go?" his father asked stiffly, cutting him off.

"I suppose so."

Robert Ambrose bent down, picked up his son's suitcase, turned on his heel, and walked impatiently from the depot. As Cole followed slowly behind, his thoughts raced with all of the words he'd wished he had heard: *How was your trip? I've got your room all made up just like it was when you left. I bet you're tired so we'll have an early supper so you can get some rest*. Instead, the only sound he could hear was their footfalls as they made their way to the pickup truck. In that moment Cole realized how wrong he had been.

Nothing had changed . . . nothing at all.

Chapter Three

THE TRUCK LEFT the depot with Cole leaning against the passenger door, staring out at the town he had called home for his first eighteen years. Located along a flat plain that dropped toward the Mississippi River in the west, Victory was mainly a farming community. The rich black earth offered up a bounty of crops, mostly corn and beans, to those who were willing to work for them. Cows and pigs were raised in abundance before being shipped northward to Chicago for slaughter.

But things had begun to change; farming was no longer the only occupation that drew people to Victory. After the lean years of the Great Depression, new businesses and homes had sprung up as easily as spring crops. Change had come to Victory, and along with it new families, each of them willing to do what was necessary to build their own American dream. As the truck drove down Main Street, Cole watched as a steady stream of businesses, the bakery, barber shop, bank, and Ambrose Hardware among them, stood as a testament to the town's growth.

Tall elm, oak, and maple trees dotted the land, their leafy branches spread far and wide. The sweet scent of wild coneflowers, prairie dock, and cut grass wafted over the town in summer. The creeks and rivers were full of fish, the woods stocked with wild game. While both the heat of summer and cold of winter could be brutal, there were plenty of days in between that were as pretty as any picture.

On this day, these sights, sounds, and colors of summer were all tinted a bright red, white, and blue; crisp, clean flags and banners hung from nearly every business awning, every porch, and every flagpole. Posters promoting the danger of waste, the virtue of savings bonds, and clear pictures of the enemy flashed by in the storefronts the pickup passed. Victory was truly representative of the American heartland, united to fight the war, regardless of the cost. It had been the same in Chicago; an America attacked was a nation now alert, ready to defend all that it so cherished.

For all of this beauty, Cole knew that Victory was made all the greater by the town's inhabitants. The people who lived on and worked the land were a hearty and God-fearing lot. From the men who gathered every morning at Marge's Diner over coffee and cigarettes to the women who organized church socials, the bonds of support between the people of Victory were as strong as iron. Lifelong friendships abounded. The sentiment of "love thy neighbor" had never rung truer. His father had always felt an intense pride to be among them.

To Robert Ambrose, Victory was the perfect, ideal America.

Cole had heard the story more times than he could count; how his father's business had played an important role in the creation of that ideal. When he had first opened Ambrose Hardware, it had been a mighty struggle just to make ends meet. He'd been a young husband and new father and had had to do it all alone, without anyone save his wife to help him or provide support, and had borne his troubles with the conviction that he would persevere. Through hard work, fair prices, and the grace of God, he'd made his way and, in doing so, had become an integral part of the community. His lumber and nails were the literal framework of each new house and business. As Victory had grown, he had grown right along with it . . . but it was not always that simple.

Driving along Victory's wide, tree-lined streets, Cole thought of the hidden cost of his father's success. Robert Ambrose had been married to his work, desperate for anything he could do to guarantee its success. In the process, he had neglected his duties as a father and husband. When Cole had needed help with his schoolwork, advice about how to deal with the bullies at school, or a friendly ear to bend, his father had been absent. Instead, he had turned to his older brother, Jason, nearly three years his senior, and full of life. It was

Jason who had been there for his small triumphs, his many disappointments, and all that fell in between.

All of this had made Cole's relationship with his father difficult, but somehow they had managed to come to an uneasy truce. Despite his handicap, they had built a relationship that was not quite father-and-son but more of cordial acquaintances, maybe even friends. But that had all changed one fateful afternoon, the day that—

"We're here," his father announced.

The Ford rounded the corner, and from behind the full branches of a large elm tree, the house that Cole had grown up in came into view. Even after all of his years away, it was exactly as he remembered. A stately Victorian that Robert Ambrose had built with his own two hands when he came to Victory in 1911, the two-story home stood on a corner lot two blocks from Main Street. Light gray in color with white framework around the windows, it had a row of stained glass windows on the upper floor that captured the setting sunlight in a kaleidoscope of colors. An enclosed porch ran along the front of the house with support beams holding up its lower roof.

Small details on the house still caught Cole's eye: the latticework framing that ran along the bottom of the porch and the colorful decorative gable trusses at the upstairs windows. His father was truly a craftsman, although his motive was not always just to strive for beauty; he hoped to demonstrate to prospective customers that any purchase they made at his hardware store could lead to a beautiful home, just like his own. All of his care and precision had paid dividends; the house, while thirty years old, looked as new as the day the last nail had been driven.

"Just as I remembered," Cole said.

Robert grunted in answer.

As the pickup turned into the short drive, Cole could see that his father still devoted as much attention to the yard as he did to the house itself. Red geraniums stood vividly together with yellow and purple pansies, although they all drooped a bit under the merciless sun. Perfectly trimmed hedges lined the walks and divided the property from the neighbors. Powerful elm trees thrust their branches high into the cloudless blue sky. No weeds sprang from the ground to mar the scene. Everything was exactly in its place.

The only thing missing was a family to live in this prettier-than-a-picture life. Cole wished that his father had devoted half as much time to being a husband or father as he had to building his home and cultivating his yard. If he had, maybe things would be different, maybe there would have been no harsh feelings, maybe what had happened to his mother . . .

A shiver of dread raced across Cole's skin as his father shut off the pickup's engine. For him, this house, while a beauty to behold, was something straight from a nightmare. His memories had scarred him and were impossible to erase, no matter how many years had passed. Now, back home after so many years away, his recollections bore down on him as if they were spring floods.

Cole could recall vividly the day when his life was changed forever. It was winter and frightfully cold, although the sun had shone high in a clear sky. The glare from the snow that lay on the ground was blinding. Frost ringed the windows and the low whistle of February wind could be heard as it passed across the frozen Illinois ground.

"Is Jason at home?" he asked his father.

"Nope," Robert Ambrose answered without bothering even to glance in his son's direction, his eyes lost out the windshield. "He's got a meeting with a fella from the draft board over in Hallam Falls. Something about his induction date. He'll be along come tomorrow."

"Oh," was all Cole could manage.

As he struggled to come up with something, anything, to say to his father, it suddenly struck Cole just how difficult it was going to be for them to live together under the same roof. He longed for Jason's company, not entirely because of his brother's warm personality, but also because he didn't want to be alone with Robert. He supposed he should get used to the idea; after all, until he found a place of his own, they were stuck together.

"I'll get your bag," his father said as he got out of the truck.

Robert moved quickly up the rear walk without waiting. Cole followed slowly behind, neither one of them saying a word.

At the back door, the screen opened with a squeak and they stepped into the small kitchen. The room was nearly dark in the fading light of day, but familiar shapes surrounded Cole. Sparsely furnished with an iron stove, icebox, attached pantry, and a small table under the lone window, the room was as comfortable and recognizable, even if it looked a bit more worn than he remembered.

"Are you hungry?" Robert asked.

"A bit. It was a long train ride."

"There'll be something in the icebox. I'm going up to my room for the night. I'll put your suitcase in your room," he said matter-of-factly and stepped toward the door that led to the front of the house.

On that cold day Cole had been only twelve years old, each year having been more difficult than the last. His sort of problem had kept him from doing the things that boys his age did; he didn't play baseball, didn't splash through creeks chasing frogs, or climb to the tops of trees. Most of his time was spent indoors, and the burden of raising him fell squarely upon his mother.

"Actually, I was hoping that we might have

dinner together," Cole offered. "It's been a while since we've seen each other and just talked. You could tell me about all the things I've missed. About what's going on in Victory and at the store, about Jason and his plans. I could fill you in on Chicago. What do you say?"

"I'm not very hungry."

"Then just sit with me while I eat."

As they silently stared at each other, Cole could see that his father was actually weighing the idea. With every passing moment, faint hope grew that his offer would be accepted. If they could just get off to a good start, if they could just talk to each other without all of the baggage between them, they might be able to start over with a clean slate! He wanted nothing more in the entire world. But as quickly as his hope had grown, it all fell away. His father's shoulders slumped and his eyes dropped to the floor.

"I'll be in my room." Robert turned and walked away.

At that point in his life, frustration had been Cole's closest companion. At twelve, he'd still been a child; unable to grasp the reality of the life into which he

had been born. His mother met that frustration with patience and understanding. They spent hours talking, reading, or listening to phonograph records, the classical music she loved floating around the house. To her son, she was infinitely dear.

For a moment, Cole could only stand dumbstruck in the kitchen. How many times had they done this? How many times had he said nothing as his father walked away from him? Was this the way it was *always* going to be? If he refused to act, nothing would ever change. As quickly as his bad foot allowed, Cole followed after his father.

Leaving the kitchen, he limped down a short, darkened hall that ended at the foyer at the front of the house. The foyer was more elegant than the rear of the house. A mirror sat atop an antique table inside the front door. A tall grandfather clock ticked in the near corner, its deep bell ready to chime the hour. A long, dark staircase rose to the second level. Lights along the stair's wall shed a soft glow. By the time Cole reached the foyer, his father was nearly at the top of the stairs.

"Wait!" Cole called. Robert stopped and

turned to face his youngest son. His face was emotionless. "Is this the way that it's going to be between us?"

"Everything between us is fine," his father said coolly.

"You know that isn't true. Things have never been fine and no amount of lying to ourselves about it is going to change that. I've been gone for six years," he declared, his voice rising with emotion. "Six long years and now I come home to find it the same as when I left!"

"Nothing is wrong with how things are."

"Damn it, there is so!" Cole snapped. "You still walk away from me as if it sickens you to be near me. No matter what I do, no matter how hard I try, you refuse to acknowledge me as your son. Don't you want to know what I've been doing? Don't you want to know what I've become?"

"I know exactly what you are, Cole."

"No, you don't!" he protested. "All that you know for certain is that I graduated from college and that I'm going to be a math teacher, but you don't know anything about the real me. You've never taken the time to ask."

At twelve, walking was still difficult. As his feet continued to grow, his clubfoot

required constant care and it seemed that he always needed new shoes. On that particular sunny winter afternoon, he'd been upstairs in his parents' room, looking at his newest pair in a tall mirror, when he'd heard a crash. He'd called out to his mother, his voice sounding small and frail, but he'd gotten no reply.

"I tried to be the best parent I could, given the circumstances."

"Those circumstances have defined everything about us for the last twelve years!" Cole couldn't stop himself from speaking; words were coming out of his mouth almost before he could even think them. He heard himself giving voice to things he'd wanted to say for years but had always been afraid to speak. "When are we going to get past this? It's been twelve long years and we still can't talk about what happened. It was an accident! I shouldn't be punished for this for the rest of my life! She would hate for us to—"

"Stop!" Robert thundered from the top of the stairs. He was usually a quiet man, but the sharp tone of his voice split the air like an axe. "You stop right there! Don't you dare speak of her!"

"We have to speak about her if we are ever going to let this go!"

"How can I let it go? Everything that I ever truly cared about in this world was taken from me! Forgetting that is impossible!"

"But why do we have to—"

"You don't have the faintest idea of what it is like. You don't know!" In his anger, Robert took a couple of steps down the stairs. He punctuated each exclamation with a jabbing finger as his hands shook with rage. "Each and every day I am reminded of her! I walk around this house and remember all of the dreams we shared, hopes that we had for the future. All of it is gone, lost to me forever! It's not something for me to forget!"

Anxiously, he'd stepped out into the hallway and called again. There was still no answer. He'd strained to hear something, anything, some familiar sound, but instead only heard the cold February wind as it moved through the trees. It was at that moment that he'd felt a fear that bordered on panic. He and his mother had been alone in the house; Jason and his father had been working at the hardware store. He'd hurried as

best he could to the steps, anxious to get downstairs, and it was then that he had seen her.

"I'm not asking you to forget her, Father!" Cole argued, the pain of his loss as acute as it had been that February day. "None of us will ever forget what she meant! But you need to forgive!"

"That's not something that I can do!"

"Why not?"

Suddenly, the anger that had clouded his father's face calmed as if sunlight had broken through a stormy sky. But Cole's slim hopes were soon dashed; it wasn't that Robert Ambrose had had a change of heart but rather that he saw no more reason to argue.

"If you wanted to come back here, back to this house and to Victory, that's your business," he said evenly. "You can stay here until you find somewhere of your own . . . I can do that much for you. But don't think that I will ever forgive you."

"She would not have wanted it to be like this between us."

"All that she would have wanted was to have lived, but you took that away from her that day, took it away from all of us," his father said, the words spoken flat and cold, each of them jabbing at Cole's heart as if they were knives. "It was because of you that she's gone. It was your fault."

His mother had lain at the bottom of the steps, her body twisted at an angle that seemed, even to his young mind, unnatural; it was as if she had been a doll, a toy tossed haphazardly down the stairs to lie as she had fallen. Blood had begun to pool near her head, coloring her blonde hair a deep crimson. What had happened was clear; by some accident she had fallen down the stairs. His mother had been badly hurt and her very life was possibly hanging in the balance. His heart came up into his throat.

But it was then that fear had overwhelmed Cole. When his mother had needed him the most, he'd crawled to the nearest corner, pulled his knees to his chest, and cried. He had been too afraid to act. Though he had been but a child, a handicapped child at that, his father had not understood. With his leg, Cole knew that he likely wouldn't have reached help in time, but that knowledge did little to erase the sting of what had happened to his father.

"Don't ever forget that it was your fault."

Robert Ambrose stared down at his son for a moment longer before going up the stairs, entering his room, and shutting the door behind him. Alone at the bottom of the stairs, the same stairs where he had discovered his mother, there was no cold February wind to keep him company.

There was only silence.

Chapter Four

I WILL NOT BE FORCED from my own home!" Hermann Heller punctuated his words by slamming his closed fist into the open palm of his other hand. The purplish black bruise on the side of his face grew even uglier as he turned a deep crimson with anger.

"But Hermann . . ." Maria anxiously pleaded.

"There will be no more running! This is where we belong!"

Sophie sat silently on the dining room windowsill as her parents argued the merits of leaving Victory. It was a scene that had been repeated every day since their barn had been burned; her father refused to be cowed by fear, adamant that they would stay on their farm as if nothing had happened, while her mother, the memory of her husband's vicious beating still as fresh as his wounds, thought otherwise.

Wiping fitfully at her eyes, Sophie stifled a yawn. No one in the house had had much sleep since that horrible night. At every creak or night sound, she bolted awake, searching for the men she was sure had returned. She was gripped by the conviction that *if the men did return*, they would almost certainly do far worse than burn a building.

And who would there be to protect her family?

Sophie looked out the window at the wreckage of the barn. Her father had cleared away some of the debris but much remained; coal black wood charred into ruin, warped nails scattered about like seed, and the somehow still standing framework of one door littered the yard. It had been many days since any smoke had drifted from the rubble, but Sophie kept expecting to see tongues of orange flame once again burst to life. Thank heaven, her father had been able to lead the animals out before they had been burned alive.

"You should have told Sheriff Carter what happened," Maria said.

"It would not have done any good."

The day after the fire, Sheriff Allen Carter had driven out to the farm to assess the damage. He had walked around the still smoldering barn, taking off his hat and wiping the sweat from his brow with a handkerchief as Hermann spun the lie the family had all agreed upon. As Sophie had watched from the porch, she'd felt the urge to run to the lawman and tell him everything about the men and their threats. In the end, she had reluctantly stayed silent. Ever since that day, she'd wondered if she'd made the right decision.

"He could have helped us," Maria continued. "He's a good man."

"Even if he were to believe what I told him, we would be no safer," Hermann explained. "Would the police stand watch over this house forever? No, they could not and they would not. The moment that they left we would be in even greater danger."

"They would catch the men who did this to us! That is their job!"

"How would they do such a thing?" Hermann asked incredulously. "There was nothing about the men that I recognized. We could not see their faces, nor did I find any of their voices familiar. Did you?"

"No, I did not," Maria admitted.

"If we go to the police, they'll kill us!" Karl paced nervously next to the doorway that led to the kitchen. Like his older sister, he'd had little peace since the fire and constantly wrung his hands. The previous night, Sophie had heard the sound of crying through the wall that separated their rooms.

"No one will kill us," Hermann reassured him.

"You don't know that for certain," Maria contradicted. "The sheriff—"

"There would be nothing for me to tell Sheriff Carter," her husband cut her off. "Nothing that would lead us to those who are guilty. I'm sure that he could think of men who could do such things, but there wouldn't be any proof. He could not simply lock these suspected men in his jail and hope that nothing happens to us.

Besides, it is too late. To change our story now, to tell him that we had lied about the lantern, would be impossible. We have always taken care of ourselves. This will not change."

"You can trust a man like Allen Carter," Gitta said solemnly from her chair, her English even more heavily accented than her son's. Though now small and frail of body, Gitta Heller's youthful spirit shone in her cool blue eyes. It had been many years since her straw blonde hair had turned white, but she appeared nowhere near as old as her true age of eighty. In most family discussions, she was happy to sit and listen, only interjecting her thoughts when she believed them to have special merit. She had watched the tragic events unfold from her bedroom window. Although struck with horror, she'd been unable to turn away. "This is not Germany."

"It most certainly is not," Hermann agreed. "That is precisely why we must help ourselves! That is why we will not run! In Germany, danger was lurking everywhere. People that I had known my entire life, people that I considered my friends, began to turn on their neighbors, to accuse them of horrible things the moment they had the chance. Here it is just three men! Three men will not drive us from the home that we have built in America. We have already run enough!"

"But what happens when they return?" Sophie asked.

"We don't know that they will come back."

"They will," Karl worried.

"We cannot be certain," Hermann said as he walked over and placed a hand on his son's shoulder. "For all that we know, they were simply talking about the war, had too much to drink, and acted without thinking. It is possible that they don't even remember what they did that night."

Sophie could not bring herself to believe what her father was saying. The three men hadn't been drinking. On the contrary, they had soberly concocted a plan and had executed it perfectly. First, they had lit the barn on fire in order to draw the family outside. Second, they had reacted calmly when Hermann had attacked them; a drunken man, a man not in complete control of himself, would simply have shot the charging man dead. The eyes of the leader she had glimpsed through the holes in his hood in the flickering lights of the burning barn were not those of a drunkard.

"But what if you're wrong? What if they do return?" Maria asked irritably.

"Then we will fight."

"How?"

Sophie already knew the answer to that question; she had seen her father cleaning a pair of shotguns in the small shed at the side of the house. When they'd first arrived in the United States, Hermann had hunted the woods and fields of their property for small game. He had done less of it in the last several years, but he was no stranger to using the guns. So intent had he been on the weapons, he hadn't noticed her watching him. The thought of her father using the shotguns on the three hooded men nearly made her sick.

"Leave that to me," he answered calmly. "I don't want any of you hurt."

"Like you were," his wife shot back. Anger at her husband's obstinacy had risen in her breast and flushed her cheeks. She was ready for a fight, as full of stormy intentions as dark clouds gathering on the distant horizon.

"Now, Maria—"

"Do you know what it was like to watch those men standing over your bleeding and broken body? Over Sophie's?" she asked, the fury of her emotion overwhelming her. "Do you have any idea how hard it was to hear their laughter as they walked away? Karl and I were too frightened to move, too scared to run to you and make sure that you were still alive, so afraid were we that they would return!"

Without a word in answer, Hermann moved to his wife, pulling her into the safety of his thick arms just as the first tears began to run down her cheeks. He held her as if she were a child, soothing her hair and planting a gentle kiss on the crown of her head.

"We can't act . . . as if nothing has . . . happened," she sobbed.

"That's not what I want either," Hermann explained, his voice empty of all of his earlier emotion. "Something did happen, but we can't let it change the way we live our lives. We must all go on. Karl starts back to school in a couple of weeks, while Sophie has her job at the newspaper. On top of that, we have plenty of work to do here on the farm. The harvest will be coming soon and the barn will need to be rebuilt before then."

"We're going to rebuild the barn?" Karl asked.

"Of course. No one's going to chase us from what we have worked so hard to create. The most important thing to remember is that this is our home. It will not be taken from us."

"But what if the men do come back?" Sophie asked. "What then?"

"We are Americans now," Hermann said simply. "We will fight."

Sophie sat on the windowsill and sighed. Outside, her father and Karl were picking through the rubble of the destroyed barn while her mother hung laundry. Were it not for the wrecked building, it would have been a day much like many that had come before, but Sophie couldn't help but feel uneasy. Despite her father's convictions, the future seemed to be filled with uncertainty and danger.

"Do you worry, child?" Gitta's voice asked from behind her. She turned to see her grandmother shuffle into the room and slowly lower herself into her favorite chair. Once she was settled, she looked at her granddaughter with a small smile full of love and concern. Sophie gave a weak grin in return.

"A little," she admitted.

"Tell your old *Oma* all about it."

"I keep thinking about all that's happened," Sophie began, searching for the words to explain her feelings. "How could . . . someone do such a thing? How could men that don't even know us do us such harm? We're not the enemy! It just doesn't seem real."

"Bad men are everywhere. The world is full of them."

"But isn't that more reason to be worried?" she wondered. "What happens if Father is wrong? Those men weren't just drunks that stumbled here to do mischief. They mean to hurt us if we don't do what they want. What do I do if they come back here or if they show up at the newspaper?"

Gitta held her granddaughter's worried gaze for a moment before lacing her thin fingers together in her lap. "Then you will do what you have always done. You will act."

"Like I did the other night?" Sophie laughed involuntarily. "I was too scared to move! It wasn't until Father had been hit with the rifle butt that I was able to take even a step." Suddenly, the words that the gunman had spoken to her came flooding back.

"The only good Kraut is a dead one . . ."

"He could have killed me," she muttered.

"Even in the face of such fear, even with the chance that you could have been hurt, you still chose to act," Gitta explained. "I saw it all from my window. You have much more strength than you know."

"I do?"

"Of course, my dear," the older woman said, a smile breaking across her wrinkled face. "You are a special young woman who cares deeply for those around you and knows what is right and what is wrong. When those men appeared, you were frightened, we all were, but you didn't let that fear paralyze you. When it was time to act, you did so to help those you care for. If the time comes where you have to do so again, I know that you will."

Sophie could only answer with a nod.

A horse's whinny drew her attention back

to the window. Karl was leading the family's draft horse, a large brown and black beast, away from the ruins of the barn. Hermann had tied a rope to its harness and its muscles rippled in the hot sun as it pulled a burnt piece of timber free from the rest of the rubble.

After all that had happened to the Hellers, the sight of her family beginning to take steps to rebuild what they had lost filled Sophie with hope. While she was not as optimistic as either her father or grandmother, she knew that some of what they said was indeed true; there were things that were worth fighting for. The life they had built in America was certainly one of them. When she had run to her father's side, regardless of the danger that it posed to her, she'd been running to fight for that life, to defend her family's right to live it.

If she had to, she would act.

The burnt yellow and orange sun had begun its slow descent toward the horizon in the west when Sophie bounded down the steps that led off the back of the Hellers' house and headed through the thick brush and wildflowers that abutted the eastern side of their property. All around her, heath aster and bush clover filled the air with the sweet scent of their flowers. Bees buzzed about, flitting from one flower to the next in their never-ending pursuit of pollen. High above, a pair of eagles soared in wide circles, their keen eyes scanning the ground for any errant field mouse not wise enough to stay burrowed in the cool, tall grass.

"Just a little more!"

"I'm trying!"

Behind her, she could hear the shouts and groans of her father and brother as they continued their work on the destroyed barn. The sound of their voices sent a slight shiver of shame racing across her heart; she'd left the house without a word to anyone as to where she was going. She knew that it wasn't the smart thing to be doing, especially alone, but she needed to get away for a while.

She needed to get to her special place!

Ever since her family had arrived in America, Sophie had been captivated by the wilderness around the farm. Nature had called to her and she had obliged by traipsing along the creek beds, climbing in the trees, watching the animals as they lived and died, and enjoying all that was there to offer. But one spot in particular had spoken to her, and she had often gone there when she needed to be alone. Now was certainly one of those times.

The tall grass fell away and she entered the tree line, leaving the heat of the summer sun for the cool interior of the woods. Scant brambly brush filled the space underneath the tall oak trees and she made her way easily. A thin creek, its water gurgling as it rushed over the worn stones of its bed, was easily jumped. Sophie had walked this way so many times that she was certain she could have found her way with her eyes closed.

Soon, a familiar knot of rock came into view. Three large crags of stone were bunched together, one rising atop the other, all bursting from a sharp drop in a low hill. Long ridges ran the length of each rock, exposing deep grays, bejeweled reds, and flecks of green. These ridges offered willing hand- and footholds, ready to be climbed and explored. The stones had always seemed out of place to Sophie; it was as if some ancient giant had forgotten his playthings behind him thousands of years ago. It was this oddness that had charmed her the first time she had laid eyes upon them.

Without a moment's pause, Sophie began to climb. She found familiar sharp points and worn indentations, pushing and pulling herself upward, straining her arms and legs. Swiftly, she rose toward the summit. Climbing one rock and then another, she finally reached the top.

"So beautiful," she muttered.

From where she stood, the forest opened up before her in every direction. Oak and maple trees spread their branches toward her, their green leaves bright in the sunlight that filtered through their canopy. The creek snaked away into the distance before being lost to sight, the sound of its water mixing with the chirping of birds and the scurrying of squirrels and rabbits.

Lying on her back, Sophie spread her arms wide and turned her palms to the sky. Thankfully, the top of the rock was as dry as a bone; water pooled in the stone's many small recesses in the spring thaw and fall rains but dried up in the strong heat of summer. As she stared at the small clouds that drifted across the blue sky above, she knew that the peaceful life she had heretofore led had been forever violated. With the attack upon her family and the threats that came with it, she would never be able to go back, to recapture the innocence of her earlier life.

What mattered now was the future, whatever it might be!

She wanted to believe her grandmother and reward the older woman's faith that, when confronted with the need to act, she would. Sophie had been raised always to do the right thing. In the calm of her special place, she knew exactly what that meant.

Whatever comes, I will be ready!

Chapter Five

UNDER THE BLAZING July sun, Cole slowly made his way toward Marge's Diner. Crossing the street in front of the bank, he cursed his bad leg; on days like this, having to hobble along, carefully turning his hip, was a real pain in the ass! Hunger had driven him into the summer heat. It was late afternoon and he was famished; over the hustle and bustle of the town he swore he heard his stomach rumble. There were only a couple of cars and a lone pickup parked in front of the small restaurant, but that was more a sign of the lateness of the lunch hour than a comment about the quality of the food. Wiping the sweat from his brow, Cole pulled open the door and stepped inside.

Marge's was small and cozy. There was hardly room enough for two people to walk side by side between the row of booths that lined the wall next to the windows on one side and the long countertop and stools on the other. Only a few seats were taken, the occasional burst of laughter was heard over the other sounds of the restaurant; the scrape of a fork, the clatter of a cup in a saucer, and the soft whir of the ceiling fan. The smell of hamburger grease and coffee clung to the air and sent Cole's taste buds salivating. The diner held some of his fondest memories in Victory.

"Well, land sakes!" a woman's voice suddenly shouted, overpowering all of the noise in the diner. "Is my eyes deceivin' me in my old age or did Cole Ambrose just walk through my door?"

Marge Stewart hurried out from behind the counter wearing a flowered apron over a white blouse, the worn stub of a pencil stuck behind one ear. Short and squat enough to appear nearly as wide as she was tall, Marge had coal black hair that was piled on top of her head in dark clouds. A pattern of wrinkles creased her face as she smiled. Marge had been a fixture in Victory for years. She ran the diner with her husband, Dick; Cole could see the back of his balding head as he manned the grill. The Stewarts knew everyone in town by both name and appetite.

"It's good to be back, Marge."

"I sure wasn't expectin' to see you! When did you get home?"

"Just yesterday."

"I'm glad to see that all those years of fillin' your head full of numbers and the like didn't push out your common sense," she crowed, cheerfully patting his cheek with her pudgy hand. "First day back in Victory and you make a beeline straight for my cookin'!"

"After all those years eating in the cafeteria, I'd almost forgotten what it was like to get an honest-to-goodness meal," Cole chuckled. "My mouth started watering on the way here."

"Now you're just butterin' me up," Marge scolded him, but her eyes quickly brightened. "But then again, I love that sort of thing! Sit yourself down right here at the counter where I can keep an eye on you."

"Yes, ma'am." Cole did as he was told.

"One cheeseburger and a glass of milk, coming up!"

As Marge busied herself fixing his order, Cole sighed. He could have just as easily eaten at home, but ever since the fateful day of his mother's accident, being there by himself had always made him uncomfortable. To make matters worse, he had only been home for less than a day but his father had done nothing to make him feel welcome. *I've been gone for so many years! You'd think there would be some part of my father that would have been happy to see me!* Cole was relieved that Robert had already left for the hardware store by the time he woke; no words at all were certainly better than the harsh ones he had received upon his arrival. He'd dressed quickly and hurried out the door. Though he'd been hungry, he wanted to get out, to get some fresh air, and reacquaint himself with Victory.

Sitting on the diner seat, he began leafing through the abandoned newspaper that lay at his elbow. The *Victory Herald*'s headline blared JAPS PUSH ON IN NEW GUINEA. Scanning through the article, Cole learned that the Japanese army had seized a couple of towns on the island and were threatening Port Moresby and the American ships at anchor there. If they didn't get reinforcements soon, they could be pushed clean off the island. Cole closed the paper in disgust. Much of the news since Pearl Harbor had been bad, but he still remained confident that the tide would soon turn. Heck, the Doolittle raid on Tokyo had proven that America would fight back. It wouldn't be long before the Japanese and the Germans would be back on their heels and in full retreat. *If only I could be in the fighting, doing my part . . .*

"Don't you pay no mind to those headlines," Marge said as she set a tall glass of milk on the counter. A golden burger, grease and cheese dripping onto the plate, soon followed. "That sort of thing isn't going to do much for your appetite. You mark my words, we'll win this war in short order."

"I hope you're right."

"I know I am," she said confidently. "It was American know-how that won the

Great War, and that same know-how will win this one, by gum! We'll make all the tanks, guns, planes, and ships we need and our boys will use them right. They'll do what needs to be done . . . just so long as they eat right."

Cole chuckled. As if he had been ordered by an officer to storm a hilltop, he bit into his sandwich under Marge's watchful gaze. The burger was delicious, exactly as he remembered. A smile of satisfaction spread across her heavy face before he even said a word.

"Still as good as you remember?" she asked expectantly.

"Better."

As he ate, Cole told Marge all about college life, his studies, and about what it was like to live in Chicago, all of the things about life in the big city he liked and disliked. She in turn told him of various bits of gossip he'd missed while away. Occasionally, she would fill a coffee cup or take an order, but she always returned eager for more.

"And now you're going to be a teacher over at the high school." Marge smiled. "It's hard to believe that the young boy who sidled up here for a slice of apple pie every summer has grown up so fast! It just don't seem possible!"

Cole chuckled. "I still love that pie."

"Your father must be so proud!"

As if dark storm clouds had suddenly appeared in a clear autumn sky, Cole's face changed. He had no idea what his father truly thought of his return to Victory, but he doubted that pride in his son's accomplishments played any part. It was almost certainly the exact opposite. He was still what he'd always been to Robert Ambrose: an embarrassment.

"I think he'd be prouder if I was a bit more like Jason."

"Don't you say such things, darlin'," Marge scolded him, her voice soothing at the same time. "Your father ain't the sort to go on judgin' you two boys the same, no matter what you got yourself believin'. Just because your brother was the one out runnin' about and playin' football and all, that don't make him more special than you."

"But—"

"But nothing," the older woman cut him off. "Your father has every reason to be as proud of you as a peacock is of its feathers! Why, it ain't just anybody that's smart enough to go off to college, to graduate and come home to teach those kids followin' on behind. Heck, I'm bettin' that if everybody had as many brains as you, this here world would be a heck of a lot better off!"

"What I wish I could do is go off and join the fight," Cole said bitterly as he slapped the newspaper with the back of his hand. "I wish I could sign up for the army just like Jason did, but I guess with a leg like mine, the only thing I'm good for is teaching."

"You'll do your part on the home front just like the rest of us will and no one will think you less for it," Marge explained. "Not your father and certainly not Jason. Your brother thinks the whole world of you and he knows you won't be a soldier because of a lack of heart."

"I just want to do more."

"You'll do the very best you can, darlin'. There ain't an ounce of shame in that."

Cole opened his mouth to argue further but fell mute as the door to the diner opened and a young woman entered. She was dressed simply in a dark blue skirt and white blouse with a small black purse hung over a thin wrist. Her dark hair fell to her shoulders. With her high cheekbones, small nose, and full lips, her beauty was truly stunning. As the door shut behind her, her blue-green eyes found Cole's and set his heart hammering. Even as she looked away from him, he worried that he had been staring too intently and felt a flush of embarrassment.

"Good afternoon, Marge," the young woman said sweetly.

"Afternoon, Sophie."

"They're keeping us so busy over at the paper that I forgot all about lunch." She laughed. "I don't have much time so I was wondering if I could have an egg sandwich to take with me, if it's not too much trouble."

"None at all, my dear. I'll be right back."

As Marge hurried off to place her order, Cole's heart pounded in his chest. *What a strange feeling!* Her beauty drew him to her as surely as if he were a moth and she an open flame. Cole wasn't the type who made a practice of approaching strange women, and he'd certainly never had much luck in love, but this was a sensation he'd never experienced before. Usually when he met a beautiful woman, he became self-conscious, achingly aware of his deformed leg. But something about this time was different. He desperately wanted to talk to her, to say something, anything, that might make her smile or laugh, but his mouth felt as dry as a desert.

Sophie! Her name is Sophie!

Cole took a deep breath, steadied himself, and turned on his stool.

Sophie hurried quickly down the street, her head to the pavement and her eyes watching her feet, trying her best not to run into any of the people she passed. One of the few times she'd glanced up, she'd checked the clock above City Hall and hadn't been surprised to find that much of the day had already passed. In the end, she wouldn't have needed to see the late hour or even notice the western placement of the sun in the sky to know she was late; the rumbling of her own stomach would have been more than enough.

I'm so hungry!

She'd gone to work at the newspaper

that morning trying to take her father's advice to heart; to act, as much as possible, as if nothing had happened. She'd dressed smartly, plastered a warm smile on her face, and gone about her day intent on making the best of it. Surprisingly, for the most part, her act had worked. The hustle and bustle of the office had been a comfort. Even though there had been a slew of last-minute changes to this week's edition that had forced everyone to work so frantically that they had forgotten to break for lunch, it had been a good day. Sophie had laughed with her coworkers, worked hard, and hadn't given much thought to her troubles.

Outside, things were different.

On Victory's streets she always felt as if she were being watched, observed by the eyes of strangers who wanted to do her harm, and worried that she was being followed. The same worries that had haunted her for days, of danger lurking behind every corner and door, returned with a vengeance. *Every man that I walk toward could be one of those from that night!* Fear teased at the edges of her mind and she wondered why she'd ventured from the safety of the newspaper office; another rumble from her stomach answered her question.

As scared as she was of running into the three men who had hurt her family, Sophie was even more ashamed of her fear. In the face of her father's words and her grandmother's faith in her, Sophie's weakness felt like a betrayal, a slap in the faces of those who had raised her. But no matter how much she scolded herself, no matter how hard she tried to be brave, she hurried tearfully toward the restaurant, glad that no one in her family could see her.

Sophie paused for a moment outside the diner. She tried to compose herself, to slow her rapidly beating heart and quiet her fright. Though she was leaving the openness of the street, those who meant to do her and her family harm could just as easily be found inside. Another growl issued from her stomach.

"You can do this," she muttered to herself.

Pushing open the diner's door, Sophie found Marge Stewart, the restaurant's owner, leaning against the counter talking with a young man she had never seen before. His face turned to her as she entered.

Beneath his short sandy blond hair, the man's eyes were a striking blue. As he took her in, his square jaw clenched tight for a moment before relaxing. His strangeness should have been unsettling, but something in his face disarmed her fear, surprising her.

"Good afternoon, Marge," she said in greeting.

"Afternoon, Sophie."

Even as she spoke, Sophie could feel the man's eyes on her, refusing to let go.

"They're keeping us so busy over at the paper that I forgot all about lunch." She laughed. "I don't have much time so I was wondering if I could have an egg sandwich to take with me, if it's not too much trouble."

"None at all, my dear. I'll be right back."

As Marge went off to fetch her order, Sophie fidgeted, her hand digging into her purse to retrieve her money, all the while aware that the man's eyes remained fixed on her. While somewhere in the back of her mind she wondered if he might have been involved with the barn fire, her intuition told her that such an idea was misguided. She worried that her face would flush, which only made matters worse.

"My name is Cole," he suddenly spoke from beside her, his voice deeper than she had expected. The suddenness of his words managed to startle her a bit. "Cole Ambrose."

Turning to face him, Sophie found a warm and inviting smile on the man's face. It seemed to her that he wanted to rise and stand beside her, but he chose to remain settled on his stool. She took the hand he had extended to her and found his grip to be firm yet welcoming.

"Sophie Heller," she offered.

He nodded. "Nice to meet you. Good choice on the egg sandwich. Between those, Dick's hamburgers, and Marge's apple pie, I reckon that I ate enough of them growing up to feed an army."

"They are delicious, aren't they?" She laughed despite her earlier worry.

"And then some."

"You seem to know where to find the best food in Victory but I haven't seen you around before," she inquired with honest interest. It wasn't a common occurrence for her to run into a strange face in Victory—the middling town just wasn't large enough—but his was a face that she felt interested in getting to know a bit better.

"That's because I've been gone for a few years," he explained with a chuckle as he ran a hand through his light hair. "I just got back into town yesterday from Chicago."

"Why would anyone leave Chicago to come back to Victory?" she asked, the words tumbling from her mouth before she could stop them. Sophie was embarrassed by her boldness, but the larger cities had always held a fascination for her, their tall buildings, loud music and voices, and bustling crowds everything that life on the farm was not. She'd hoped to live in one someday, so the thought of someone leaving Chicago willingly was a strange one.

Cole certainly didn't take any offense at her blurted question; his response was warm as the day. "If I had a dime for every time I've asked myself the same thing, I'd be rich! Quite frankly, I'd always wondered if I'd ever return. After all, that's why I left in the first place, to get as far away from here as I could. But things have a way of changing, I guess. After finishing up at the university, I was offered the job of math teacher at the school and somehow here I am."

"You're going to be a teacher?"

"Hard to believe, I know." He winked.

"I didn't mean it like that," Sophie stammered, suddenly fearful that she had accidentally insulted him. "It's just that most teachers are usually either old maids or stodgy balding men and you're . . ."

"I'm what?" he prodded her.

Sophie held her tongue, unsure of what to say. What she wanted to be able to tell Cole was that he didn't look like any schoolteacher she had ever met; not with those blue eyes and tight jaw. She was about to crack a joke, to try to laugh her slip-up casually away, when she heard the barest whisper of a voice from somewhere behind her.

". . . nothin' but a goddamn Kraut."

Sophie spun around quickly, the hateful words already seamlessly blending into the other noises of the diner, but it was already gone as surely as smoke caught in a breeze. Her heart thundered in their absence. For the briefest of moments, she wondered if she had imagined the voice, but then her eyes found a booth at the far end of the diner and she knew that what she had heard was every bit as real as the fire that had destroyed her family's barn.

Three men sat in the booth, two of them staring directly at her and Cole, their eyes boring holes of murderous intent. As her knees grew weak and a choking gasp racked her chest, Sophie was certain she knew their identities.

They were the hooded men who had burned the Heller barn!

Chapter Six

. . . NOTHIN' BUT A GODDAMN KRAUT.

Shivers of emotion raced across Sophie's skin as she stared silently toward the rear of the diner. Over and over, the hateful words she had heard echoed in her head. Her heart thundered relentlessly, her small fists clenched so tightly that her nails dug deep into the soft flesh of her palms.

These are the men that attacked my family!

Though she had spent every day since that horrible night in fear of just such an encounter, she was surprised to find that it was not fright that filled her; it was anger. Raw and blazing anger! Memories roared in her thoughts as brightly as the flames at her family's barn; she thought of her mother's piercing scream as the butt of the rifle was brought down on her husband's head, the soft sobs of her brother, and the helplessness she had felt as she held her bleeding father in her arms, staring daggers at the hooded men.

"Sophie?" Cole asked as he followed her gaze to the rear of the diner. He'd been waiting for her answer to his prodding question, but as he waited, his smile slowly fell. "Is something the matter?"

Somewhere in the maelstrom of her mind, Sophie was aware of Cole's words, but they were as lost to her as if they were whispers in the teeth of a thunderstorm. All that she could see and hear were the three men. The two who were facing in her direction met her stare silently, unblinkingly, as if challenging her to do something, anything, to them. Her father's words argued against her growing fury, asking her to simply turn the other cheek and act as if nothing had happened, but the sound of his voice swiftly began to dim. In its stead, she heard her grandmother telling her that she would know what was right and would act accordingly.

What surprised Sophie was *what* she felt was right. With no hesitation, she put one foot in front of the other and began to walk toward the three men, fully aware that with that first step, she could never go back, could never erase what was about to happen. From that moment forward, the consequences would truly be damned.

"Sophie?" Cole asked again, his voice filled with concern.

With each step, Sophie drew ever closer to the strange men. Their booth was the last that lined the long windows looking out onto the street. Thin tendrils of cigarette smoke rose lazily toward the ceiling from ashtrays that sat crowded among the plates of half-eaten food. Two of the men sat facing toward her; the man opposite them gave her only his back. As she neared, two pairs of low-slit eyes followed her intently, their hostility as clear as if they were wolves lying in wait inside the coop for the chickens to come home to roost.

She recognized them both. Riley Mason sat nearest the aisle, his long, dirty fingers drumming a rapid cadence across the tabletop. Barely twenty, with scraggly blond hair that hung limply over a lean, pockmarked face, Riley had a reputation about Victory as a bit of a brawler, more apt to end a disagreement with his fists than with common sense. While he was small of frame, his slight stature hid a whirlwind of violence raging to be set free. His crooked nose and a couple of chipped teeth were testament to that. His deep-set hazel eyes darted over her body in a way that made Sophie's skin crawl.

Beside him, Ellis Watts leaned back into the corner casually, one arm draped along the windowsill. Only a couple of years older than his companion, Ellis had been blessed with movie-star good looks: a chiseled jaw, high cheekbones, broad shoulders, and hair as black as coal. Though he had a name as a charmer, his eyes betrayed him. They were a deeper green than would be found in a forest, and pools of anger and disdain bubbled and festered in their deepest recesses, occasionally overflowing. As sly as a fox, he still had a temper that was hard to reckon with. He'd spent time in jail for a number of offenses, most recently for beating poor John Bauserman to within an inch of his life after an altercation at the tavern. Sophie hadn't known he'd been released. As she looked into those harsh eyes, she knew without a doubt a particular truth.

It was Ellis Watts's eyes that I saw through that burlap hood!

"Just go on and march your pretty self right on back from where you came," Ellis warned before she had come to a stop before their booth. "There ain't nothin' you're gonna find here that's gonna be to your likin'."

"Best do what he says," Riley added.

Hearing Ellis Watts's voice was unnerving. Just like his good looks, his words sounded smooth and alluring, but she could hear the sharp edge lying at the back of his voice as if it were the serrated edge of a saw.

"I heard what you said," Sophie answered as defiantly as she could, straining to keep her voice steady. Though her anger still burned brightly, fear had begun to fray the edges of her courage. Still, she didn't dare look away, instead keeping her eyes locked on the men. "Don't act as if you didn't say it, because I heard every horrible word!"

"And what would that have been?" Ellis challenged, a wisp of a smile curling his lips.

"You must take me for some kind of fool!" Sophie gave right back, her finger punctuating the air with every word even as she struggled to keep it from shaking. "I won't stand to have you saying such things about me or my family! Do you hear me? I won't stand for it!"

"I'll show you what you won't—" Riley barked as he began to push himself up from the table before one of Ellis's hands clamped down on his arm and forced him roughly back to his seat.

"Sit down, Riley," Ellis ordered.

"But, I ain't gonna—" the other man began to argue.

"Don't give me none of that arguin' shit," Ellis hissed sharply through teeth clenched as tight as a steel drum. With his jaw locked tightly, his eyes held Riley as he waited to see if the younger man would find the spine to have any more argument in him. Satisfied that he did not, Ellis turned back to look at Sophie with a sudden smile on his face, a change she found more unsettling than his open menace.

"I can see that whatever you thought you heard got your skirt in a snit," he disagreed, "but you ain't got no idea what we was goin' on about. Hell, for all you know we was talkin' about the war."

"Don't lie to me," Sophie snapped. "I heard what you said."

Rather than anger at being cut off, Ellis's eyes regarded her with amusement. "Now, I know I ain't gonna have no trouble speakin' for Riley and myself when I tell you we ain't the sort of fellas that take too kindly to bein' called liars." He shrugged. "But I can't say the same about Graham here. What about it? You the sort that can stomach that sort of talk?"

For the first time since she had approached the table, Sophie's attention was drawn to the third man. An audible gasp escaped her when she found it to be Graham Grier sharing a booth with the other two ruffians. As clean-cut as the others were rough, Graham had blond hair cut high and tight over his icy blue eyes and thin nose. Broad-shouldered and tall, he wore clothes that were as neat as the rest of him, starched and pressed to perfection. He glanced at her for only a moment, his eyes darting over her face faster than lightning forking across a stormy sky, before his gaze found his plate and stayed there.

Sophie was beside herself with confusion. *Why is Graham Grier sitting at a diner with Riley Mason and Ellis Watts?* She couldn't imagine a stranger gathering. While the other two's exploits around town were well-known and frowned upon, Graham was one of Victory's favorite sons. Not only was his father the mayor, but his mother played the organ at the Lutheran church. Sophie had known Graham and his family ever since the Hellers had first arrived in town. The same age, they'd attended school together, sharing laughs and smiles, never a harsh word between them. Just two years earlier, Graham had nervously asked her to the movies, and though she had politely declined, it hadn't been because of lack of interest, but rather a shyness she had instantly regretted.

"Graham?" she shakily asked.

"Afternoon, Sophie," he mumbled in answer.

"What in heaven's name are you doing with these two?"

Graham's mouth opened slightly as if he were about to answer, but before he could make a sound, Ellis's smooth voice cut him off. "Ain't nothin' wrong with a fella havin' lunch, now is there?"

Sophie never heard Ellis's smart-mouthed question, her gaze still locked upon Graham. When she had first heard the hateful words, the same words she had heard the night her family had been attacked, Sophie had been positive that the three sitting in the booth had been one and the same as the hooded men. Now, looking at her friend, she wasn't as sure. *Could Graham Grier have been one of the men at the barn? Could he have stood by and done nothing as my family was threatened and attacked?*

"Did you have anything to do with it, Graham?" she asked him.

"He ain't got nothin' to say to you," Riley growled, his voice full of danger.

Despite the warning, Sophie persisted, her eyes never leaving Graham. Even though he refused to move his gaze from his half-finished plate of bacon and eggs, she wished he would just glance up, to let her see his eyes, certain that if he did she would see the truth in them. But no matter how hard she wanted him to do as she hoped, Graham refused to budge.

"Graham?" she prodded again. "Did you help these two burn down our barn?"

"Ain't you heard what I said?" Riley barked, his hand snapping out to latch her wrist between his thin fingers. His grip was like a vise and a sharp pain raced up the length of Sophie's arm.

"Ouch." She winced, trying to pull away from Riley's grasp.

A filthy grin spread across the man's face at her discomfort and he gave her an extra squeeze for good measure. "Bitches like you ain't the sort to listen," he snarled. "The only thing you'll mind is a man that ain't got no fear of puttin' his hands on you."

Though both fear and pain filled her, Sophie was surprised to find her anger still remained. It sizzled and then suddenly blazed, raging at the racist slur uttered toward her and her family, against Riley Mason for daring to put his filthy hands on her, and even at her confusion toward Graham. *I refuse to be treated like this!*

"Let go!" she ordered.

"Go to hell!"

Without warning, Sophie's free hand shot out and slapped the brazen man across the face. She struck him hard, the clap of her blow cracking around the diner. For a split second it was as if all of the air had been drawn from the restaurant; even the fans seemed to fall silent. Riley's face was momentarily as shocked as her own, but fury filled his features faster even than the color that had begun to mark his cheek.

What have I done?

Cole sat dumbfounded on his seat as Sophie ignored his question and purposefully walked to the rear of the diner. *She walked away like she was in some kind of trance!* One moment they were laughing easily, getting to know each other a bit, even doing a bit of good-natured teasing, and the next it was as if he didn't even exist. He'd never been good with the ladies, but this was a bit ridiculous, even for him!

"Sophie?" he asked again, but still no answer.

If that isn't a woman for you!

Still, there was something about her

demeanor that was a bit strange. He tried to look past her, to get a glimpse of the men at the table she was approaching, but from where he was sitting, she blocked his line of sight. He hadn't paid much attention to the other patrons when he'd entered and couldn't recall anything about the men. Whoever they were, they certainly attracted her interest more than he had!

Turning back to his meal, Cole couldn't help but sulk. Try as he might, he couldn't drag his attention away from Sophie and the men in the booth. He sipped at his milk and took a bite of his burger, but he could not stop the nagging feeling that something wasn't quite right.

Glancing back at the booth, he caught a glimpse of Sophie's face in profile as she looked down at the man sitting with his back to Cole. Her eyes were wide with surprise, her brow wrinkled in thought.

What the heck's going on back there?

Shifting on his stool, Cole once again tried to get a better look at the men. The only one he could see was the one facing him and nearest to the window. While not a bad-looking sort, he didn't like the way he was leering at Sophie; something in his eyes had long since gone rotten. Vaguely, Cole thought he knew the man. Willis or Wilkens. No, it was Watts.

Ellis Watts!

Something soured in Cole's stomach at the realization that Sophie was talking to one of the biggest bastards in Victory. Ellis Watts had been bad news all the way back in their first school days and time had done nothing to change him. Thankfully, Ellis had been several years older and far too preoccupied with his own hoodlum shenanigans to care much about the disabled boy. Still, he was a cancer upon the whole town. Cole turned to look for Marge, to see if she knew what was going on, when the sound of Sophie's curt voice shot across the diner.

"Let go!" she barked.

"Go to hell!" a man's voice answered.

Without a moment's thought, Cole was off his stool and making his way as quickly as he could to the rear of the restaurant. Even over such a short distance, the going was hard. He struggled to make his left leg swivel and plant before propelling himself forward. He was only halfway there when the sharp crack of a slap momentarily slowed him.

"You goddamn bitch!"

Willing himself to move faster than he had ever moved before, Cole managed to hobble the remaining distance between him and Sophie. Snatching her by the arm, he quickly pulled her behind him, freeing her from the grip of the other man while nearly yanking her from her feet, and took her place before the stranger's fury.

The man had risen from his seat, his eyes dancing wildly with both anger and surprise. He was shorter and smaller of build than Cole, but appeared no less dangerous, his fists balled and cocked as if he were more than ready to throw the first blow.

"Don't even think about it," Cole said.

"Who the hell are you?" the man snorted derisively.

"You better put your hands down or you're going to find out that I'm not as easy a target as she might have been," Cole warned. It had been a long time since he'd been in any type of scrape, but he was no stranger to using his fists; growing up with his bad leg had brought him a lot of unwanted attention and he'd had to defend himself often. If the stranger wanted to throw down, he'd get more than his share in return. *I may not come out the winner, but this son of a bitch is going to know he was in a fight!*

"This ain't none of your concern," the man said, his eyes uncertain.

"You made it so."

Before another word could be spoken, deep, rich laughter rang out from Ellis Watts's mouth. He cackled wildly, slapping one palm down on the table with so much force that all of the silverware jumped.

"Now, don't that just beat all," he hooted. "We got us a war involvin' the Krauts breakin' out right here in the middle of Victory!"

Cole opened his mouth to argue but fell silent as the sound of sobs reached his ear. He spun on his heel to find Sophie breaking down into tears behind him. Her hands rose to her mouth, covering her trembling lips. Her gaze held his for a long second before she ran back down the length of the counter, her shoulders shaking.

"Sophie!" he shouted. "Wait!" But she was already out the door and gone.

"Now ain't that just like a woman."

Cole turned back around at Ellis Watts's words. The man was casually sipping at his coffee but his wolfish eyes never left Cole.

"What did you say to her?" Cole demanded of him.

"The three of us was just enjoyin' a bite to eat when she came over, accusin' us of somethin' or other, and got all out of shape," Ellis explained, waving to his other companions. For the first time, Cole took stock of the third stranger; staring downward at his plate, the man gave off the air that he wished he were somewhere else.

"I bet her story is a mite different," Cole suggested.

"A woman's always is."

"Stay away from her."

"Or you'll do what?" the younger man asked, some of his bravery returning.

Though he prided himself on being a man of intelligence, a man who would not jump to using his fists easily, Cole knew with certainty that he would do whatever he could to protect Sophie Heller from these men. He was equally certain that

that was precisely what it would come to. He wouldn't leave her to their mercy.

"You don't want to find out."

Before they could offer an answer, Cole turned and walked away as steadily as he could, all the while waiting for them to start laughing at him, to make fun of his disability, but was instead met with a silence that chilled him straight to the bone. These were dangerous men, of that there was no doubt.

"We'll be seein' you, hero," Ellis called after him. "You can bet on that."

Chapter Seven

TEARS STREAMED DOWN Sophie's cheeks as she hurried from the diner, crossed the empty street, and rushed down the opposite sidewalk. The wetness in her eyes made it hard to see where she was going and she nearly collided with an elderly man as he left the barber shop. Mumbling her apologies, she kept on. More than a few heads turned to watch her pass but she paid them no mind, rushing on as more sobs racked her body.

The encounter at the diner had unnerved her. She knew in her heart that Ellis Watts, Riley Mason, and, as hard as it was for her to truly believe, Graham Grier had been the hooded men who had attacked her family. The three of them had burned the barn, beaten her father, and threatened her own life. Though she felt sure of the horrible truth, she could not stop the questions that raced across her confused and distraught mind.

Why do they carry such hatred for my family?

Now that I know who they are, to what lengths will they be willing to go to keep me silent?

How could Graham have become mixed up with such men?

When Cole Ambrose rescued her from Riley's grasp, pulling her behind him and out of harm's way, her relief had been great. Not only had her wrist been freed from that wild man's painful grasp, but she had also been removed from Graham's side. Only then had her confusion been temporarily broken. She wished she had thanked Cole for rushing to her aide, for selflessly standing up for her, but it was a sentiment that would have to wait.

With every step, the memories of her past with Graham pummeled her: how they had played down on the dry creek bed as children, soon after the Hellers had arrived in America; helping him with his arithmetic in school; and the anxious look on his face when he had finally given voice to his feelings for her. *Was all of this because I rejected him?* On many a late night she had lain in bed, staring at the blanket of stars outside her window, wondering what would have happened if she had answered differently. But now it was too late . . . far too late for all of them, it seemed.

Soon, Sophie found herself in front of the *Victory Gazette* office, but instead of heading inside and returning to work, she kept on walking. It had been hard enough to go about her business that morning; now, with what had happened at the diner, she knew it would be impossible. She wouldn't be able to hide her tears from her coworkers, and lying to them would only make her feel worse.

But if not work, then where do I go?

Sophie knew that she couldn't stay in town, not with every face searching hers, wondering why she was so upset. Surprisingly, she didn't fear the three men chasing after her; confusion and shame had completely replaced her fright. Though her father wasn't supposed to pick her up from work for hours, she set her feet toward the edge of town, determined to walk the four miles to her family's farm. Once she got outside of Victory's limits, she was certain there would be no one to hear her cry.

Cole Ambrose burst from the diner's door, looked up both sides of the street, and gave a silent curse that he could see no sign of Sophie Heller. Where in the heck had she gone? He'd hurried from the three men's table, slapped a few coins on the counter to settle his bill, and headed outside as fast as he could, but it appeared that he hadn't moved quickly enough. *Damn my leg!* Still, he was determined to catch up with her and make sure she was all right. For a moment he hesitated, unsure of which way to turn, before deciding upon the center of town, and he began to hobble off in his search.

Try as he might, he couldn't make heads or tails of what had happened in the diner. It had been hard enough to understand why Sophie had walked away from him as she had, but it had been made all the more confusing when he had recognized just *who* sat in the rear booth. Ellis Watts was not the sort of man he expected an intelligent and vivacious young woman like Sophie to know; approaching a no-good thug like him was even further out of the question. His companion, the scraggly man who had grabbed her by the wrist, looked to have been cut from much the same cloth. Though he hadn't taken a good look at the third man, Cole couldn't imagine him to have been much better.

What had they said or done to make Sophie so upset?

Why had that son of a bitch put his filthy hands on her?

Even if he were to find Sophie and offer her his help, would she want it?

What further confused Cole were the strange feelings stirring in his own gut. Though he'd only spoken to Sophie for a couple of minutes, he had felt *something* for her. He liked her smile, the sound of her voice, her laugh, and especially the way she looked. It had been a long while since he'd felt comfortable around a woman, comfortable enough to not be painfully aware of his own handicap; it was a feeling that he wanted to get to know a bit better. To do that, he would have to find her.

Where the heck had she disappeared to so fast?

Hurrying as fast as he could on his bad leg, Cole rounded the corner near the Victory Bank and Trust and slowed to a stop. Sweating under the glare of the blistering sun, he sucked air in ragged gasps, his shirt clinging tightly to his skin. His bad leg throbbing steadily, he peered up both ends of the street, hopeful for some sign of Sophie. But strain as he might, he couldn't find her tear-streaked face among the few people hearty enough to brave the Victory summer.

"Damn it," he muttered.

He was just about to give up and trudge back home when he caught sight of her off in the distance, nearly lost among the heat shimmers. Though she was little more than a speck approaching the horizon, he was sure that he recognized her white blouse and dark skirt. She was heading east on Colvin Road toward Baker's Corner; her family must live out that way. She was farther in the distance than he had estimated, but thankfully she hadn't completely vanished from sight.

But what am I supposed to do now?

Even if his leg hadn't been deformed, she was far enough ahead of him that he would have a hard time catching up to her. Certainly, it would do no good for him to shout her name; he'd have better luck being heard over the roar of a tornado! Indecision racked him, but slowly the realization of what he needed to do dawned on him.

Cole turned on his heel and headed for home as quickly as he could.

Wiping sweat from her brow, Sophie gazed down the long road that stretched out before her. A scattering of thin clouds scudded across the distant horizon, the only stain on an otherwise perfectly blue sky. The sun hung fat above her, having just begun to dip toward the west, its heat as intense as it was relentless. The faint smell of wildflowers drifted on a lazy breeze far too light to offer any relief.

She had already walked most of the way home; she guessed that she'd covered three of the four miles since she'd just passed the Moores' farm. Up ahead, the road began to fall away as the countryside dipped toward the river, but she swore that she could see the charred remains of the family barn in the distance. Though she was tired and thirsty, she'd soon be home.

And safe . . .

Since leaving Victory, she'd been able to do little else than replay her awful confrontation with Ellis, Riley, and Graham. It had been nothing short of a nightmare! Every step recounted harsh words, menacing stares, and the paralyzing fear she had felt upon being grabbed. But while she had been truly shaken by the whole ordeal, shedding more salty tears as she solemnly walked, she had soon found herself unable to cry any further.

She worried about what she would say to her father when he asked why she wasn't at work. As much as she hated to admit it, Sophie thought that Hermann Heller might just have been right all along; if she'd only turned the other cheek at the diner and not approached the men when they'd hissed at her, nothing would have happened. Instead, she'd gone against her father's advice and it had cost her.

Now she would have to explain why she was home from work early; she certainly felt sick enough to her stomach over all that had happened that it wouldn't be much of a fib to say she wasn't feeling well.

I don't feel right about lying to my family, but how can I possibly tell them the truth?

If she were to tell her family of her tale in the diner, it would do nothing but cause them more worry. To give faces and names to the hooded men would make the night-mares that terrorized Karl worse and would cause her mother and grandmother to fret even more. Her father would snort, bellow about how he would not be forced from his home, and then proceed to chide her about her foolishness in approaching such men. She needed to stay quiet, to keep her story to . . .

From somewhere far behind her, a horn honked. Turning around to look up the road, Sophie could see a pickup truck approach-ing in the distance, dust billowing up in clouds from the gravel road. Though it was a little less than a mile back, it was closing quickly. *Could it be Ellis Watts, Riley Ma-*

son, or even Graham Grier coming after me?

With every quickly passing second, Sophie weighed what she should do. Far too tired to go bounding from the road into the cornfields, she knew that she wouldn't truly be safe even if she made it that far; the men would certainly hunt her down in minutes. Besides, if the driver of the truck was someone who meant to do her harm, why would he honk and announce his presence? It would have been much easier to just run her down without warning and be done with it.

Resigned to learning the driver's identity, Sophie stepped to the side of the road and waited as the truck steadily approached through the shimmering heat, finally revealed to be well kept and black in color, though covered in dust from the road. It slowed as it neared her, its engine rumbling.

Through the dusty windshield, Sophie could see that the driver was Cole Ambrose and her heart made a soft flutter that surprised her. He brought the truck to a stop and smiled easily at her through the open window on the passenger side. Even in the glare of the bright summer day, she thought his blue eyes shimmered as he regarded her. Still, a simmering anger suddenly bubbled over within her and Sophie found she could only scowl in return.

"Were you following me?" she asked accusingly.

Surprise wrote itself across Cole's face just as clearly as the words in a book. He was momentarily taken aback, his warm smile vanishing, and he stammered his answer. "It's . . . it's not like that, Sophie," he said defensively. "I tried to hurry after you once you'd left the diner, but I only managed to see you walking in the distance. I drove out here to see if I could give you a lift."

As grateful as she was for Cole's help in the diner and, as equally relieved as she was to find him behind the pickup's wheel, something prevented Sophie from meeting his answer with a smile. Too much had already happened to her, too many fears had become far too real, for her to be so trusting. She could only think of her father's words, of how not listening to them had cost her dearly, and she found herself resigned to bearing her burden alone.

I cannot trust anyone!

"I'm fine," she answered. "I'm almost home."

"It's still awfully uncomfortable in the hot sun," he offered, his smile slowly returning as he looked out the windshield at the road ahead. "You're the only one out here under it. Everyone else has enough sense to stay in the shade where it's cool. Heck, even the cows know better! If I were in your shoes, I believe I'd be more than a bit grateful to get out of this heat, even for a short while."

"I don't have a problem with walking."

Once again, Sophie began to head up the road, intent upon leaving Cole and his offer of a ride far behind her, but she hadn't gone more than a couple of steps before she heard the crunch of gravel under the pickup's wheels. She stubbornly stared straight ahead as he came alongside her, matching the speed of the truck to her own.

"You're covered in sweat," he observed.

"I don't even notice it."

"Come on now," he chided her. "Don't be stubborn!"

"I'm not being stubborn," she shot back, giving him a quick sideways glance. She saw that he was watching her intently, his lean but muscled forearm resting easily on top of the steering wheel. The sudden thought struck her that he was handsome and she turned away for fear she would blush.

"If you're not being stubborn then you're being silly," he kept on.

"Maybe I am."

"Where's the harm in accepting a ride?"

"This from the man that admits to following me," she gave back. "You're a nearly complete stranger I've never met before today. For all I know, you're the sort of man that likes to follow young women home in order to abduct them and have your way with them."

Cole jammed on the brakes and the pickup ground to a sudden halt beside her. The unexpected abruptness of his action startled her and she couldn't help but do the same, jumping away from the road, her heart thumping wildly in her chest. When she turned to him, his smile was gone, replaced by a piercing gaze of seriousness.

"I'm not going to hurt you, Sophie," he said, his voice determined and firm. "My intentions in coming after you were just as

I said: I only wanted to check if you'd needed a ride. After everything that happened at the diner, I think you have plenty of reasons to trust me."

The sincerity in his voice gave Sophie pause. Though she had met Cole Ambrose only an hour earlier, she could feel that there was a depth to him, a strength in the way he carried himself that put her at ease. While she felt betrayed by Graham's actions, confused by the way he had broken her trust, she found herself believing what Cole told her.

"I don't think you'll hurt me," she heard herself answer.

"I'm not like the men at the diner," he added.

"No, you're not."

"Then you've got nothing to lose in letting me take you home, do you?"

Sophie could only nod as she glanced at the painted sign on the truck door: AMBROSE HARDWARE. Wiping the sweat from her eyes with a sigh, she pulled open the door to the pickup and climbed inside. Though the inside of the truck was as hot as an oven, she felt relief to be out of the sun. She gave Cole a quick smile as he put the truck into gear and they began to head down the road, a cooling breeze rushing through the open windows.

Sophie expected Cole to ask her about what had happened at the diner, about how she had come to be mixed up with such men, but he surprised her by doing nothing of the sort. Though the drive to the farm was short, he instead inquired about her and her family, about how long she had worked at the newspaper, and he even spoke more of his trepidation of returning to Victory from Chicago. She was so intent on what he had to say that she nearly let him drive right past her home, telling him so late that the truck skidded a bit before stopping.

She blushed. "Sorry."

"Not a problem."

Cole pulled the truck into the long drive that fronted the farm and followed the route as it twisted past a pair of apple trees before bringing the whole of the property into view. The two-story farmhouse sat quiet around the bend, laundry hanging limply on the line, drying quickly in the summer sun. A quick wave of relief washed over Sophie when she saw there was no one else around the property; accepting Cole's offer had been awkward enough without having to introduce him to the rest of the Hellers. Still, she felt uneasy. Though it had been weeks since the barn had been burned to the ground, seeing its charred remains sent a shiver racing across Sophie's skin and her hand involuntarily rose to the spot on her head where her bump had once been. *It still seems so real!* Cole drove up to the farmhouse, shut off the engine, and whistled as he caught sight of the black skeletal frame of the barn.

"That must have been one heck of a fire."

"It was."

"What happened?" Cole prodded. "Was it lightning?"

"My father—" she started, beginning to tell Cole the story that her family had stuck to ever since that fateful night, that her father had simply tipped over a lantern, but something stopped her. Shame colored Sophie's cheeks at the thought of so blatantly lying to the man who had shown her nothing but kindness. "—wants to rebuild," she said instead, finishing with a truth that still didn't answer his question.

"That won't be an easy task."

"My father is the sort of man who doesn't shy away from hard work."

"I'd imagine not." He chuckled. "What with raising you, and all."

This time, Sophie was certain she had blushed.

"Just make sure that he speaks with my father down at the hardware store," Cole explained. At the reference to his father, Cole's smile appeared to falter, but only for a moment. "It's going to take an awful lot of wood and nails to put that back together again!"

"I should probably get inside," Sophie explained, desperately wanting to stop talking about the barn, her head still dizzy from learning the identities of the men who were responsible. "I don't want my mother . . ."

"Let me get the door for you."

Before she could tell him that it wasn't necessary, Cole was already getting out of the truck. Oddly, he stood still for a moment as if he were steadying himself before heading around the front of the pickup. His pace was slow, almost labored. As he went along, he kept one hand on the hood, his gait unseemly and awkward, his left shoulder dipping lower with every step.

What is going on here?

Finally, when he reached her door and pulled it open, beads of sweat lined across his forehead. As he shut the door behind her, she couldn't help but glance down at his feet. She had to stifle a gasp at what she saw; his left leg seemed smaller, almost shriveled underneath his trousers, and his foot lay at an awkward, unnatural angle. Until that very moment, Sophie hadn't realized that he had any infirmity; when she had first met Cole at the diner, and even when he had come to her defense at the rear of the restaurant, she simply hadn't noticed. She hoped he hadn't observed her glance, but when she looked back up, his eyes held hers and he smiled knowingly.

"I'm . . . I'm sorry . . ." she stammered.

"It's all right," he assured her, though she thought she could see in his eyes that it wasn't. "It's nothing I'm not used to."

Sophie didn't know what to say. She knew that she shouldn't look upon this kind man any differently for his infirmity, but she couldn't help herself. She'd never met someone with Cole's particular handicap, though she knew that this was hardly an excuse for gawking. After the way he had risen to her defense at the diner, she knew the last thing she should do was judge him, but she found it impossible to do otherwise. Shame caused tears to well in the corners of her eyes. She was about to try to apologize further, to somehow make up for her embarrassment, when he spoke.

"Given the circumstances, it was awfully nice to meet you, Sophie Heller," he said as he offered her his hand. "And thank you kindly for trusting me enough to give you a ride home."

She took his hand as a tear loosened and coursed down her cheek. "I'm the one who should be thanking you," she managed before the dam of her emotions collapsed and she found herself rushing away from the truck toward the farmhouse.

She was so upset with herself that she never once looked back, never noticed Cole limping back around the front of the pickup, and was never aware of the curtain of her grandmother's upstairs room slowly swinging shut.

Chapter Eight

WHERE IN THE HELL'S Graham?" Riley Mason barked.

"Keep your shirt on."

Ellis Watts leaned back in his chair and took a long drag on his cigarette before blowing a thick plume of smoke toward the ceiling of his small shack on the outskirts of Victory. The milky cloud wafted lazily around the lone naked bulb that lit the room.

"He's late!"

"He'll be here," Ellis insisted.

He reached for the whiskey bottle that sat on his makeshift table and hoisted it to his lips. He took a lengthy slug of the dark liquor, then dropped the bottle to the table with a clatter and absently wiped his mouth with the back of his hand.

Goddamn, that whiskey burned all the way to his toes!

"He knows we was countin' on him showin' up," Riley groused as he ran a thin hand through his scraggly blond hair. He paced like a caged animal before the cracked and dirty window that looked back toward town. "I ain't likin' a-waitin'. If he ain't here right quick, he's gonna find himself with a fat lip!"

"What's got your ass up?"

"It's on account of that shitty Kraut bitch, that's what," the wiry man said with a snarl, his nostrils flaring and his eyes wide. "Walkin' on over to us in that damn diner! She knowed we'd not put up with it."

Ellis hardly needed to close his eyes to see Sophie Heller walking the length of the diner, approaching their booth with a look on her pretty little face that was equal parts anger and fear. He had to admit that she had surprised him; he hadn't figured on her being quite so brave. He was sure that he hadn't shown his surprise, but it shamed him a bit just the same. If she wasn't one of them no-good Krauts bent on destroying his country, he reckoned he might even begrudgingly respect her.

"I shoulda just slapped her," Riley argued.

"What you should have done was stay planted on your ass and not said even one goddamn word," Ellis gave right back, rehashing an argument they'd been having ever since they'd left the diner. "That would have been the smart play but we both know that ain't your way. Instead, you had to get all uppity and ended up actin' the fool. Just like I done told you a dozen times already, it was your big mouth that got her attention in the first place."

"I didn't say nothin' that you hadn't said before."

"And that's why now she knows who did it," Ellis growled, utterly exhausted of having to explain himself over and over, especially to a fool like Riley. "Even after all that, if you could have somehow managed to hold your tongue, she woulda just walked away without much fuss. Now you might have done screwed it all up."

"Sorry, Ellis," the younger man whined. "I just thought I was doin' what you wanted."

"Then you should quit thinkin'."

Ellis's eyes drifted over Riley Mason. With the scant hair on his face and his patched-up clothing, he resembled a boy more than a man. Lean and nervous, his hands constantly fidgeting, Ellis had never met someone so eager to please. He was just like a faithful dog; only this mutt had just as much chance of biting someone's hand off as it did of actually doing what it was told. Still, he had to admit that Riley had his uses. So far, he'd managed to hold his own. *I've just gotta keep him on a tight leash.*

"It's too late to change it now, anyways," Ellis offered by way of reconciliation.

"Then where do we go from here?"

"That's what we're waitin' on Graham for."

The sorry truth of the matter was that Ellis didn't know what they should do next. When he'd first come up with the idea of driving the damn Germans away from his town, everything had seemed to come easy: planning when they should strike, what they should wear, and just how far they were willing to go seemed as simple as falling out of bed. But now, after the confrontation in the diner, that ease seemed to have changed for the worse. Indecision racked his thoughts, urging him to lash out, to strike faster and harder than before, but something also nagged at him, warning him to be smart, not to take any unnecessary risks.

"Is Graham gonna be all right?" Riley asked.

"All right with what?"

"With what it is that we're doin'," the younger man said with a shrug. "When that bitch done come by the table, he didn't seem too right . . . like he was soft or somethin'. He gonna be able to hold his own if it comes to it?"

"You leave the worryin' to me."

"I'm just sayin' . . ."

"Graham ain't gonna have much choice in the matter," Ellis snarled. "Not on account of what we know. If he finds himself gettin' a little weak in the gut, it ain't gonna take much to remind him of what he stands to lose. The last thing he is gonna want anybody to know is that he ain't as perfect as he looks. Believe me, a warnin' will be more than enough to get him right back in step."

Ellis might have talked a good show in front of Riley, but he knew that what his fellow conspirator said was the plain truth; that Graham Grier was the weak link in their plan. But he also knew that they needed his help, his money, and most important, his influence in Victory. Without it, they were doomed to fail. That was why he'd put up with Graham's shortcomings; he'd just have to take pains to remind the man of what they knew, and remind him of all he had to lose.

"What's to keep her from goin' to the police, then?" Riley asked. "She knows we was the ones that done it."

"She won't."

"How can you be so sure?"

"Because she ain't nothin' but a scared woman, that's why," Ellis explained, his voice as edgy as his mood. "Provin' that we did it ain't gonna be easy. She'll be too worried about what we'd do to her family to take the chance."

"I hope you're right," Riley worried.

"I am."

"I couldn't go to jail."

"You ain't gonna," Ellis said. "You're gonna have to trust me on that."

"But now that the Kraut bitch knows it was us, we ain't got no choice but to go ahead and finish the job," Riley said, giving voice to Ellis's own baser instincts. "How hard would it be for us to make our way back out to that farm and catch her unawares? Hell, it ain't like we got much choice. Like I said, she already knows it was us!"

"And that's just why we can't do nothin'."

"What do you mean?"

"There were other people in that there diner," Ellis began to explain, hoping that Riley would be smart enough to follow. "When you stood up and grabbed her by the wrist, well, people just ain't gonna forget seein' that sort of thing. If anything were to happen to that bitch now, it wouldn't take much for folks to tie it to what you done to her in that diner. Before you knew it, the police would be on you like stink on shit."

"So we can't do nothin'?"

"Not for now."

"Goddamn it," Riley complained. "Why the hell did she have to come over?"

Because you opened your big mouth, that's why!

Ellis turned his frustration at Riley toward

himself. In hindsight, it hadn't been a good idea for all three of them to be seen together in town; they'd just been asking for trouble. His error now meant they would have to be extra careful and bide their time even if that was the last thing they wanted to do. Though he'd just been trying to do his part, to drive the Nazis out from their midst, he wasn't fool enough to believe that all of his fellow townspeople would see it the same way. No, it was best if they didn't draw too much attention to themselves. Once things quieted down, then they could act.

"What about the cripple?" Riley asked.

"What about him?"

"Who in the hell was he and what was he doin' stickin' his nose where it just don't belong?" Riley pulled a pack of smokes from his shirt's breast pocket and proceeded to light one, striking a match on the heel of his ragged boot. "I ain't been in this here town but a couple of years and his ain't a face I recognize."

"That's Jason Ambrose's brother," Ellis explained. "If I remember right, his name is Cole. He must have been sweet on the Kraut. Thought that playin' the hero might be how he could charm his way into her pants."

"He gonna be trouble?"

"Naw," Ellis chuckled. "Not if I remember him the way I think I do."

"What are you sayin'?"

"Cole Ambrose ain't the sort of fella that measures up. What with that bad leg of his, he's the kind that stands to the side and watches as things get done. That's the way it was when he was a boy and that's the way it's gonna be now he thinks he's a man. He's gonna get in our way about as likely as he's gonna go off to war."

"But what if that ain't the way he thinks about it?" Riley argued, small lines of worry knitting their way across his forehead. "Sure didn't seem like the sort that's accustomed to watchin' this afternoon."

"That's on account of the German," Ellis snorted. "Hell, it ain't as if you and I ain't never gotten in over our heads because some cheap twitchy twat raised her skirt and gave us a whiff. He's just gone and bitten off more than he can chew is all."

"And suppose that he wants another bite?"

"Let him take it." The older man shrugged. "What harm can he do?"

"I'm just sayin' . . ."

Ellis Watts took another long pull on his whiskey and didn't speak until the last drop of alcohol had landed in the bucket of his gut. His thoughts swam with the booze but he was able to find land. When he finally spoke, his eyes were little more than slits and his words a growled whisper.

"If Cole Ambrose interferes in our business, it ain't gonna make no goddamn difference if he's an American and a cripple," he warned. "I promise you it'll be the last thing he ever does."

Graham Grier hurried down the road in the scant light left to the day. The last rays of the setting sun clung to the far horizon, leaving blazing reds and purples that colored the hazy low clouds. A curious wind sniffed at his feet, chasing along behind him and stirring the dust. The impending gloom of nightfall was appropriate; it more than matched his mood.

As he quickened his already fast pace, Graham kept his eyes on the road and his shoulders hunched. Though darkness was falling, the chance of his being recognized heading to Ellis Watts's shanty was still greater than he would have liked. If someone were to see him now, if he were to be recognized . . .

Why in the hell am I doing this?

Loath as he was to admit it to himself, Graham already knew the answer to his unspoken question, and the truth nearly made him sick. In a moment of weakness, Sophie's words of rejection still echoing in his mind, he'd turned to another woman in solace. But that had just been the beginning. He thought about that fateful night often; he often marveled at how fast his excitement had turned into abject shame, and he still had a hard time accepting responsibility. Coming to grips with what he had done was harder than he would have imagined. The results had been disastrous. Even if he wasn't entirely certain of his own guilt, he knew that simply being accused of his crime would be a wound from which he and his father's honor would not be able to recover. That one moment, that one instant of weakness, had led directly to his current predicament.

No matter how you look at it, you know what you did!

Still, the events of the last couple of weeks haunted Graham. Everything had gone faster than he had thought possible; it was as if he were rushing down a steep hill in the midst of a heavy spring rain, unable to get his footing, let alone stop. It had all felt inevitable; from his reckless actions in another woman's arms to the burning of the Hellers' barn. It seemed to have happened in little more than the blink of an eye. Even now, he couldn't believe he had been part of it.

How could I . . . how could I have done this to Sophie?

Try as he might, Graham could not erase the image of Sophie in the diner. When Ellis had first noticed her coming in the door, Graham had uttered a silent prayer that she wouldn't notice them. But when Riley had opened his big mouth, the slur that came out made Graham's skin crawl, and he'd known his wishes had no chance to be answered. When she approached the table, he'd tried to remain perfectly still, so as not to draw her attention, but she had noticed him just the same, just as he supposed he deserved.

"What in heaven's name are you doing with these two?" she'd said.

Graham hadn't been able to so much as look at Sophie, so great was his shame. It was already enough to hear the shock and disbelief in her voice; if he had had to gaze into her eyes, he would not have been able to bear it. As painful as it was for him to admit, he was still in love with Sophie Heller. He supposed he'd been in love with her from the first moment they met. Even the bitter sting of rejection had done little to quiet the intense feelings he had for her. He had been dejected, even a bit angry, but he still believed that Sophie would eventually return his romantic longings and that they would be together . . . together forever. What he had done next was supposed to have been temporary, nothing but a ripple in the long and wide river of his life . . . but he had made a mistake.

A mistake that costs me to this very day!

Ellis Watts had discovered his secret. Graham didn't know how the bastard had found him out, but the answer hardly mattered. Armed with such knowledge, it took little effort for a man such as Ellis to entice Graham into doing his bidding; the threat of his secret being revealed was enough to force him to toe the line. He knew that it was his closeness to Sophie that Ellis and Riley needed, that and the fact that his father was Victory's mayor and wouldn't want to see his son locked up behind bars. Graham was absolutely certain that the Hellers were no more Nazi agents than he was, but squeezed between a rock and a hard place, he had little choice but to go along with the men's plan.

I'm nothing but a goddamn pawn!

That fact had never been clearer than the night the Hellers had been attacked. Graham had done nothing but stand silently by as Sophie's father had been bludgeoned into a bloody mess. He'd been too frightened, too interested in protecting his own skin to even move. Some part of him had wanted to stop it all, to protect the woman he truly loved by putting a stop to Ellis's madness, but in the end, protecting his secret had been more important. After all, his own life, as well as that of his father, had hung in the balance.

Slowly, the outline of Ellis Watts's home came into view in the scant light left to the day. Little more than a shack, its doorway sagged as if it were an elderly woman, and the roof was covered in pieces of tin that had been haphazardly patched together to provide a ramshackle defense from the elements. Just looking at the dump gave Graham a shiver of disgust. The light from a bare bulb shone dully through the cracked windows that fronted the place.

How in the hell do people live this way?

Graham paused outside for a moment, composing himself and gathering his thoughts in the prayer that he could somehow endure another meeting with these despicable men. Sighing deeply, he knocked three times and entered.

"Where in the hell you been?" Riley barked before the door had even shut behind him.

"I'm here, aren't I?" Graham shot in answer. His contempt for Riley was obvious. Ellis Watts was a dangerous man in his own right, but Riley Mason was nothing but a follower, a pistol needing only to be aimed and fired.

"Don't you dare take that tone of voice with me! I'll show you—"

"You ain't gonna do a goddamn thing," Ellis snapped. He leaned back casually in his chair, savoring the lingering taste of his whiskey with the air of a man enjoying a Sunday afternoon social, even if his choice of words suited a whore more than a preacher. "Save all that rotten piss and vinegar you been storin' up for them Nazis and what I got planned next."

"What are we going to do?" Graham asked, sick to his gut that there would be more violence.

Ellis Watts leaned forward and smiled as he lightly rubbed the fresh stubble on his square jaw. His eyes danced and Graham came to the sudden, sickening revelation that Ellis enjoyed all of this; terrorizing helpless people and inflicting pain upon them was his pleasure.

"I do believe," Ellis said, "that these folks just ain't scared enough."

Chapter Nine

COLE'S FIRST THOUGHT upon waking was of Sophie. Bright yellow and orange sunlight flooded through a crack in the drawn curtains of his eastern window, announcing the day to the accompaniment of the noisy chirping of birds. He absently ran a hand through his tousled hair, stretched, and gave one last yawn before getting out of bed. All the while, his head was filled with the memory of the easy smile she had given him at the diner, the sweet sound of her voice, and even the woman smell of her as she rode beside him in the truck.

Still, his wonder was tempered by the

many questions that continued to roll around in his thoughts . . .

What did Ellis Watts have to do with Sophie Heller?

Who was the man who violently grabbed her by the wrist?

Was it the confrontation at the diner or the sight of my crippled leg that sent her running to the house in tears?

Would she tell me the truth were I to ask?

The most difficult question for Cole to answer was how he was going to meet her again; that he wanted to spend more time in Sophie's company was a given, he just had no idea how to go about making it happen. He knew where she lived and where she worked, but he felt uncomfortable with the idea of simply showing up at either place uninvited. Confusion raged in his head as he dressed and made ready for the day.

At the head of the tall staircase, Cole sighed deeply. Every day held the same problem; to slowly and carefully descend the treacherous steps, making sure to set his bad leg before moving, for fear he would tumble forward and be seriously injured. It would take only one wobble, one misplaced step, and he would be gone. Though it would have been much easier to stay in the small guestroom on the ground floor, he took a measure of pride in refusing to leave the room in which he had grown up. Going up and down the stairs was a time-consuming and arduous task, but one that he deliberately overcame. Cautiously, he began to descend the steps.

Halfway down the staircase, Cole paused. His eyes held fast to the still distant bottom of the steps and he could not help but be assaulted by memories of his mother, of the horrific sight of her lying broken and bleeding on that very floor. As long as he lived, this image would haunt him. Even after all of the intervening years, he had never fully healed from that day, but being back in his father's home made the pain feel as raw as an open wound. Not for the first time, he wondered how his father managed to bear his grief; after all, he had to look upon that spot every day.

What if I had gone for help? What if I hadn't been so afraid? No wonder he hates me so . . .

Robert Ambrose sat silently at the kitchen

table. Dressed for work in a shirt and tie, his hair slickly pomaded, he stared over his small glasses into the newspaper, a plate of bacon and eggs half-eaten before him. When Cole entered the room, he didn't look up.

After pouring himself a cup of black coffee, Cole leaned back against the stove and looked at his father. He'd been back in town only a couple of days, but it was long enough for him to realize that little or nothing had changed between them. For the most part, it was as if each was living alone, but when they did happen to run into each other, no more than a few words were exchanged, often less than between complete strangers on the street. If he were to remain silent, Cole was certain that this morning would be no different. He resigned himself to change that.

"Do you know the Hellers?" Cole asked. The question sounded awkward in the previously silent room. "They have a farm out to the east on Colvin Road, just before Baker's Corner."

"I do," his father answered, his eyes never leaving the newspaper.

"Did they come to you for supplies for a new barn?"

"Hermann placed an order with me right after the fire," Robert explained in a tone that Cole thought contained no small amount of weariness. "They're waiting for one last delivery from Springfield before they start building. It shouldn't be more than a few days before the order is filled."

"That's good to hear."

"What interest do you have in the Hellers?" Robert asked, looking up from the table for the first time, his hazel eyes locked upon his son.

"I met Sophie Heller in town yesterday afternoon and gave her a ride back out to their farm," Cole explained, happy to have finally garnered some attention from his father. "She seemed like a nice girl. I wondered if her family traded with you. It's a shame their barn burned. I suppose I was a bit worried about her is all."

"You should worry less about a girl you just met and more about your job," Robert shot back in answer. "Such a thing isn't becoming to a teacher. You have enough on your plate without running after Sophie

Heller. All that'll come of it is that you'll set tongues to wagging."

The venom in his father's words momentarily stunned Cole. The hope that he'd had that they would finally be able to find some common ground on which to speak, to begin the slow process of healing their many wounds, vanished. It was as if his father was itching for a fight and choosing his words to ensure that one occurred.

How can he possibly be happy being so bitter?

Cole's blood began to heat up. Ever since the day his mother had been tragically taken from him, he'd felt as if he'd been unfairly judged by his father. The fear in seeing his mother's broken body had overwhelmed him. He'd been a child! Now the anger and resentment that he'd felt upon returning to Victory rose with a vengeance. When he'd first voiced his displeasure to his father on the staircase, he'd been met with a stinging rebuke. This time, he promised himself that he wouldn't let his father simply walk away.

"You've no need to speak to me that way," he defiantly declared.

"I'll stop doing so only when you've started to use your head."

"I'm no longer the boy I was when I left."

"You won't be much different as a man."

"How would you know?" Cole barked, his anger rising to color his face. "It's only been a couple of days since I returned and you still haven't taken a moment's time to talk with me!"

"And I told you then . . . I know exactly who you are, Cole."

"No, you don't," he snapped, bringing his coffee cup down on the stove with a bang. "Don't you dare suppose that you know anything about me! I'm not a kid. Through nothing but my own hard work, I've clawed and fought to build my own life. I'm going to be a teacher . . . something to be proud of. Why is it so wrong of me to expect you to respect what I've done?"

"Then why did you come back here?" Robert asked, setting down the paper and turning all his attention on his son, refusing to answer his question and instead asking one of his own. "If you'd managed to build this new life, why not just stay in Chicago? Surely you could have found a teaching job there. Why return to Victory?"

"Because this is my home! Because—"

Cole was cut off in midsentence by the sound of a car door banging shut and footsteps on the back porch, approaching the house. Before the knob was turned, Cole knew who their visitor was . . .

Jason was home!

Jason Ambrose sprang through the back door with all of the energy of a summer storm. Tall, broad-shouldered, and every bit as fit as a mule, he had blue eyes that sparkled beneath his close-cropped brown hair. Jason's face was a younger copy of their father's, with higher cheekbones and a smaller nose. As soon as he saw his brother in the kitchen, an ear-to-ear smile spread across his broad jaw and he dropped his bags on the floor with a heavy thud.

"Is that my little brother I see?" he shouted.

Before Cole could so much as lean away from the stove, Jason had bounded across the room and taken him in his thick arms, hugging him so tightly that it nearly drove the breath from his chest.

"Are you so happy to see me that you're going to kill me?" Cole wheezed.

"Quit your whining!" Jason kidded good-naturedly.

"I didn't know when to expect you," Cole said when he'd finally been set free.

"What are you talking about?" his brother asked with confusion. "I told Dad to make sure to let you know I'd be back from Hallam Falls this morning. Heck, as soon as the draft board meeting was over, I lit out of there and drove half the night to make sure I'd be here about the time you hauled your sorry butt out of bed. You always were one heck of a sleeper!"

"Still am." Cole chuckled, but he wasn't laughing on the inside.

He turned an expectant look toward his father, but the older man didn't seem to be paying him any mind. A sickening feeling spread across Cole's gut. When he'd first arrived back in Victory, he had made a point of asking when Jason was supposed to return, but his father hadn't given him an exact time, only that he'd return later.

Does he really think so little of me . . . ?

Before he could even entertain the idea

of mentioning his displeasure to his father, Robert rose from his seat and took his plate to the sink. "I believe I'd best get myself to the store," he explained. "I'm sure you boys have much to talk about without me getting in the way."

"But what about my induction date?" Jason asked. "You said we'd—"

"It'll wait till evening," Robert cut him off, and before either of the brothers could say another word, he grabbed his worn hat from a peg on the wall and was already heading out.

"What's his problem?" Jason asked as the door banged shut.

Cole wanted to tell Jason what had happened since his return, to ask his advice about their father's behavior, but knew in his gut that it was neither the time nor the place; it would have to wait. Instead, he simply said, "He must have gotten up on the wrong side of the bed."

"I figured he'd want to know how it went," Jason said with a shrug as the pickup truck chugged down the drive and out of sight. "Now let me get something to eat before I starve to death!"

"Don't let me stop you."

As Jason fixed himself a heaping plate of bacon and eggs, he told Cole all about his trip to the draft board in Hallam Falls, of standing among all the other men seeking to join the armed services, and particularly of his excitement and nervousness at signing his name to the dotted line that would induct him into the United States Navy.

"I never figured you for a boat," Cole said.

"Me neither," his brother heartily agreed. "But looking at all of those pictures of planes made me hope that I could be a flyboy. According to the docs, I've got the eyes of a hawk. But hell, for all I know I'll fail some other test somewhere down the line and the only thing I'll be good for is peeling potatoes!"

"I wonder if you could even do that right," Cole teased.

"Keep laughing, funny guy!"

Cole couldn't help but smile at his brother. Jason had always been confident and self-assured in ways that his younger sibling could only imagine. People were instantly drawn to Jason's warmth and wit. That strength of character had always served him well. If Jason had set his mind on being a navy pilot, Cole had no doubt that he would succeed.

Jason frowned. "It's too bad I've only got a couple of weeks before I have to report."

"That soon?"

"I'm afraid so. Uncle Sam can't keep Hitler and Tojo waiting, I guess."

Cole frowned as well. He'd known that it would only be a matter of time before Jason was shipped out, like the soldiers he'd seen on the train. Still, he'd hoped for more than just a couple of weeks. They'd seen each other infrequently over the last couple of years and he figured they had much catching up to do. The idea that his brother was only months from facing enemy fire was unsettling.

"Are you afraid to go off and fight?"

"Yes and no."

"What do you mean?"

"I can't say I'm too excited about looking down the barrel of some Jap's gun or a Nazi tank," Jason answered between bites of egg, "but I know it's the right thing to do. After Pearl Harbor, there isn't any choice but to go off and fight for the country I love.

That feeling, the certainty that I'm right, makes the fear a little less."

"I understand what you're saying," Cole said.

"I just have to do my part, is all."

The familiar feelings of inadequacy that had plagued Cole for years returned with a vengeance at his brother's words. While able-bodied men such as Jason suited up as soldiers, pilots, and sailors, there was no uniform that he was capable of wearing. His shame felt as sharp as a knife's blade. "I wish I could do my part, too," he muttered. "I wish I wasn't a cripple."

"Don't you dare say such a thing, Cole," Jason snapped. "Don't you dare!"

"But it's true!"

"The hell it is!" his brother spat back, his brow furrowed in exasperation and anger. "There isn't a person alive that knows you who thinks you wouldn't fight if you could! You've got every bit as much heart as I do, if not a lot more!"

"A lot of good it's doing me here."

"Don't think that I'm going to stand here and let you feel sorry for yourself, little brother," Jason scolded him. "That leg is only a handicap if you let it be one! Take pride in what you are, not in what you think you're not. So you can't be a soldier, so what? Be what you are! You're one of the smartest men I've ever known and there are a lot of kids who will benefit from your teaching. Filling their heads full of numbers is going to do them more good than anything I could do for them."

"Stop joking around."

"Who's joking?" Jason asked with a shrug of his wide shoulders. "We both know you're the one in this family that got all the brains! You're just too stubborn to see it!"

From their childhood, Jason had been more than willing to look past his younger brother's disability. When they were out with friends and Cole had struggled to keep up, he had patiently waited for him, even if it meant that all of his other companions ran off. When Cole had inevitably been picked on, Jason had been the first to defend him, even with his fists and even if that meant he received the beating. They had rarely fought each other, choosing instead to be especially close, a closeness that persisted to this very day.

"I still wish I could fight alongside you," Cole said.

"That's nothing to wish for."

"I can't help it."

"Don't worry. You'll do your part."

With talk of the war out of the way, they joked about Cole going back to their old school as a teacher instead of a student, about how hard it must have been to leave a city as exciting as Chicago for one as quiet as Victory, about some of the gossip around town, and even about how nice it had been to taste one of Marge's cheeseburgers again.

"Even if you're leaving in a couple of weeks, we'll still have plenty of time to get caught up," Cole said.

"You'll get your share, but you can't have it all."

"Why not?"

"Because if I did that, Mary Ellen might never speak to me again."

"Mary Ellen?"

"There are a couple of things that have changed since you left town." Jason chuckled. "Do you remember Mary Ellen Carter? I think she might be a couple of years younger than you."

Cole clearly remembered Mary Ellen; when they had been kids, she was the only person that had been picked on more than he had. Short, with stringy blonde hair, dumpy clothes, and eyes perpetually turned to the ground, she'd been teased mercilessly. There had been many times Cole had wanted to console her, but every time he had approached her, she'd run away screaming.

"Pig Patch?" Cole asked, using the nickname with which she'd been saddled.

"If you call her that now, she's likely to kick you."

"So . . . wait . . . are you saying what I think you are?"

"Yep."

"You and Mary Ellen?" Cole asked incredulously.

"She's my gal," Jason answered proudly. "She's not quite the ugly duckling she used to be. Now she's got curves in all the right places with plenty of beauty and charm to spare."

"Weren't you the one that made her eat mud pies one summer?" Cole asked.

"One and the same," his brother admitted.

"I can't believe she forgave you."

"That makes two of us," he said, and they both laughed.

In that moment, Cole was truly glad to be home.

Chapter Ten

HOW CAN YOU stand this heat? It's unbearable!"

Sophie wiped heavy beads of sweat from her brow with the back of her hand as she watched Walter Deets type words into the hulking Linotype machine in the rear of the *Victory Gazette* building. Large and foreboding, the black metal contraption seemed to take up the whole room. They'd been at it for hours; Sophie's blouse clung to her body like a second skin and her knees felt wobbly, nearly as unsure as those of a newborn calf.

"You say that now, but come winter you're gonna be pretty glad about it!"

"I doubt that very much."

The newspaperman chuckled. "Trust me. When the snow flies, this is the place to be."

Sophie sighed. For the past several days, she had been paired with Walter as he explained the ins and outs of his job at the newspaper. In his early thirties with hound-dog eyes, an overbite, and a nature as easy as a Sunday breeze in June, he would soon be shipping out for the United States Army and some distant foreign land, leaving behind responsibilities that someone would have to assume. To that end, Sophie had been chosen.

Prior to the outbreak of the war, Sophie's duties at the *Gazette* had been to run copy, do some proofreading, and even, on the rarest of occasion, take a grainy photograph or two. She knew that the men who worked in the rear of the building were important to the well-being of the paper, but their jobs had always seemed beyond her. Though she had often joked with Walter in passing, she'd had no idea what his work had entailed. Now, exhausted, overwhelmed, and covered in sweat, she had begun to know all too well.

"You want to give it another try?" Walter asked.

"I suppose I can't be so lucky as to hope it would just manage without me."

"Let's hope not." He laughed heartily, his voice still loud and strong over the heavy clanks and bangs of the Linotype machine. "Otherwise I'll not have a job when I get back."

"I already can't wait to give it back to you!"

Taking the page of text that Walter handed her, Sophie sat down at the odd keyboard of the machine. Though she still wasn't completely sure of the process, she knew that the large contraption was essential to the publication of the newspaper. By typing on the keyboard, which, to her chagrin, did not remotely resemble that of a normal typewriter, characters that created sets of words and letters were selected and placed in the order in which they would be needed. Once a line had been completed, a lever was pulled and the text was plunged into molten hot metal, a combination of tin and lead, creating a mold that could be used for printing. Sophie's discomfort came from the Linotype's melting pot, many hundreds of degrees hot.

Carefully pecking away at the keyboard, Sophie tried to concentrate on her task, but her mind kept wandering back to Cole Ambrose and their brief time together. The memory of him was a powerful thing, coming unbidden yet not unwanted. She thought of the sound of his voice, of his gallantry in coming to her aid at the diner, of his easy smile, but try as she might, she could not keep her thoughts from returning to the sight of his crippled leg.

I'm so ashamed that I ran away from him!

Her face already flushed from the heat coming from the Linotype machine, she couldn't help but fear that it grew a deeper crimson from the shame that raced throughout her body. Why did that one moment have to color how she felt about Cole? Up until the moment when she had first looked upon his leg, she'd felt a strong, growing interest in the young teacher. He'd been charming, witty, and undeniably well-intentioned. Did it matter that he was crippled? Was she truly so shallow that her feelings could be changed so quickly?

Somehow, she managed to finish typing her line without any errors and now faced the task she most hated: pulling the lever that plunged the text into the molten metal. The tension of the lever was tremendous. It had seemed so easy the first time she had watched Walter pull it, but while he effortlessly did it with one hand, she could barely manage with both, straining with every ounce of strength she could muster.

"You can do it," Walter said, sensing her unease.

"I'm glad one of us thinks so."

"Ain't but one way to find out, now is there?"

Taking a deep breath, Sophie grasped the lever in both of her sweaty hands, said a silent prayer, and pulled back hard enough to make her shoulders ache. Unlike her previous attempts, she immediately felt the lever begin slowly to move, and soon she heard the metallic bang of the characters dropping into the liquid metal. With much of the remaining process automatic, she felt an instant rush of both success and relief.

"Wasn't that easier?" Walter crowed with an obvious pride in his pupil.

"It was," Sophie had to admit.

"Before long, you'll be snappin' that thing just as easy as you open a door."

"I doubt that very much," she said with a sigh, although she could not deny that her heart felt a bit lighter. "Besides, with as slow as I type this out, being a little faster with the lever isn't going to make much difference. You can do six or seven lines in the time it takes me to do one."

"No one will be pressuring you, Sophie," Walter tried to explain, his voice reassuring. "Heck, the first time I sat in front of this contraption, I felt about as outta place as a hog at a high-society dinner! But I just kept at it and learned as best I could. 'Fore long, I wasn't half bad. It will be no different with you."

Sophie knew that no matter how difficult it was for her to learn to use the Linotype machine, she had no choice but to figure it out! When the Japanese attacked Pearl Harbor, she had known it would only be a matter of time until all of the able-bodied men were rushed into duty. In their absence, it was every citizen's responsibility to make up the difference. If the Linotype was to be her burden, then so be it. Still, she couldn't help but feel that with Ellis Watts, Riley Mason, and Graham Grier still in Victory, mastering this piece of machinery was the least of her troubles.

"Let's try it again," Walter said, gently coaxing her out of her thoughts and back to the machine.

And so she did.

It was shortly after lunch when Carolyn Glass burst into the *Gazette*'s main office like a tornado. Sophie and Walter had been sitting at his desk, going over ways to avoid errors in the printing process, when the front door flew open and every head turned to witness the woman's certain-to-be-ensuing theatrics. After all, as the wife of their boss and publisher, Carolyn was someone they simply could not afford to ignore.

Twenty-nine-year-old Carolyn was a pretty woman to look at, but as cold as ice on the inside. With high cheekbones, a modest nose, and tight-pursed lips, she carried the air of a movie starlet with a personality every bit to match. She had a way of looking down her nose at anyone she thought was beneath her, which ended up being nearly everyone she met. The first time she had encountered Carolyn, Sophie felt as if she were invisible. Still, being noticed was sometimes even worse. Her tongue was as lethal as a snake. Her platinum blonde hair was swept up into the latest fashion and she made regular trips to Chicago and St. Louis to purchase whatever hat, blouse, or purse might catch her fancy. No makeup was too excessive, no bauble too expensive for Carolyn Glass.

To make matters worse, she was nearly five months pregnant. While she had always been difficult for the employees of the *Gazette* to stomach, being with child seemed to make her even more irritable. She acted as if no other woman in history had ever had to endure such agony. As the summer progressed, her complaining seemed as constant as the whirring fans strategically placed to cool the office.

"A woman in my condition shouldn't have to be out in such heat!" she shouted as she dropped her growing weight into a chair set just inside the door. Her gaze expectantly surveyed the faces nearest to her, her brow furrowed as if she were wondering why they hadn't fallen all over themselves in a race to see who would be first to wait on her hand and foot.

"Carolyn, do you—" Harriet Connor began but was cut off.

"Get me a glass of water!"

"I just wondered—"

"I don't give a damn what you might be wondering," Carolyn swore, her body half rising from the chair in indignation. "What on earth could there be to wonder about? Only a fool wouldn't know when a pregnant woman needs a drink!"

"I'm sorry, Carolyn," Harriet stammered. "I just—"

"Stop talking and get me a drink!"

Before Carolyn could heap any more abuse upon the poor woman, Augustus Glass hurried from his office, crossed the newsroom, and knelt at his wife's side. Approaching his late fifties, nearly thirty years older than Carolyn, Augustus clearly looked his age, with a balding head barely covered by wisps of whitish blond hair that had been teased hopefully across the top, deepening wrinkles that had begun to canvass their way across his face and hands, and an impressive gut permanently perched atop his beltline.

"What's the matter, darling?" he asked, his heavy, watery eyes never leaving her face, his hand gently finding her own for only an instant before she yanked it away in anger.

"How did you ever manage to hire so many idiots?" Carolyn snapped.

"But, sweetheart," he stammered. "No one ever—"

"I don't know how this rag manages to stay open in the face of such complete and utter incompetence!"

While not a single citizen of Victory doubted Augustus Glass's devotion to his wife or their marriage—one look in his hazel eyes as he gazed upon her would have cleared up any misconceptions—there was more than a little concern when it came to Carolyn's motivations. Though no one would have dared to utter the word in her presence, Sophie had heard the woman described as a gold digger on more than one occasion. She was young and vivacious and Augustus was, with the noted exception of his wealth and standing about town, not considered much of a catch; such a discrepancy naturally set tongues wagging.

Sophie felt pity for the *Gazette*'s publisher. From the very first day she had started at the paper, he had been patient and kind, encouraging her to learn as much as she could. Around the office, he was known to have a firm but fair hand. Still, Sophie had always noticed the loneliness that filled his eyes. So desperate to believe that a woman like Carolyn could truly be attracted to him, Augustus had chosen to ignore the obvious and had had to pander to his wife in order to maintain the illusion ever since. That she was pregnant with his child had given him a much-deserved sense of pride, but Sophie worried that Augustus's servitude to Carolyn was only the beginning of the misery she would someday inflict upon him.

He's a much better man when she isn't around!

"Here you are, dear," Augustus said as he handed her the glass of water that Harriet had finally brought. Carolyn snatched it from his hand and, in her reckless haste, dribbled a bit of water down the front of her blouse.

"You old fool!" she screeched as if the fault had been her husband's instead of her own. The way that her face scrunched up in disgust, the offending liquid might have been ink instead of water.

"It's only water, honey," Augustus said.

"You should still be careful!"

"It will dry, darling," he added as Sophie's stomach curdled in equal parts of disgust at Carolyn's childishness and Augustus's desire to make her worries disappear.

"How did he ever marry such a catty broad?" Walter asked out loud at her side.

"Hush!" Sophie whispered. "She'll hear you!"

"And so what?"

"You'll get yelled at, Walter!"

"There's no way it can be worse than what some drill sergeant's got in store for me," he said with a shrug. "Besides, if there's one thing that there woman needs, it's the truth."

Part of Sophie believed Walter; it had surely been a long time since someone had tried to put Carolyn Glass in her place. She was the sort who demanded her every wish be met without pause. In Augustus, she had found her perfect match; in his desperation to end his own loneliness, he was all too happy to bend over backward for her, even if it meant that he would be made to look like a fool. Still, if the day were to come when someone told Carolyn exactly how they felt about her behavior, Sophie hoped she would be nowhere near.

"Come along now, sweetheart," Augustus said as he helped his wife to her feet and gingerly led her between the desks of the newsroom toward his own office. Sophie couldn't tell if he wished to end her suffering or put an end to his own embarrassment.

"Slower, you oaf!" she snapped. "I'm pregnant, remember?"

"Yes, dear."

As they neared Walter's desk, Sophie could not bring herself to tear her eyes from them. Something about Carolyn was mesmerizing; maybe it was the shock and indignation that anyone could act in such a manner, least of all in public. With every step they took toward her, she knew she should turn away, follow Walter's lead and look down at the desk, but she found herself frozen, unable to move.

Much to Sophie's horror, Carolyn's green eyes suddenly rose and found her own, holding her as easily as if she were small game in the talons of a ferocious predator. Though Carolyn and Augustus were still several feet from where she stood, Sophie felt that they were much closer and shivers of unease and fear raced wildly across her skin. A sneer grew from the corners of Carolyn's lips and she shook herself free from her husband's grasp, a look of pure disdain upon her face.

"What are you staring at?" she snapped. "Why do you always stare at me?"

"I'm not . . . not . . ." Sophie stammered.

"Don't think that I haven't noticed you looking, little missy," she barked, her voice dripping with contempt. "Every single time I come in here, it's the same thing!"

"What . . . what are you talking about?"

"Don't even try playing innocent with me, honey," Carolyn said, with a smile less inviting than any Sophie had ever seen. "You're judging me! Always measuring your looks against mine!"

"I'm not!" Sophie said, suddenly bathed in a nervous sweat. "I swear!"

"I suppose you think that because I've gone and gotten fat and pregnant that you'll be the belle of the ball in these parts, but think again!" Carolyn boasted, quickly looking around the small office to ensure that every eye was back where it belonged—on her. "No matter how hard you try, no matter what you do, you'll never be half the woman I am!"

Dumbstruck by the woman's accusations, all that Sophie could do was stare blankly. It was as if she had been transported back to Karl's side, watching their family's barn crumble into cinders, unable to do anything to stop the carnage unfolding before her; Carolyn's words had been so destructive. Thankfully, she was saved from any further scolding when Augustus again grabbed his wife's arm and gently pulled her toward his office.

"Sophie isn't like that, darling," the newspaperman soothed.

"Don't think for one minute I'm not watching, you hussy," Carolyn said over her shoulder, choosing to ignore her husband's words to the contrary. Her icy gaze never left Sophie until the oak door to Augustus's office shut behind her and she turned her fury back toward her husband, her voice still audible from behind the closed door.

For a moment, Sophie stood silently, wondering if by some trick of her mind she had imagined the whole thing. But then Walter spoke and any illusion she might have had was shattered.

"Maybe you should have let me run my mouth, huh?"

When Sophie left the *Gazette*'s offices at the end of her workday, summer heat still pressed down on the day like a blanket. Though she knew that a strong storm would eventually break the heat and bring some coolness, she wished it would hurry up and arrive.

Her father leaned casually against the hood of his truck. His hat sat low on his ears and sweat ringed both arms of his shirt and stained the chest. Picking her up from work had been a daily routine ever since the night of the fire; even with her father's desire to act as if nothing had happened, he had proven unwilling to leave his daughter's safety to chance. Still, she couldn't help but feel a bit sad upon seeing him. To Sophie's eyes, he had looked older ever since the night he'd been struck by Ellis Watts's rifle butt; she supposed it was the first time she had ever witnessed her father in a state of vulnerability.

"Are you ready?" Hermann asked.

"I am, Papa."

"Then we should be going," he said. "Your mother makes a big dinner."

Making her way to the passenger door, Sophie felt a trickle of unease shiver up her arms over what had occurred with Carolyn. She had been worthless to Walter the rest of the afternoon; try as she might, she'd never been able to shake the image of the pregnant woman berating her in front of the whole office. Walter had told her to keep her chin up and not to worry, but she doubted she would be able to follow his advice.

Why couldn't Mr. Glass have found a nicer woman?!

She had just placed her purse inside the truck's cab and was getting ready to slide into her seat when she noticed Riley Mason watching her intently. He was across the street, leaning lazily against the wall of

McKenzie's Barber Shop with the air of a man who didn't have a care in the world, a half-eaten apple in his hand. He looked every bit as dirty and disheveled as when he'd violently grabbed her wrist in the diner. When he realized he had been seen, he tipped his hat and gave her a lewd wink.

Surprisingly, Sophie's first thought was of Cole. Though she felt secure with her father beside her, she still found herself wishing that the young teacher was once again at her side. For a moment, the thought struck her as odd; if Riley were suddenly to come charging across the street intent on hurting her, Cole would certainly be hindered by his bad leg. But as soon as she had birthed that thought, Sophie found it replaced by another; disabled or not, Cole Ambrose was the sort of man who would do anything in his power to protect her. He had come to her aid in the diner, and if he had to, he would do so again.

"Cole," she whispered softly under her breath.

Her mind held no shortage of schemes for Ellis Watts to concoct. Her earlier fears of being watched now seemed to have merit; she would have to assume that every move she made was being observed. Now that she knew the identities of her family's attackers, her life was in danger. If Riley were watching her now, he would be doing so under Ellis's orders. They were undoubtedly planning something. *But what?*

Doing her best to ignore Riley, Sophie got into the truck beside her father and he brought the engine to life, reversed into the street, and headed for home. The sudden sound of his voice startled her.

"How was your day, Sophie?" her father asked. "Were you busy?"

"It was fine, Papa," she lied. "Just like any other."

"That is good."

When they neared the end of the street, Sophie stole a quick glance over her shoulder to find that Riley was no longer in front of the barber shop. Desperately, she searched the street but could see no sign of the man. Instead of being relieved, she felt a slow, sinking feeling fill her gut. Somehow, she would feel safer if she knew where a man such as Riley Mason or Ellis Watts was; if they were out of sight, it was then that they would be at their most dangerous.

". . . nothin' but a goddamn Kraut . . ."

Sophie and her father headed out of Victory under the colorful fluttering of dozens of American flags and the grim resolve of propaganda-poster soldiers staring out from under the brims of their helmets.

Chapter Eleven

SO HOW ON EARTH did a nice girl like Mary Ellen Carter ever wind up with a guy the likes of you?"

Cole leaned back in a chair in his brother's bedroom, his fingers drumming tunelessly on the windowsill. Outside, the sun had just disappeared for the night and a thick blanket of stars had begun to stretch across the ever-darkening sky. A gentle breeze stirred the curtains through the open window but did little to staunch the still oppressive heat.

"That's a question I've asked myself more times than I can count."

"I bet you aren't the only one."

Jason stood before the mirror, applying a dollop of pomade to his hair. He was dressed smartly: crisp-pleated trousers hung over freshly shined shoes, his knotted tie was loose but ready to be pulled taut at the throat of his button-down shirt. Though naturally good-looking, Jason wasn't the sort to spend a lot of time fussing over his clothes. Mary Ellen, and their impending date to the movies, clearly made for an exception.

"Are you sure you don't want to tag along?" Jason asked.

"The last thing you need is me being a third wheel."

"Well, I sure could have used you the last time we went."

"How do you mean?"

"A couple of weeks back I took Mary Ellen to see that new Jimmy Stewart picture," Jason explained as he brushed the unruly hair at his temples. "We were running a bit late but somehow we luck into a cherry spot right out in front of the theater. I'm thinking we've got it made . . . heck, I can practically taste the popcorn already! But just as I'm getting out of the car, I hear this ripping sound and I know, much to my horror, that it's the seat of my pants."

"You've got to be joking!" Cole exclaimed.

"Don't I wish."

"What did you do?"

"The only thing I could," Jason said with a shrug. "I kept my rear end pointed away from Mary Ellen at all times and just went on with our date. I tell you what . . . I had quite a time crossing that lobby!"

"You didn't tell Mary Ellen?"

"Heck no! I was too embarrassed! I kept my mouth shut, although in the end, it turned out I didn't have to."

"She found out?"

Jason nodded and gave a heavy sigh. "I don't know just when she figured out what had happened, but she didn't say a peep until our date was over. There we were on her doorstep with me wishing her good night. She rises up on her toes, gives me a peck on the cheek, and tells me what a gentleman I was not forcing her to look at my hind end all night."

"Oh, that's rich!" Cole exclaimed, slapping his knee.

"'Thank you for not forcing me to look at

your hind end,'" Jason exclaimed, mimicking the high pitch of his sweetheart's voice. "What the heck kind of talk is that, anyway? The way I see it, my hind end is one part of me I want her to see!"

"It'd be better than your face."

"Very funny, wiseass!"

"So how could you have used me?" Cole asked.

"You could have run home to get me another pair of pants," he said, and they both laughed.

"Thank goodness that wasn't your first date."

"No kidding," Jason agreed. "If it had been, I'd have to wonder if I would've gotten another."

Listening to his brother talk about his dates with Mary Ellen, Cole couldn't help but think of Sophie. He wanted the same thing for the two of them, even if it meant that he had to rip out the seat of his pants to have it! It wasn't that he was jealous of Jason, just slightly envious. It surprised him how easy it was to imagine he and Sophie together romantically, even though they had just met, and not under the best of circumstances. He wanted to believe that the two of them could go to the movies, share a good-night kiss, and laugh about a split seam in his pants.

I just have no idea how!

"What was your first date?" Cole asked, eager for any help he could get.

"A picnic."

"Really?"

"I'd had my eye on her for a while and finally decided to hell with it," Jason said, laughing. "So I showed up at her door one day with a picnic basket in hand and asked her whether she wanted to come along. You know, really put her on the spot. By some stroke of luck, she said yes! From there on out it was pretty easy."

"What would you have done if she'd said no?"

"I suppose I would have had one huge lunch to eat."

It was hard for Cole to imagine taking such a bold step with Sophie; he had always been far more cautious than Jason, but much of that was due to his handicap. Maybe this time could be different? What if he were to show up out at the Hellers' farm? What about the *Gazette* office?

Hadn't Sophie mentioned that she worked there?

"So what's got you so interested in first dates?" Jason asked, interrupting Cole's thoughts. He studied his brother intently in the mirror's reflection, his eyes hooded with a mischievous interest. "Don't tell me there's someone you're sweet on?"

Cole blanched, his heart hammering like a rabbit's. For the briefest of moments, he thought about telling his brother about the enchanting Sophie Heller; about the strange way in which they met, about the ride in the truck out to her family's farm, and even about the sweet sound of her voice.

But something stopped him.

The sudden realization struck Cole that he wanted to keep Sophie all to himself for a little while longer. Once he had worked up the nerve to approach her for a date, once he'd finally taken a chance, then he would be ready to tell Jason the whole amazing story, but only then.

"Just curious about you, Romeo," Cole kidded his brother.

"You sure you're not just trying to cover your butt?"

"Sure as sunshine."

"It's about time you started thinking about your own love life."

"Don't I know it," Cole agreed.

"Who knows," Jason said with a shrug, turning his attention back to his hair, the movie, and Mary Ellen, "the girl of your dreams might be just around the corner."

With a little luck, Cole hoped to prove his brother right.

Sophie labored beside Walter in the sweltering heat produced by the Linotype machine, her face screwed up in concentration as she pecked at the odd keyboard, trying desperately not to make a mistake, when Harriet Connor entered the room and told her she had a visitor.

Her first thought was that it was Carolyn Glass, returning to give her even more of a tongue-lashing, but she quickly dismissed the idea; if there was one thing that Carolyn did not need, it was to be announced. As quickly as that thought diminished, a prickly unease teased at the corners of her mind that it might be Ellis Watts or Riley Mason.

"Who is it?" she asked cautiously.

"I'm afraid I don't know, dear," Harriet answered. "I've never seen him before."

Tentatively, concern written large on her face, Sophie moved to the door and peered toward the front of the office. There, standing just inside the door, his hat in his hand, was Cole Ambrose. He looked in her direction, his blue eyes easily finding her own, and gave her a smile and nod.

"Cole?" she whispered in surprise.

Without even being aware that she had begun moving, Sophie made her way across the newspaper office, weaving among the chairs and desks, finally standing before Cole. Warmth spread across her chest, her heart fluttering from intense delight. It was as if no time had passed since their last meeting, and she suddenly realized that she had been waiting for this very moment, anxious and eager to see him. But then she remembered the way she had left him, running to the farmhouse in tears.

"It's nice to see you again, Sophie," he said warmly.

"I'm sorry about how I left you the other day," she offered, a tinge of shame rising in her cheeks. She wanted to apologize just as quickly as she could, the words rushing out of her mouth. "It's just that . . ."

"There's no need," he quieted her. "I'm not here for an apology."

"Then why?"

"You might find this hard to believe, but I just happened to find myself wandering aimlessly around town carrying a picnic lunch," he explained, raising a wicker basket that she hadn't noticed. "I suddenly had this crazy thought that you might want to join me."

"Wandering around town with a picnic lunch?" she asked with a sly grin.

"Strange, isn't it?" he chuckled. "It's never happened to me before."

Sophie couldn't help but smile. She liked the way Cole joked with her and she felt more than comfortable playing along. "That sounds like an awfully unlikely story."

"I was afraid you might say that."

"So what happens if I call your bluff?"

"Then I suppose that I'd have no choice but to tell you the truth," he said.

"Which is?"

"To be honest, it's pretty simple," he explained as beads of sweat broke out across his forehead; though they were nowhere near the Linotype machine, Sophie was certain that it was not entirely due to the heat. Standing there before her, Cole carried the air of a confident man, but she could see that it was an image with which he struggled. He seemed somewhat shy, very nearly bashful, and because of it, she found herself liking him even more intensely. "I brought this picnic because I enjoy your company and wondered if you might like to share a bit of mine."

"Now was that so hard?" she asked, giving him one last bit of ribbing.

"More than you'd ever imagine," he admitted and they both laughed.

At the sound of their laughter sounding around the newspaper office, Sophie suddenly found herself feeling more than a little self-conscious. She looked around the room and saw every face in the room turned in their direction, though none of the looks were disapproving; most all were smiles. Unable to help herself, she blushed at the attention.

"How about it, Sophie?" Cole asked.

"It's just that . . ." She trailed off, unsure of what to say.

"Don't you worry none about me and this old girl," Walter called from the back of the office as he thumbed toward the Linotype machine. Leaning in the doorway, he'd clearly been listening to their entire conversation. "I hate admittin' to it, but there ain't nothin' gonna come up that I'll not be able to handle. You go on and have a nice lunch."

"Are you sure?" Sophie asked.

"As sunshine."

Turning back to Cole, Sophie could clearly see the expectant look in his eyes. There was no use in denying that she desperately wanted to go with him, but the paralyzing fear that had gripped her since the burning of the barn was still powerful. Ever since the confrontation in the diner, she hadn't felt safe enough to leave the *Gazette* office for lunch. Whenever she set foot outside, dread filled her at the thought of running into Ellis, Riley, or especially Graham. If she were to find one of them waiting for her, as Riley had been when her father had picked her up from work, she didn't know what she would do.

But now things feel different!

Sophie found that she wasn't quite so

scared. Looking at Cole's square jaw and broad shoulders, she knew that he was a man willing to rise to her defense, just as he had at the diner. If she were to meet any of the men who meant to harm her, she felt sure she would be safe as long as she was in Cole Ambrose's company.

She smiled. "I'd love to have a picnic with you."

"Then let's go," he answered. He held open the door, and they were off.

Cole led Sophie around the side of the *Gazette* building and down a short street toward Watkins Creek, a thin burble that ran along the west side of town. Majestic maple trees offered cool shade, but Sophie found herself reveling in the feel of the sun on her skin; too many of her recent afternoons had been spent indoors.

They walked along slowly, Sophie adjusting herself to Cole's pace. She found that it was a struggle not to look at his disabled leg. She tried to fix her attention upon her own feet, but she couldn't help but steal a glance, her eyes drifting to watch him plant his disfigured foot, his hip lurching awkwardly to heave his weight forward.

"It's all right if you want to look," he said suddenly.

"I'm sorry . . . I didn't . . ." Sophie stammered with flustered embarrassment. She felt the urge to say more, to explain to Cole that she hadn't been staring at his disfigurement, but she held her tongue; to say more would be to lie, and that was something she did not want to do . . . not to him.

"Don't worry, Sophie," he offered. "It's always been that way."

"Your leg?"

"Well, yes, but what I meant was that people have always stared at my leg," Cole said with a shrug. "Heck, it's not as if I blame them. It's not every day that you come across someone with a problem like mine."

"It's rude."

"Not really. I think it would be stranger if people didn't look."

"How can it not be rude?" Sophie asked, a flare of anger rising in her heart at all of the people who had ever stared a moment too long at Cole's leg, herself included. Shame still colored her thoughts at how she had run from him at her family's farm, even if he had told her not to worry about it. "Doesn't it ever make you angry?"

"Once in a while, I suppose," Cole admitted. "The only time it really bothers me is if I see pity in someone's eyes. That's when it's the worst. The last thing I want is to think that I'm any less than a normal man. Just because my darn leg isn't the same as everyone else's doesn't mean that I can't manage on my own. My father—" he started but suddenly fell silent, his jaw tight and his eyes locked on the road before them.

In the short time that she had known Cole Ambrose, Sophie had found him to be every bit of a man, in many ways even more so than any other she had ever met. Just because he had a handicapped leg, he'd had to spend his whole life wondering if he measured up, when it was others who should have been worrying if they were as strong and decent as he was.

"You're right." She nodded. "You aren't any different."

"Except that I can't do the one thing I truly want."

"What's that?"

"I wish I could go off and fight."

Sophie frowned. After the attack on her

family, after the horrifying way that the conflict had been brought to her home, any talk about the war and the men going off to fight it disturbed her. That this man longed to be a part of such carnage made her uneasy. Even in his presence, even though she didn't want to offend him, she found that she couldn't suppress her feelings. "I can't imagine why anyone would wish such a thing," she said with no small measure of disgust.

"Whyever not?" he argued. "We were attacked!"

"Just because we're fighting in a war that is just, doesn't make it something that anyone should want to do," she explained. She felt his eyes searching for her own but couldn't bring herself to look at him. "It's not right that someone should want to go off to kill other men."

"Are you saying we shouldn't fight this war?" he asked incredulously.

"No, not at all," she explained. "But it shouldn't be something we want to do but rather something we feel we have to do."

"All I want is to do my part."

"And you will," Sophie reassured him. "You'll do your part the same as I'll do mine, but that doesn't mean that we should find any joy in our burden. We'll just scrape and sacrifice, all in the hopes that our lives can go back to what they were before the fighting started."

"I just wish I could do the same as other men," he insisted.

"I'd hate to think that you're in a hurry to die in some foreign land," she said, and the harshness of her words startled her. Cole did not offer more and they walked on in silence.

They soon arrived at the small footbridge that spanned the narrow creek. On the far side, the broad canopy of an old elm tree spread its cool shade, beckoning to them. They crossed the rickety bridge, the creek's flowing water little more than a trickle in the oppressive summer heat, and Cole spread a blanket, set the picnic basket on it, and offered Sophie his hand to help lower her to the ground. With no small amount of effort, he joined her and began to empty the basket's contents: egg salad sandwiches, a handful of grapes, a couple of apples, and an empty milk bottle filled with water.

"I doubt that it'll hold a candle to what

you'd find at Marge's," he explained, handing her one of the sandwiches, "but I did the best I could."

Sophie took a bite and was pleasantly surprised to find that it was very tasty, better than she would have expected. Still, she couldn't help but tease him a bit. "I like it, although I hate to say that Marge doesn't need to worry about any competition."

He laughed. "Then I guess there's no need to quit the teaching job and open a restaurant."

They ate leisurely, enjoying the meal and each other's company. For a while, Sophie forgot about all of her problems. They talked at length about Victory, her family's farm, and her job at the newspaper. She told him about learning to use the Linotype machine and, for a brief moment, even came to believe that she knew what she was talking about. He, in turn, told her about his love for mathematics, his brother's impending entry into the army, and his nervous excitement about beginning a new job.

Suddenly, a serious look crossed Cole's face and he pushed his hat back on his head. He lay on his side on the blanket, his body lazily propped up on one elbow, gazing into her eyes with such intensity that Sophie couldn't bring herself to look away, even though she felt certain that she had begun to blush. Taking a bite of his apple, he said, "Tell me about what happened at the diner."

Taken aback, she stammered, "It . . . it was nothing . . ."

"That was much more than nothing, Sophie," he insisted. "That sorry cuss had his hands on you. If you're being bothered, I want you to tell me."

Sophie stared hard at Cole's face, her blue eyes searching his for some sign of what she should do with his request. On the one hand, she didn't want to burden him with her problems, nor did she want to go against her father's wishes that she hold her secret. Still, though she had known Cole for only a couple of days, she felt in her heart that he was a man of honor, of integrity, and she had no doubts that he could be trusted.

"All right," she said softly.

Words fell from Sophie's mouth as if they were rain. She told Cole about the burning of the barn, about the three hooded men who had suddenly appeared and threatened her family with violence if they didn't leave Victory, and about her father being struck with the rifle butt. She spoke of the horrific slur that had been uttered just before she had been battered with the same rifle and of how she had heard the slur spoken again in the diner.

"Those were the same men?" Cole asked, his face taut.

Sophie could only nod.

"Why would they think that you and your family are Nazis?"

"I have no idea!" she exclaimed. "My family came to America to escape all that Hitler and the Nazis represented in Germany! From the very moment my father set foot in the United States, he has done everything that he could to be an honorable citizen, to stand proud for his adopted country! How could he be mistaken for a Nazi?"

"The fact that you're German seems to be enough."

Sophie knew that Cole was right, as much as it disgusted her.

"If they're the sort of men capable of what they did to you and your family, you shouldn't have approached them," he continued. "Lord only knows what they'd do if given another chance. I don't believe I would put anything past them."

"I couldn't help myself," she said. "I just had to show them I wasn't afraid."

"Even though you are . . ."

"Yes," Sophie admitted.

"You need to take this to the police," Cole argued, his voice firm. "That's the only thing that men like Ellis Watts are going to respect. He shouldn't be allowed to get away with what he's done."

"But I can't!"

"Yes, you can," he prodded. "You can't let them make you live your life in fear!"

"It's not because I'm afraid of them!" she pleaded, her voice rising. "It's because I have to honor my father's wishes. He told all of us that we should act as if nothing has happened! He wants us to be good Americans!"

"Telling the police what those bastards did to your family won't make you any less of a good American, Sophie, no matter what your father believes. You must know that I'm telling the truth."

Sophie was certain that Cole *was* right;

she had known all along that turning Ellis Watts and the others in to the police was the only thing she could do to make certain that her family was truly safe. Still, she couldn't get the image of Riley Mason standing outside the newspaper office out of her head. With such dangerous men, there was one truth that she simply could not ignore.

Anyone near me is in danger!

Before Sophie had told Cole what had happened to her family, it had never occurred to her that he could be hurt. Now the image of him lying broken and bleeding at the three men's hands intruded into her thoughts, horrifying her. If anything were to happen to him because of her, she doubted that she would ever be able to forgive herself.

"You can't tell anyone what I've told you, Cole," she fretted.

"I cannot stand by and let those men threaten you."

"Please, Cole," Sophie begged. "You have to give me your word."

Cole did not answer, his eyes remaining flat and hard.

"I trusted you enough to tell you the

truth," she pressed him. "After the way you defended me in the diner, it was the least I could do. But I can't betray the trust my father placed in me not to tell the police. I know that you're right, that it's probably not the right thing to do, but it's my family I would be placing in danger. For that reason, you mustn't tell!"

Cole's mouth opened as if he wanted to argue the point further, but instead he remained silent, swallowing his unspoken words. Gravely, he nodded his head. "I don't like what you're asking me to do, but I give you my word that I won't tell the police."

"Thank you." Sophie exhaled with obvious relief.

"But that doesn't mean that I'm going to stand by and let them walk all over you and your family," Cole explained as he reached over and took her by the hand. The tenderness of his touch set Sophie's heart to hurrying. "They won't hurt you further. That's something I won't allow."

"I believe you."

Warmth raced over Sophie's body at the thought of being watched over. She had been brave enough to face Ellis, Riley, and Graham in the diner, but she had needed

Cole's help even then. Now, as he offered his protection to her, she felt far safer than she had in a long time.

At the thought of Graham, Sophie couldn't help but think of how she had always wondered if it would be the two of them, sitting under a tree, having a picnic, laughing and talking about each other's lives. But now, sharing just such a moment with Cole Ambrose, she was surprised to find how natural it seemed, how completely at ease she felt at his side.

Chapter Twelve

ELLIS WATTS SAT in the near dark at the back of Victory's lone tavern, far out of reach of the blazing midafternoon sun and any unwanted attention. He had wandered in irritable and more than a fair amount thirsty. Two fingers of amber whiskey sat in a tumbler in front of him, the third glass that he could account for since he'd arrived. He knew there would be others to follow.

Such an early hour ensured that the joint would be mostly empty; there were only two other patrons who had needed a drink as badly as he had. One man sat listlessly on his stool, with one leg flopped over the other, his head down on the bar-rail and a lit cigarette dangling between two tobacco-stained fingers, smoke curling toward the ceiling. The other was engrossed in playing cards with the bartender at the far end of the long bar, the occasional snippet of their talk or belt of raucous laughter the only sound in the place.

Ellis paid them no mind, his attention given over completely to the crisp piece of paper spread out on the table before him; his draft notice. It had come in the morning mail and had been weighing heavily on him ever since. He had been waiting for it, in some ways hoping for months that it would appear, and had known exactly what it was the moment the postman had handed it to him. But now that it had arrived, he was utterly shocked and horrified by the emotion that swirled in the pit of his stomach.

He was afraid.

Ellis reckoned that it was normal to be frightened of such a thing; an order to pick up a weapon and traipse halfway around the world to fight and kill men he had never met. After all, he had no more wish to die than the next man. But his fear shamed him. Snatching up his glass, he drained his drink in a quick gulp and struggled to settle himself; no matter what, he'd never let anyone else see what he felt inside.

The worst part about receiving his draft notice was that he hadn't managed to deal with those damn Nazis living in Victory's midst, the Hellers. His stomach tightened at the thought of leaving town, his work undone. It wouldn't be long before Riley and even Graham got their notices, and then what?

They were running out of time . . .

He'd meant what he had told Riley after the encounter at the diner; they had to be careful to not draw attention to themselves. To that end, they needed to be patient. Sending Riley to keep an eye on the girl had been a risk; he had wondered if the dumb bastard could keep his tongue in check, but so far he'd behaved. The plan had been to keep her good and scared, and in that, Ellis knew Riley would succeed.

Thinking about Sophie Heller, frightened out of her wits, brought a sly smile to the corners of Ellis's mouth. Though she was undoubtedly in cahoots with that bastard of a father of hers, intent upon sabotaging America, he had to admit that she was something of a looker. In the diner she had proven feisty; he had admired the way her chest had thrust out as she had argued with him, and it had caused a stirring in his pants. He supposed that if all of the girls in Germany looked like that, maybe being shipped out wouldn't be so bad.

Ellis was lost in this lustful daydream when Cole Ambrose stepped in front of the open doorway. The man took a tentative step inside—but what other kind could he take?—peering first at the men clustered along the bar and then into the murky gloom at the rear of the tavern. His eyes soon settled on Ellis's table, and even in the thick shadows that covered his face, Ellis knew that Cole was there with a purpose.

Awkwardly, Cole made his way over to where Ellis was sitting. Ellis watched without humor the ungainly way he moved his leg; he'd seen the way Cole had snatched up Riley's hand close enough to know that the man was much more of a threat than might first be believed. Looks, in this case, weren't everything. After his last pained step, Cole stared down at Ellis, his shirt stuck tightly to his body with sweat.

"You look like a fella in need of a drink," Ellis offered.

"Why did you do it?" Cole asked in return, his voice heavy with accusation.

"Just sit down, Ambrose."

"Tell me why you burned down that barn!"

"Keep your goddamn voice down," Ellis hissed. Out of the corner of his eye, he could see the bartender's head rise from his card game and turn in their direction. The last thing he needed was a pair of flapping gums getting hold of what he had done; if that were to happen, he'd have as much chance to hold on to the secret as he would to shoot out the sun. "Either you sit your ass down or I swear to Christ I'll get up and knock you down."

Cole stared at him for a moment longer before reluctantly sliding out a chair and sitting down. Ellis waited until the bartender returned to his card game before turning his attention back to the angry man opposite him. "You sure you don't want somethin' to drink?" he asked. "Hell, I'll even buy.

A day like this, it's 'bout the only thing that'll beat the heat."

"I'm not here because I want to share your company."

"I reckon that's fair enough."

Now sitting up close to him, Ellis took a long measure of Cole Ambrose. He was no longer the scrawny runt tagging along behind his brother, accepting of the fact that he would constantly stumble and fall, picking up just as many bruises as he did insults. Now, things were different. Even with that bad leg of his, he was clearly the sort of fellow who was capable of handling himself. No wonder he'd been able to hold his own with a scrapper like Riley.

"This ain't none of your business," Ellis said, looking him dead in the eye.

"You made it my affair."

"You said that before," Ellis chuckled easily, remembering the defiant way in which the young teacher had rushed to Sophie Heller's defense. "Back in that diner, you done got it in your head you was gonna play the hero. But you ain't got no idea what it is you're stickin' your nose into, boy."

"Snakes like you never change, Ellis," Cole said contemptuously. "Even if I didn't already know what you bastards have done, I'd have been certain that you were up to no good."

"All the more reason for you to back off now."

"Then your thinking is just as rotten as the rest of you. Just as bad as the ridiculous thought that you acted upon," Cole said with an angry shake of his head. "The Hellers aren't Nazis! Any sane person would see that! They're no less Americans than you or me."

"Bullshit!" Ellis spat. "You think that just 'cause you came back to town one of them college-educated fellas that the rest of us are just dumb hicks, too damn ignorant for our own good, but I'm keen to what's goin' on. This war done began long before them Japs bombed Pearl Harbor. Them Nazis been plannin' this whole thing for years, puttin' their agents in America and tellin' 'em to just go and act like they was normal folk. Ain't no one gonna even notice until it's too damn late! That's what them Hellers are . . . third columnists! I sure as shit ain't gonna just sit by and do nothin' while them Nazi rats turn Victory over to those stooges in Berlin!"

"You're crazy," Cole whispered incredulously. "You're completely insane."

"You're the fool if you don't believe me," Ellis argued as he brought a closed fist down onto the tabletop with enough force to make his nearly empty whiskey glass jump. "Mark my words, once all the men are up and gone, them Hellers is gonna poison the water supply or light fire to the whole damn town! Ain't gonna be nothin' left of this place 'cept some name on a map! They mean to kill us all for Hitler!"

With every word that he spoke, it became increasingly clear to Ellis that Cole Ambrose chose not to believe him. Frustration and anger roiled in his chest at this latest rejection. He'd tried to convince a scant few others in town, people that he thought might be receptive to his message, but most all of them had proven to be just like the cripple sitting before him; too blind and ignorant to see the truth. Only Riley had believed him . . . Riley and one other.

"You ain't a good enough American," Ellis snarled in accusation.

"There's nothing good about what you're doing."

"I would've thought a smart fella like you might have had a shred of sense in him." Ellis shrugged, leaning back in his chair. "Hell, your brother's gonna put on a uniform and go hunt down some Huns on their own land. Since that bum leg of yours ain't gonna let you fight over there, I done reckoned you might want to do your part over here."

"Go to hell, Ellis," Cole growled.

"I'm just sayin' is all," he said with a smirk. "Pains me to think I was wrong."

"I'm nothing like you!"

"Then I suppose we're at a stalemate. That little split-tail up and told you what it is we done but you ain't enough of a man to see we done it for all the right reasons." Ellis's eyes searched Cole, carefully gauging him as he gave voice to the worry that had been nagging him from the moment the cripple had first told him that the Heller bitch had squealed. "I suppose the only thing left for you to do is go and tell what you know to the police."

Cole paused, only for an instant, before he said, "I might."

"Bullshit," Ellis cursed, reading the young

teacher as easily as he might read a book. "If yellin' to the cops were your intentions, you'd have already done it, 'stead of sittin' here and refusin' my hospitality. There wouldn't been no need to seek me out. The way I see it, you ain't got the guts."

"Stay away from the Hellers," Cole warned, a redness rising in his face.

"Or what?"

Cole rose to his feet much faster than Ellis would have imagined possible, his hands gripping the edges of the table so violently that Ellis's near-empty glass tipped and rolled, sending the whiskey crashing to the floor, where his drink lay dead and wet. Neither man turned to it, their eyes fixed on each other.

"There a problem?" the bartender called.

Out of the corner of his eye, Ellis saw that their commotion had managed to attract some unwanted attention; both the bartender and his card-playing companion were staring at them. Even the lone drunkard had raised his head from the bar top. Without a word, Ellis raised his hand to the bartender and scowled. Such an act was more than enough to squelch any curiosity; his brutal reputation was enough for all three of the men to suddenly act as if he were not even in the room.

"Don't think for one second that I'm just going to stand by and let you three bastards have your way with the Hellers," Cole said, glaring down at him. "Knowing what you're up to, I'll be watching you like a hawk. You can bet on it!"

"So you've decided to play the hero, huh?" Ellis smirked.

"I'll do what I have to."

"You're only going to get yourself hurt."

"We'll see about that. It'd be a mistake to underestimate me."

"I'm already learnin' that very thing."

"You'll find that I'm full of surprises."

"Like the fact that you're sweet on poor Sophie," Ellis said, suddenly rising up from his chair and stepping around the table, stopping only when he was a matter of inches from Cole's face.

Cole seemed taken aback both by the bluntness of Ellis's claim and the way in which he had risen to face him. Shaken, he took an uneasy step back, but his eyes never left the other man's face. His hands balled into fists, certain that it was about to come to blows.

"You ain't never been with a woman, have you?" Ellis asked.

Cole refused to give him the satisfaction of an answer, holding his tongue.

"I've known a couple of fellas like you," Ellis said softly, his voice little more than a whisper. The faint smell of whiskey hung in the air, wafting up from the floor below. "All of 'em shy and more than a little unsure of themselves. With your leg, wouldn't be nobody that'd blame you for it. Ain't never had no attention from a lady. Then some pretty girl starts talkin' in your ear and you start thinkin' with what hangs between your legs instead of usin' your head."

"It's not like that," Cole said defensively.

"Sure it is. It's *always* like that," Ellis contradicted, moving even closer to the other man. "But the mistake you're makin' is that you're too blind to see you're flirtin' with the enemy. You take her to your bed and you're gonna be doin' just exactly what them Huns want. The sooner you realize this, the better off you're gonna be."

Cole stared at Ellis, his face a mask of smoldering anger. Though he remained silent, Ellis could see that he could be provoked; all it would take was a push here, a tug there, and he could be brought to blows. And that would be his undoing . . . But now was neither the time nor place. It was enough to know he was vulnerable.

"But it's your pecker, I suppose." Ellis chuckled, backing away from their face-off and bending to pick up his wayward glass.

"Stay away from her, Ellis," Cole warned him. "Or you'll be sorry."

By the time Ellis rose, Cole was already ambling toward the door, measuring each movement carefully, his hip jutting awkwardly. He stepped from the gloom of the tavern into the summer heat and was lost to sight. He never once looked back.

Ellis Watts felt uneasy; Cole Ambrose was clearly more of a man than he'd given him credit for. He would have to be accounted for if they were to deal with those damn Nazis. But unease wasn't fear; it was impossible for him to believe that a one-legged nothing could stand in the way of his plans. He knew that he could end the man's life just as easily as snuffing out a match. Still, as with the Hellers, he would need to be patient. Just as when he'd decided to burn the barn, the time to act would reveal itself and he would not hesitate, he would not show any mercy, and then that damn cripple would be in for the fight of his life.

"We'll see who's gonna be sorry," he muttered to himself before signaling the bartender for another drink.

Cole hurried down the sidewalk as quickly as he could manage, distaste roiling in his gut at having been so near to Ellis Watts. Warm sunlight washed over his skin and he couldn't help but feel he was being cleansed; after learning the horrible truth of what had happened to Sophie, after sitting in the murky gloom of the tavern, he felt he had been tainted, covered in filth as surely as if he'd been pushed into a mud puddle.

Having to listen to Sophie speak of the heinous acts that Ellis and his two hooded companions had committed was nearly more than Cole could bear. The fear in her voice had been paralyzing, a raw pain that felt as real to him as a slap in the face. Still, he'd given Sophie his word. But while he would not go to the police, that didn't mean he was going to do nothing. To that end, he'd gone in search of Ellis Watts.

No-good rotten son of a bitch!

Finding the bastard had been easy; stomaching his presence long enough to learn the reasons for what he had done had been something else entirely. Having to look at the smirk plastered on his face, having to listen to the self-assured way he spewed his insanity, had made Cole both sick to his stomach and angry as hell. When Ellis had shot to his feet, he had steeled himself for a confrontation that, to his surprise, had never come. Still, Ellis Watts had proven himself to be just as Cole remembered him; as dangerous as a coiled rattlesnake.

From the moment that he had set foot inside the tavern and leveled his charges against Ellis, Cole knew that he had crossed a line he could never erase. For better or for worse, he had inserted himself into the middle of the whole sordid affair. To Ellis's way of thinking, he was one with the Hellers; enemies who had to be dealt with, violently if need be. It would inevitably come to a fight; of this Cole couldn't be more certain.

Though Cole knew that Sophie would be upset with him if she knew what he had just done, he didn't regret it. He simply couldn't bear the thought of seeing her hurt. If he had even a single ounce of strength left, he would use it to protect her, no matter what the cost. It was impossible for him to know what was growing between them, but he knew in his heart that it was truly special, maybe once-in-a-lifetime.

What could be more worth fighting for?

Chapter Thirteen

GRAHAM GRIER STOOD down the street from the *Victory Gazette* office, peering anxiously around the corner of the grocery store, his eyes locked upon Hermann Heller and his pickup truck. He'd been watching the man for nearly ten minutes, the afternoon slowly inching closer to five o'clock, as his stomach busily tied itself into knots. Even though he was in the shade, he constantly needed to wipe his brow, his dark hair plastered to his forehead.

I can't believe I'm lurking out here like some common criminal!

Unlike Riley, Graham couldn't bring himself to simply wait for Sophie from across the street, watching in plain sight; the very last thing he wanted was for her to see him. He was still so embarrassed about being tied up in the whole scandalous mess that he wished he could hide under a rock. From down the street, he could still keep an eye on the newspaper's door.

After all, Sophie isn't the only person I want to avoid . . .

Standing so close to the newspaper's office dredged up all of the memories that Graham constantly struggled to repress: the liquor he'd consumed that fateful night, the full moon shining outside the bedroom window, and even the soft feel of the woman's skin beneath his fingers. Though the pleasure of that moment had been exciting enough to send his heart to racing, the agony Graham had experienced ever since weighed on his heart as if it were a blacksmith's anvil.

Carolyn . . .

Guilt still gnawed at him over his having lied to his father. Calvin Grier had asked him to attend a meeting with Franklin

Sweeney, the president of Victory Bank and Trust, but Graham had begged off, claiming that he hadn't been feeling well. He knew that his father wished to groom him to someday take over his duties as mayor, but Graham simply could not risk angering Ellis; the danger to his and his father's name was far too great. While Graham knew that Riley could just have easily continued his duties of watching Sophie, he was certain that Ellis had given the task to him as a means of reminding Graham that he was under the man's thumb, that he was being kept on a short leash that could be yanked tighter at a moment's notice.

Chafing at his own foolishness, Graham silently cursed himself. It was as if he were an animal that had been caught in a trap. To do nothing meant that he would undoubtedly starve to death, full of fear as he resolutely waited for the inevitable. To fight against the bonds that held him meant to shred his body against the metal of the trap, a horribly painful end. In the real world, his choices didn't seem any better. If he were to disobey Ellis, he would never recover from the damage that would be inflicted. But to go along with Ellis and Riley made him every bit the lowlife they were . . .

He simply didn't know what to do.

Nervously, Graham checked his watch. It was just after five; he knew Sophie would be appearing soon. He was nothing short of a mess; sweat ran down his face in rivers just as shivers raced across his arms. He was startled to realize that he had been holding his breath in anticipation of seeing her and forced himself to exhale. It felt as if he had been waiting for hours.

Suddenly, there she was. Sophie stepped from the newspaper office, heading straight toward her father. But unlike her terror that Riley had described as her reaction upon seeing him, she didn't seem the least bit worried. Not once did she glance around, looking for a menacing face. Instead, she seemed happy, even elated, as if she didn't have a care in the world. Smiling brightly, she was more beautiful than he'd ever seen her. Confusedly, Graham watched as she laughed at something her father said, slid into the battered old truck, and headed out of town.

Graham was so surprised by her demeanor that he blindly stepped out from the shadowed safety of the building and out onto the sidewalk. He watched, slack-jawed, as the truck drove past him, Sophie chatting cheerfully with her father. Squelching the sudden urge to call out her name, to obtain the attention he had been so carefully avoiding, Graham's heart pounded in his chest. Helplessly, he stared at the truck until it was completely swallowed from his sight. Sophie never once looked back.

"What the hell?" he muttered.

A cascade of worry crashed through Graham's thoughts. Try as he might, he simply couldn't find any rational explanation for what he had just witnessed. He had dreaded seeing her overwrought with fear, but this . . .

Why had she been so happy?

Hermann pulled the truck into the long drive that led to the house, bouncing over every hole and divot. Lacking rain, the ground had hardened as if it were cast in concrete. The truck lurched hard to the left, then forward, and then left again.

"Uppsie-Daisy," her father said, as he did every time.

Sophie clung tightly to the doorframe, smiling every bit as warmly as the sun; not even being bounced around the inside of the truck as if she were in an earthquake was enough to dampen her mood. *Cole Ambrose took me on a picnic lunch!* Pleasantly, she wondered if she would ever stop smiling, a thought so wonderful that she let out a laugh.

From the moment that the young teacher had returned her to the newspaper office, she had felt as if she were walking on air. Spending time with Cole had proven all of her thoughts about him to be true; he was well-spoken, kind, considerate, and certainly easy on the eyes. She'd been certain that everyone in the office had known exactly what she had been thinking. For his part, Walter had taken one look at her, chuckled, and said, "I do believe I'd have to be a blind man not to know you had yourself a good time, and even then I ain't too sure I wouldn't know!"

For a short while, all of her many problems had vanished as if they were so much smoke. Though it had been difficult, relief had flooded her upon telling Cole the truth about Ellis, Riley, and Graham. Although part of her still worried that he would feel compelled to tell the police, she believed Cole to be a man of his word. He had promised to protect her, to watch over her and her family, a thought that brought her no small amount of comfort. When they had parted, they had vowed to see each other soon, a timeframe that both beckoned and taunted her all at once.

I cannot wait for it to be soon!

Up ahead, Karl continued to clear away the last remnants of the burned-out barn, sweat glistening on his brow and bare forearms as he strained to pull a long, twisted piece of blackened metal free from its entanglement. Sophie was surprised to see how little of the barn remained; every day, more and more of it vanished. Now only a few charred beams, the odd farming tool, and the scorched earth remained to speak of what had happened.

"It will not be long now until it will be time to build again," Hermann explained as he brought the truck to a halt and shut off the engine. "Soon, it will be good as new."

For once, Sophie found herself agreeing with her father's belief in the future.

"Does Mother need help with dinner?" she asked.

"I think that all is ready," Hermann said, grunting softly as he got out of the truck. "Go and wash up. Karl and I will be there soon. You know how your mother gets when food starts to grow cold."

Sophie hurried to the house and headed indoors. She had hoped that there might be time for her to rush to her special spot in the woods before dinner; the day had been so wonderful, so full of possibility, that she wanted some time alone to revel in it. But just as she was about to rush up the stairs that led to her room, her grandmother called to her. "Sophie, my dear," she said, her voice carrying both the frailty of age and the richness of surety. "Could you join me outside for a moment?"

Following her grandmother's voice, Sophie found Gitta sitting quietly on the long porch that wrapped around the rear of the Hellers' home. From such a vantage point, the view gave nearly as rich a bounty as the land: gently rolling hills of cornstalks stretching skyward toward the sun; stands of majestic trees, their gnarled limbs now thickly covered in leaves; and even the roughly cut path that Sophie followed from the house to her special place among the tall rocks, gurgling stream, and peaceful quiet.

Gitta loved the porch. Even on the hottest days of summer, sticky afternoons when the air felt thick enough to touch, she liked to sit in the meager shade the porch offered and simply watch the world go by, content to bear witness to the subtle shifts of the seasons; for Sophie, seeing her grandmother on the porch was as much a part of the landscape as any of the trees, rocks, or fields. Now, sitting in a wicker chair that faced all the beauty nature had to offer, she looked serene. Gitta's wrinkled face brightened when she saw Sophie.

"You seem very happy, my granddaughter," the older woman observed.

"I am," Sophie admitted. Her heart skipped a beat at the thought that her happiness was so obvious, clear enough to be seen without a single word being spoken.

"I suppose this has something to do with that young man who drove you home."

The perceptiveness of her grandmother's words startled Sophie, leaving her momentarily stunned.

"When someday you become my age, dear, you will find that very greatest of pleasure you have is watching life go on around you," Gitta explained, knitting her wrinkled hands together. "When that day comes, then there you will sit, as quiet as church mouse, and no one will notice."

"You saw us?"

"I did."

Color rose in Sophie's cheeks at the realization that her grandmother must have seen her running away from Cole, tears streaming wildly down her cheeks. The burden of her shame pressed down upon her and though she and Cole had spoken about what had happened, she could not bring herself to completely forgive herself for how she had acted.

"Is he the reason you feel so happy?"

"Yes." Sophie nodded. "He is."

"Then why were you so upset that day?" Gitta asked. "I may have somehow become old, but I still know tears when I see them . . . I am not so deaf that I cannot recognize sobs behind closed door when I hear them."

Sophie didn't know how to answer her grandmother. After all of the horrible things that had occurred that day, from hearing the hateful slur in the diner to being grabbed by Riley Mason, her emotions had been as shaken as if they had been trapped in a tornado. Looking upon Cole's disfigured leg after he had painstakingly made his way around the truck had simply been the last straw, breaking her will and sending her running to the house in tears.

"Is it because of his leg?" Gitta asked as if she were reading Sophie's mind.

"Yes . . . no," Sophie tried to answer. "At that moment, right there and then, it might have been, but now it's not like that at all. Now, I'm ashamed of how I acted. Now, it's not important."

"Because now you know who is this man on inside."

"Yes, I believe I do."

Gitta sat silently for a moment, a gentle breeze rustling the air, carrying with it the myriad smells of the farm. She regarded her granddaughter curiously, as if weighing some hidden truth. "Would you like to hear a story?" she finally asked.

"Yes, *Oma*," Sophie answered softly.

"When I was young girl in Cologne, I met man who makes my heart swim and my knees shake," she explained, her thin lips lifted in the gentlest of smiles. "The first time I see him, he tells me that he is to marry me someday, and I laugh and tell him he is fool, but he sees that I am not quite telling the truth. He is man who makes me smile, laugh, and when he is not there I cannot wait until I see him again. He feels same way for me that I feel for him. We are falling in love together. Do you know about these feelings?"

Sophie could only nod.

"But it is not meant to be easy." Gitta frowned. "My father is too strict man. To him, all that matters is standing, what kind of family my suitor is from, what money they have. To my father, they do not have enough, are not good enough. My mother understands but she cannot go against the wishes of her husband. At first, my heart breaks and I cry and cry. It all seem hopeless. But then I start to think different.

I start to feel different. Do you know what I did?"

"What, Grandmother?"

"I decide to fight," her grandmother said proudly. "I decide that I will live my life as I want, as I choose. My father have to accept. It was then that I married Konrad Heller, your grandfather. Every day of our marriage, I know that I am right. Through many good times and some bad, through marriage, through birth of our children, and until Konrad passes, I have no regrets for what I have done. Even now, an old woman living in America, there is nothing that I would change. No mistakes. My love for Konrad is greater than all."

"I didn't know," Sophie said. "You never told me this story."

"That is because it does not matter," Gitta said as if it were the most obvious truth in the world. "From the moment that I fall in love with Konrad, nothing else mattered. Not that his family make less money than my own, not what anyone thought, nothing but our want to be together." Her eyes held Sophie's for a tender moment, letting the weight of her words sink in. "Do you understand what it is that I am saying to you, Sophie?"

Sophie knew with certainty what her grandmother was trying to tell her; that the handicap that ravaged Cole Ambrose's leg did not matter if she could find it in her heart to love him. What was truly important was the man he was on the inside; decent, hardworking, possessed of a true heart that clearly returned her feelings. For an instant, she thought of Ellis Watts and how his movie-star good looks hid an inside that was rotten straight to the core. Though she still found Cole to be a very handsome man, she knew that others would see only his flaw. She doubted that there would be anyone who had ever met him who would deny that his inside was a thing of beauty.

"Thank you, *Oma*," Sophie said as she leaned over and gave the older woman a kiss on her cheek. "Whether I knew it or not, that was exactly what I needed to hear."

Gitta's hand found Sophie's and held it tightly. "Always remember that you are special, Sophie," she urged. "Knowing what is right is something that will always serve you well, even in love."

Sophie blushed, the tiniest welling of tears coming to her eyes.

"Supper!" her mother suddenly called from the kitchen.

"Come now, dear," Gitta said, rising on tottering legs. "You know how your mother gets when food gets cold." Sophie did not immediately follow, choosing instead to watch as the elderly woman slowly made her way across the porch and into the house.

"You're the one who's special," she whispered.

For the first time, Sophie was glad she hadn't gone to her special place.

Chapter Fourteen

COLE PAUSED from his task to wipe the thick sweat from his forehead with the back of one gloved hand. High above in the cloudless sky, the sun relentlessly pounded down upon him with the persistency of a hammer driving a nail. *It has to be nearly one hundred degrees!*

"We haven't been at this for even three hours!" Jason barked.

"What's your point?"

"That here I am working my ass off and you're already quitting!"

"Can't a guy take a break?" Cole snorted.

"This close to lunch?" his brother shot back. "Hell, no!"

Cole chuckled as he bent back to his work. He and Jason had spent the bulk of the morning unloading a flatbed truck of supplies just arrived from Springfield into the fenced storage yard just behind their father's hardware store. While Jason grabbed the long beams of wood, hoisting them effortlessly up onto his muscled shoulders, Cole busied himself picking up heavily laden sacks of nails, hammers, and other smaller tools; with his bad leg, it was too difficult to balance the larger items. Cole knew that much of what they were unloading was destined to become part of the Hellers' new barn.

Initially, his father had asked only Jason for help, but the older Ambrose brother had shown no reluctance to drag Cole into it. Cole was thankful that he had; even though they were out in the blazing heat, their once white shirts rolled tightly at the sleeves and filthy from dust and sweat, there was no small amount of pleasure to be found in each other's company. They'd been trading needling barbs from the first load, a playful whack on the arm here, a brotherly insult that would make a preacher blush there. He couldn't help but love every minute.

"How many hours were you spending in those Chicago libraries, anyway?"

"What the hell are you talking about?" Cole asked.

"You're as soft as a boiled egg!" Jason teased as he headed back to the truck for another load. "I've made at least four trips to every one of yours! Mary Ellen could have done just as much as you in only half the time! Are you even trying at all?"

"No wonder I'm the one that's going to be a math teacher," Cole shot back. "You never could count for a damn!"

Scarcely a week had passed since Cole had taken Sophie on a picnic and he had been surprised to find that he was growing used to being happy. They'd managed to see each other a couple more times since, and during each meeting, Cole felt his feelings for the dark-haired beauty growing in leaps and bounds. They had made plans to see a movie later in the week, a date he was looking forward to with great anticipation.

But today was a time to be given to his

brother; Jason would be leaving on the next morning's train, bound for California, the navy, and finally some distant foreign shore. Who knew how long he would be gone? Cole couldn't believe that their time together had passed so quickly; it seemed as if it were only yesterday that Jason had burst through the kitchen door, fresh from Hallam Falls, his induction date still a moment set far in the future. But somehow, the weeks had fallen away as surely as the rising and setting of the sun. Come tomorrow, Jason Ambrose would be off to war.

For as long as he could remember, Cole had wished that he were the one that would be sent off to fight, but now that Jason was about to leave, he found his thoughts to be uncertain. Sophie's words still echoed in his head, that no one should wish to go to war but simply accept it as an unwanted but necessary responsibility, and he felt a bit ashamed of his earlier bravado. Still, he felt secure in the knowledge that his brother, as well as all of the other Americans who had answered their country's call, were fighting the just fight and would be home just as soon as their duty was fulfilled.

"About time to eat, I reckon," Robert summoned them from the rear of the store.

"Truer words have never been spoken!" Jason shouted.

Their father had sent out for bagged lunches from Marge's; thick-cut turkey sandwiches piled high with lettuce and tomatoes, ice-cold bottles of milk, even generous cuts of apple pie. Cole had hoped that Robert might join them while they ate, but he had no more than set the lunches on the steps when he headed back inside the hardware store. The two of them sat in the shade afforded by the rear door's overhang, their legs dangling over the side of the steps as if they were much younger children, and ravenously dug into their food.

They ate in silence, each brother more than content just to share the other's company. But as Cole finished his meal, his intentions began to nag at him a bit. He had already decided that this would be the day he would tell Jason all about Sophie and had begun to realize that this was a time as well suited to the task as any. Though he was no longer working under the direct gaze of the summer sun, he nonetheless began to sweat.

"There's something . . . something I wanted to tell you about," Cole struggled.

"Yeah?" Jason answered, popping the last bite of his apple pie in his mouth.

Cole took a deep breath. "I'm seeing a girl."

"What?" Jason barked, leaping to his feet so quickly that anyone passing by on the street would have been convinced that his rear end was on fire. With a beaming smile stretching from ear to ear, words poured from his mouth as quickly and surely as spring rain. "Who is she? How did you meet her? Don't you dare leave out even one detail or I swear to Christ I'm going to punch you so hard you won't wake up until the middle of next week!"

Though Jason had threatened him with physical violence, Cole found that he had to fib a bit as he recounted his first meeting with Sophie Heller. When he recounted their time at Marge's counter or the ride home in the pickup, he left out all mention of Ellis Watts and his two companions. He further neglected to tell Jason about the burning of the Hellers' barn. As badly as he wanted his brother's advice about what he should do, he had given Sophie his word, and that was a bond he was not willing to break.

Jason smiled. "Sophie's a nice girl."

"She definitely liked your picnic idea."

"I knew it!" Jason exclaimed, playfully punching his brother in the arm. "I would have bet the farm that you weren't asking me about first dates because of some interest in my love life!"

"So you caught me! I'm guilty!"

Cole told Jason about how he had picked Sophie up at the newspaper office and taken her to Watkins Creek. He spoke of how nervous he had been but was then just as honest about how easy it was for him to be in her company and of how effortlessly they had talked of their lives, all the sorts of moments that he had never before shared with a woman. Recounting their meetings since that day, Cole felt as if he were experiencing them all over again, and his heart could not help but swell with joy.

"I'm happy for you," Jason said, and Cole knew his brother truly meant it.

"It's still hard for me to believe it's true."

"But it is," his older brother said as he threw a sweaty arm around Cole's shoulder and gave him a squeeze. "If there's anyone who's ever deserved to be happy, truly happy, it's you, Cole."

"I just don't want to screw it up."

"You won't."

"That's easy for you to say." Cole laughed. "But I'm still new at all of this."

"Just be glad you don't have to leave her."

The smile that creased Cole's face fell flat at his brother's words, replaced by a sickening feeling that rumbled in the pit of his stomach. The one worry that he had had about speaking of his newfound relationship with Sophie was that it might cause Jason to reflect on his own feelings for Mary Ellen Carter, a fear that now appeared to be justified. Tomorrow, Jason was not only leaving Victory, he was also leaving his girl.

"How's Mary Ellen taking it?" Cole asked carefully.

"About as well as can be expected, I suppose," Jason said. "At first, after I'd gone and volunteered for the war, it was pretty easy for both of us to just put it out of our minds. We just sort of denied that it was even happening. Going off to fight was this faraway thing that we didn't have to worry about, even though we both knew that it was coming, no matter how much we tried to pretend otherwise.

"But then things changed. Mary Ellen started crying a lot. She tries to hide it from me the best she can, but every once in a while I'll catch her just staring at me, her eyes all swollen and wet with tears. Whenever this happens, all I can do is tell her that I'm sorry, even if I'm not sure what I'm supposed to be apologizing for." Jason sighed deeply; in that moment Cole could see that he was struggling to control his own emotions. "I don't think she'll be able to make it to the station tomorrow. I'm afraid it might kill her to watch me go."

"I'll watch over her," Cole offered. "I promise."

"I know you will."

"It's kind of hard to admit it, but I know how she feels."

"How so?"

"For about the last week, I've found myself worrying about you going off to the war," Cole explained. "Every time I pick up the paper, I end up closing it without reading a single word. Now that you're going, now that the day is finally here, it all seems more real than before." There was much that Cole found himself unable to say; particularly that he was afraid for his brother. He kept trying to convince himself that Jason had always been a careful sort and he tried to cling to the belief that everything would be fine. Just like Mary Ellen, all he wanted was for Jason to come home safe and sound.

They sat in silence for a while, unable to speak to each other. Cole couldn't help but wonder just how long Jason would be gone; the war in Europe had been raging for nearly three years already with no sign of letting up. *Surely, it can't last much longer!* With the Japanese now involved, it seemed that the whole world was a powder keg just waiting to be lit. Cole already knew that every time he ran into Mary Ellen, it was going to break his heart; he was the one person in Victory who would know just how lonely and scared she was.

"I'm going to come home," Jason suddenly said.

Cole put his hand on his brother's knee

and gave it a pat. Turning his head, he looked carefully at Jason's profile, marveling at how much he looked like their father; his green eyes and tight jawline were nearly the spitting image. Still, Jason possessed a special sort of warmth, of character, a spark of life that Robert Ambrose had never had or had somehow lost along the way. Cole knew that it was this spirit that would carry Jason back to Victory, back to his family, and back to Mary Ellen Carter and their future together.

Jason suddenly sprang from the steps and began to trot back to the truck, then turned back to face his brother. All the sadness and worry had gone from his face, replaced by a look of good humor and mischief. "We best get back to work," he said with a smirk. "After all, if I leave any of this to you, it'll still be waiting for me when I get back home!"

Cole could only smile.

Cole was sitting by his bedroom window, trying to read a book, when he heard a light knock on his door. It was late, nearly one o'clock in the morning, but he'd long since given up trying to sleep, unable to stop thinking about his conversation with his brother. He'd picked up the book in the hope that it would distract him from his worries, but he'd read the same page five times and was getting no closer to understanding its meaning.

He crossed the room quickly, fearful that it was his father; he'd tried to be as quiet as he could, but with his bad leg, there was always the chance that he'd managed to interrupt Robert's sleep. But when he pulled open the door, he found Jason awaiting him, his shoulders slumped low and his mouth set in a deep frown.

"Is everything all right?"

Jason didn't give any answer, but simply entered Cole's room and dropped onto his back on the bed, one hand absently running through his light hair. His eyes were bloodshot and wet and it looked to Cole as if he could break down again.

"Mary Ellen?" Cole asked softly.

Jason gave a nearly imperceptible nod. "I did everything I could think of to make her smile, cracked every dumb joke I knew, even the ones I knew weren't funny, but she just couldn't get past the fact that this was our last night together," he explained, his voice cracking. "No matter what I tried, I couldn't get her to stop crying. With the way she was carrying on, you'd have thought tomorrow was my funeral!"

"She's scared."

"So am I," his brother admitted.

"I'm sure she knows that."

"There's a part of me that's glad she's not going to be at the train station in the morning. As bad as it would be for her, it sure wouldn't be a picnic for me to see her all upset."

"Even if she's not there, Mary Ellen will be thinking of you all the same."

Jason exhaled and sat up on the edge of the bed, trying his best to put up a good face but not doing the most convincing job. "Anyway," he said. "I didn't come in here to jabber on about my love life, but to give you something."

For the first time since he had opened the door, Cole noticed that his brother was holding something in his hand; a long, ornate walnut box that teased at his memories. "What is it?" he asked.

Opening it with a soft cry of its hinges, Jason held the box out so that Cole could see its contents; there, nestled elegantly among several sheets of thin crepe paper, was a pearl necklace. Clasped to the necklace was an elaborate brooch; delicate golden tendrils spread out from a sapphire center as if they were rays of light being shed from the sun.

"It belonged to our mother," Jason said, and in that very moment, the spark of recognition spread across Cole's memory; he saw her elegantly standing before the window as she wore it, just as plain as the day, and he couldn't help but feel a touch of shame at ever having forgotten such a sight.

"Where did you get it?"

"I suppose you could say that I stole it," Jason shrugged.

"*Stole it*?!"

"I took it out of a box that Dad had put in the attic right after she died," he explained. "I'm sure that the old man would be more than a bit furious to know that it was no longer there, but I figure that what he doesn't know won't hurt him. I just couldn't bear the thought of it being locked away."

"I remember her wearing it," Cole said, and his brother smiled.

"I want you to have it while I'm gone."

"Why me? Why not Mary Ellen?"

"Someday I do want her to have it," Jason said, and as he spoke, Cole could see just how much he truly loved the girl he used to pelt with mud. "When I'm finally back home and all the fighting is over, I'll work up enough nerve to ask her to be my bride. On our wedding day, she'll wear our mother's necklace. But until that time, I want to know that it's in your hands. If I know you have it, that it's being looked after, then I'll have something else to come home for."

Jason handed Cole the jewelry box. Gently, Cole pulled the necklace free and draped it loosely across his fingers. Turning it first this way and then that, he stared at the brooch, certain that if he looked at it hard enough, his mother might somehow look back.

"I'll take good care of it," Cole promised.

"I know you will," Jason said. "Just like you'll look out for Mary Ellen."

"I still miss Mom, you know," Cole murmured, his voice barely a whisper.

"We all do."

"It's just that I . . ." he began, but trailed

off, his memories of that fateful day getting the best of him. He had been standing in this very room when he'd heard the crash, so startled by the noise that he had been unable to move, listening for some further sound. Tentatively, he'd gone out onto the landing, tears welling in his eyes when he'd seen her. He'd tried to move quickly, to make his bad leg act as it never had before, but . . . "It's just that I still can't help feeling that it's my fault she's gone."

"You can't torture yourself over this for the rest of your life," Jason said as he rose to his feet and placed a consoling hand upon his brother's shoulder. "No one blames you."

"Dad does."

"No, he doesn't," Jason disagreed. "He blames himself."

"What are you talking about?" Cole asked incredulously. "I'm the one . . ."

"Who was here when she fell," Jason finished, cutting him off while finishing his thought. "That's true, but one of the reasons she was alone in this house with you was because he was always at the hardware store. Maybe if he hadn't been so focused on the business, he might have been home at that moment. When he looks at you, he doesn't just see your failure to go and get help, he sees his own."

"But he couldn't have known—"

"It doesn't make any difference," Jason said. "He feels it all the same."

"But I didn't go for help! I didn't—"

"You were a child, Cole," his brother explained. "No one could have expected you to do more than you did. Dad knows that you should never have been in that position."

Cole found himself momentarily speechless. In all of the years he had played the events of that tragic day over and over again in his mind, he had always interpreted his father's reaction to his mother's death as *his* fault. But what Jason said shook him. If it was true, that meant that every time Robert Ambrose looked upon his younger son, he was reminded of his own guilt as well as his loss.

"Maybe I should go, leave the house," Cole said. "It would be easier if I wasn't here."

"No," Jason argued with a shake of his head. "This is his problem, not yours. Eventually, he's going to have to understand that accidents happen and there's simply nothing we can do to prevent them. No one wanted her to die, but she was taken from us just the same. We have to accept that, as uncomfortable as such a thought is. Both of you need to realize that fact instead of beating yourselves up over things you can't fix."

"I'll try," Cole offered.

"Give Dad some time," Jason said. "He'll eventually come around."

Standing there in his room, Cole was once again struck by just how much he was going to miss his brother. His arms found Jason and he hugged him tightly, wishing he could stay in that moment forever. Though he knew that Jason would be leaving for foreign lands and unknown dangers on the morning train, he wanted to cling to this memory, to hold it in his chest where he could treasure it every day that Jason was gone.

Finally, Jason let him go, tousled Cole's blond hair, and stepped to the door. "Try to get some sleep," he said with a wink. "After all, tomorrow's going to come soon enough."

Chapter Fifteen

COLE STOOD NEXT to his brother and father under the short awning of the train station and cursed the weather. Unlike every other day since he had returned to Victory, the morning had dawned every bit as unpleasant as his mood; a light pitter-patter of raindrops fell ceaselessly from the leaden sky, steadily drumming upon the earth. Peeking out from under the cover afforded to him, Cole looked up into the solid mass of gray clouds that spread like a blanket from horizon to horizon as rain struck his hat and wet his chin.

Jason shrugged. "It could be worse."

"How do you figure?"

"I could have been sent off in a blizzard, I suppose."

"At least there's no thunder or lightning," Robert added sullenly.

Cole was as startled by the sound of his father's voice as he would've been by the very thunder the man spoke of. It was the first time that day he had heard him speak. The ride to the train station had been spent in silence, save for the creaking of the truck and the never-ending drumming of the rain upon the windshield. Cole hadn't been able to find his tongue; it had been as if he were in church, a place where even a cough seemed inappropriate, listening to the preacher lecture from his pulpit about eternal salvation. They had sat in the cab of the pickup stiffly, the three of them packed as tightly together as sardines.

Inside the depot, there was a similar quiet. Occasional sounds echoed off the brick walls or concrete floors grown slick with rainwater. Most of the wooden benches that lined one wall of the depot were empty, their middles permanently sagging from weight that had been visited on them long ago. A cracked clock dutifully marked the passage of time. Across the glistening tracks, a dirt road ran along the rails and beyond that an open cornfield, now covered in a veil of rain and a haze of fog as thick as a curtain. A fitful breeze rose and then fell, swaying the heavily laden branches of maples and oaks. Above them, a pair of bare light bulbs momentarily sputtered to life but just as quickly extinguished, keeping them in a gloomy dark.

Few people milled about inside the depot or stood out near the rails; a young couple cooing over a sleeping infant, a middle-aged man methodically stuffing his pipe with tobacco, and an elderly woman profusely thanking one of the depot's porters for helping her with her luggage. Cole couldn't help but think that Jason's earlier premonition about the day seemed right: it had the air of a funeral.

"What time do you have?" Jason asked. "It must be getting close."

"Give it a look."

Cole checked his watch; still nearly ten minutes remained before the train was expected to arrive. Out of the corner of his eye, he could see his father looking at his older son appreciatively. Cole wondered what his father was thinking at a time like this; it saddened him that he had no idea if the man was filled with pride or racked by nerves.

For a moment, the two brothers stood silently, watching the rain endlessly fall.

"I'm sure as spitfire gonna miss baseball," Jason said, breaking the quiet.

"They'll keep you posted on who's in the running for the pennant."

"You reckon there's even going to be a season next year, what with all of the players getting called up?" Jason asked, as if he'd never before given the idea a moment's thought.

"I can't imagine a summer without baseball," Cole answered.

"You suppose a guy like Ted Williams would have to go and fight?"

"I can't imagine why not. If there's someone more able-bodied than him, I'd be hard pressed to tell you who he is."

"Wouldn't it really be something if Teddy Ballgame became a flyboy just like me?"

Jason exclaimed. "Heck, since I'm already daydreaming, we could even end up in the same unit!"

"Maybe then he could finally teach you how to hit a curveball."

"Still a wiseass, I see."

"You're only sore because it's true." Cole smiled.

"Who do you suppose would play left field for the Red Sox if it isn't him?"

Cole shrugged; though he was still enjoying their talk, his heart felt as heavy as a boulder. While it was certainly true that Jason was passionate about baseball, it was clear from the sound of his voice that he was nervous. For this, Cole certainly couldn't blame him; his own stomach was roiling, and he wasn't the one about to board a train bound for war.

Suddenly, the piercing whistle of the approaching train sounded in the near distance. Every head in the depot braved the miserably wet weather, necks craning to peer down the tracks for first sight of the locomotive. Cole was riddled with disappointment; he realized that he had never wanted a train to be late as much in his entire life.

Still, as the train slowly began to make its way into the tiny station, Cole found the sight of the looming black locomotive to be impressive: billowing clouds of thick black smoke pouring from the engine's tall stack; the first glimpse of the conductor, his white beard stained with soot; the hissing of rain as it steamed against the heat of the furnace; the shrill, sharp cry of the brakes as they slowed the iron horse; and even the expectant thrill of the passengers, contemplating journeys that were coming to an end and those that had yet to begin.

Cole's eyes found those of a young soldier sitting alone in the first passenger car as it slowly drifted past. Their gazes met for only a brief moment, but it was enough for him to remember his return to Victory. There had been soldiers on that train as well; it was hard to believe that his brother was heading off to become one of them. He wished that there were more people to see Jason off, a band or the mayor, perhaps, but this was the new reality of war; men would do their duty with little or no fanfare.

The train finally came to a halt and a handful of people got off. Most of those who had been waiting in the depot happily rushed to greet the new arrivals, curse the weather, and rush away. In a matter of moments, the depot emptied, the Ambrose family the only ones left.

Cole felt a tightness grip his chest. It was all happening too fast! Turning to his brother, he expected to see the same anxiousness, but Jason was silently regarding the train.

"I guess this is it," Jason said.

"Don't forget you promised to write."

"Each and every time I come across paper and a pencil."

"I'm sure they'll have plenty of both at Camp Parks."

Jason was scheduled to arrive at the United States Naval Training Yard at Camp Parks outside of Oakland, California, in three days' time to begin his boot camp.

"Just make sure you do it."

"Yes, sir!" Jason barked, throwing Cole a salute for good measure.

"It's not a joke!"

"Who thinks it's funny?" his brother shot back with a chuckle. "I'm under the impression that if I don't rush off a strong and steady stream of letters telling you about every last detail of military life, there's going to be a special kind of hell to pay. Does that sound about right?"

"It does, at that."

"That's why I'll keep my promise," Jason said as he clasped Cole's shoulder.

"You'd better."

Cole pulled his brother close and they embraced tightly. Tears began to well in his eyes and he had to struggle to stifle them; he'd sworn to himself that he would manage to be strong for Jason's sake, no matter what. Memories of their lives together raced through his head; they had always been close as children and their affection for each other had only become stronger as they had grown older. Though he held his brother in his arms, Cole couldn't help but feel that Jason had already gone, and that sudden fear made him hold on all the tighter. In that moment, he was ashamed of how he had felt the last time he had been at the train depot; the wish to go to war struck him as absurd.

Breaking their embrace, Cole was momentarily surprised to find his father standing beside them. He was even further startled to see Robert Ambrose take his departing son close to him and hold him tightly. Cole couldn't recall a moment where his father had demonstrated great affection toward him or his brother; he was a man more likely to offer words of encouragement or an occasional pat on the back. But now, as Jason was about to be whisked away to an unknown future, he was clearly struggling to control his emotions. It may have been the rain, but Cole watched what looked like a lone tear slowly fall down the man's cheek.

"You be careful now, son," Robert said, his voice cracking.

"I will, Dad," Jason promised. "I'll keep my head."

"Remember what I told you."

"I couldn't forget if I tried. I'll do just as you taught me."

"You do that. It'll get you through."

"Don't worry about—" Jason started, but the words quickly died in his throat as his eyes fell upon something over his father's shoulder, something in the distance. An audible gasp burst from Jason's chest as he stood transfixed. Cole and Robert followed his gaze to find a woman standing at the other end of the platform.

"Mary Ellen . . ." Jason whispered.

Cole couldn't help but gawk at the change in Mary Ellen Carter. Gone was the dumpily short, stringy blonde-haired girl, her gaze perpetually turned to the ground, fated to be picked on and mercilessly teased. In her place stood a stunning beauty, dressed in a flattering white blouse and dark skirt, her curled blonde hair covered by a pillbox hat, her pale arms pressed tightly to her chest. This was the woman that Jason had once pelted with mud, the woman who had somehow forgiven him and instead stolen his heart.

For a long moment, Jason and Mary Ellen stared silently at each other, neither capable of taking even a single step. Finally, it was she who could resist no longer, breaking from her trance and running toward Jason, sobs racking her chest, a mixture of rain and tears streaming down her pretty face. When she reached him, she threw her small body into his arms and buried her face in the crook of his neck. He lifted her off the ground effortlessly, as if she were little more than a doll.

"I can't believe you came!" Jason rejoiced. "I can't believe it!"

"I couldn't . . . stay . . . stay away . . ." Mary Ellen struggled to say through her sobs.

"But you told me that you couldn't bear to see me leave!"

"I guess . . . I'm not . . . a very good . . . liar . . ."

"I love you, Mary Ellen!" he said as he twirled her above the ground.

"I love you, too!" she cried in answer.

Through all of the joy of his brother and Mary Ellen's reunion, Cole tried to give them what privacy he could; both he and his father moved quietly away, their eyes locked upon the ground, leaving the young lovers alone on the platform for their parting moments.

Eventually, the couple managed to untangle from each other's arms, though Jason continued to gently hold Mary Ellen's face in his hands. He spoke softly to her, whispering as if he were explaining something that could only pass between the two of them. When he had finished, he looked at Cole and motioned for him to join them. "I reckon I should reintroduce the two of you," he said. "After all, it has been a few years."

"I remember you," Cole said to Mary Ellen. "Although I'd be one heck of a liar if I didn't admit you've changed a bit."

She smiled through her tears. "We all have." Up close, even though her face was still racked by emotion, Cole could clearly see why his brother was so attracted to Mary Ellen Carter; she had blossomed into a natural beauty. If Jason were so over the moon for her, Cole had no doubt she was even more beautiful on the inside.

"Cole's going to look out for you while I'm gone," Jason explained. "He'll be there for anything you need, even if it's a shoulder to cry on. He'll do just about as good a job as I would."

"I'll be there for whatever you need, Mary Ellen," Cole echoed.

"Thank . . ." was the furthest she got before again dissolving into tears.

Before Jason could offer her any comfort, the conductor blew his whistle and called for all passengers to board. With a resigned sigh, he picked up his heavy canvas bag, gave Mary Ellen a soft kiss on her forehead, his father and brother one last clasp on the shoulder, and climbed the steps to the train's passenger car.

Their eyes followed him down the aisle until he found a seat and threw open the window. He leaned out, rainwater falling down onto his head, just as the locomotive's whistle blew and the engine came chugging back to life, its wheels churning ever faster, destined to take him away.

"I'll be back!" he shouted. "I promise I'll come home!"

Watching his brother being borne away from him, Cole started to realize just what he would be missing without Jason at his side. While they had been apart during his years in Chicago, he'd never so much as entertained the thought that they would *never* see each other again. Now that thought was as real as an enemy soldier's next bullet. Though his future held much to look forward to, his budding relationship with Sophie Heller and his new job as a math teacher, Cole understood that there would be a void in his life until Jason made good on his word and returned to Victory.

Jason never moved back out of the rain into the safety of the passenger car, never stopped waving to them, and was soon lost to sight as the train took a gentle turn westward. Soon, all that remained was the billowing black smoke of the engine, and then that too was gone. At this final loss, Mary Ellen collapsed against Cole, crying unabashedly, her shoulders quivering with every sob. Cole did the only thing he could think might help; he held her gently and whispered that everything would be all right, even if he wasn't sure quite how.

Chapter Sixteen

SOPHIE WALKED HAPPILY down the street next to Cole, her heels clicking along the wet pavement. The sun had already set on the day, leaving behind lazy, dark clouds to ominously drift across the nearly full moon that was bright enough to erase the stars. The last couple of days had been filled with occasional streaks of rain and the side-walk was spotted with puddles, the breezy night air just cool enough to send a shiver racing down her bare arms.

The changing weather was something that Sophie paid little mind to; this was the night that she had been looking forward to for a whole week. Tonight was the night that she and Cole were to go to the movies, an event she supposed was their first *real* date. Walking the short distance to the theater, Sophie felt as if she were walking on those slowly drifting clouds high above.

"Too bad we couldn't find a closer spot to park," she said.

"That's all right," Cole answered. "A night as nice as this is just made for a bit of a walk."

They'd parked the truck behind the hardware store, but it'd still been a little more than a block away. Thankfully, they had arrived early enough that they didn't need to hurry. In the days since their first picnic lunch, it had become much easier for Sophie to walk beside Cole, matching her stride to his own. The problem with his leg was no longer an embarrassment to her, but rather a concern that she needed to take into account.

"It could be worse," Cole said.

"How do you figure?"

"The truck could just have easily broken

down when I picked you up at the farm. Four miles is a heck of a long way to walk just to see a movie."

"If that had happened, my father would have brought us into town."

"That's only if I managed to make a good impression."

"You would have known it if you hadn't."

Cole had arrived to pick Sophie up for their night out at exactly the time he had told her to expect him. He'd come into the farmhouse, taken off his hat, and proceeded to charm her parents. Sophie had noticed that her mother had stolen a glance at Cole's bad leg, her smile faltering for only an instant, but her eyes had been those of a mother caring for another's child, more full of sympathy than pity. Her father had shaken Cole's hand stiffly, but she could hear in his voice that he didn't begrudge anything to the man who had come to take his only daughter out for the evening. Gitta and Karl had chosen to stay out of sight. Much as Sophie would have liked to introduce them to Cole, there had been a part of her that was relieved.

"Maybe they'll even let me take you out again," he said hopefully.

She laughed. "If you're lucky."

The Majestic Theater's marquee brightly lit up the gloomy night; yellow, white, and red bulbs shone brilliantly against the dark sky. THE TALK OF THE TOWN—STARRING CARY GRANT AND JEAN ARTHUR was written in large letters. Sophie's heart leaped at the sight; it had been a long time since she'd been to the movies. The fact that she was going in the company of Cole Ambrose made it all the better.

After Cole purchased their tickets, they managed to make it to their seats just as the projector sprang to life and the first black-and-white images began to dance across the screen. Sophie slipped off her light coat and relaxed contentedly.

"I hope you'll like the movie," he whispered.

"I'm sure I will."

After a short cartoon that set the whole theater laughing uproariously, the mood grew much more somber as the first newsreels began to roll. Before Sophie's wide eyes, the war was everywhere; images of President Franklin Roosevelt sitting behind his desk at the White House, the American flag snapping briskly at the top of a flagpole, and a long convoy of warships steaming far out to sea. Watching most of these images set Sophie's heart racing with pride. But there were two different vignettes that set her heart pounding in a very different way.

First, there was a series of pictures that depicted the increasing readiness of the American serviceman: soldiers firing their new weapons, columns of men dressed in their crisp uniforms and shiny helmets as they marched in unison, a sailor being inoculated with a shot against some unknown disease, and an officer giving a crisp salute. The voice-over spoke of the willingness of all able-bodied American men to step to the forefront and defend both their native country and the promise of liberty throughout the world.

Through it all, Sophie could feel Cole holding his breath. She knew this was what upset him about his leg, what made him feel that he was not doing his expected part, and her heart went out to him. He'd told her about watching his brother leave on the train, about how he had come to the unexpected realization that war did nothing but destroy lives, but she could still see his jaw clench and his hand grip the armrest tightly.

The second series of images struck much closer to home. In them, the hordes of Nazi Germans continued to cut a swath across Europe, leaving nothing behind except death and destruction. It was as if the entire continent were to be bathed in the colors of the swastika. Hitler was shown giving a fiery speech, his shaking fist punctuating every word as spittle flew wildly from his mouth. Tanks, planes, and soldiers were then shown carrying out their Führer's orders. But the most disturbing image to Sophie was that of children crying in Britain, their homes blasted to pieces by bomber planes, their innocence in similar shambles, their lives forever changed.

It galled Sophie to believe that there was anyone in Victory who believed her family could be considered part of the same evil as the Nazis. Hitler and his followers were an affront to all of mankind! Though her family's roots were in Germany, the Hellers were every bit as appalled by the actions of their native land's citizens as any other decent, caring person. Images of Ellis, Riley, and Graham, their hoods covering their faces but not their intentions, swam through her memory. It had been much easier to forget all that had happened when she was at Cole's side, but even now, with him sitting in the seat next to her, the fears that had plagued her returned.

The movie itself proved to be quite entertaining. In it, Cary Grant played a man on the run named Leopold Dilg, who is unjustly accused of a crime he did not commit. Taking refuge in the summer house of a vacationing law professor, he tries to prove his innocence. In the end, he is defended from an angry mob and eventually cleared of all charges. Both funny and intelligent, the love triangle between the two men and Jean Arthur's character was witty, if not completely believable.

Though Sophie often found herself laughing loudly at the film's antics, there was still a nagging feeling that remained at the back of her thoughts. Beside her, Cole seemed to be enjoying the movie just as much as she was, but she couldn't help but notice that he was also a bit reserved, quieter than she expected, as if he were not letting himself go completely.

"Did you enjoy the film?" Cole asked once the credits had rolled and they were out in the lobby.

"Very much," Sophie answered him, content that she wasn't truly lying, even if she wasn't being completely honest, either. "I was worried the judge wouldn't let him go in the end."

"That would have been one heck of a way to end a comedy," he remarked.

Sophie was just about to answer with a joke of her own when, up ahead, she caught sight of Carolyn Glass. Standing just inside the front doors to the theater, she waited impatiently beside her husband as he spoke with Ernie Kennedy, the owner of the grocery store, a look of utter and complete boredom written plainly across her face. Much as she had been on the day she had verbally accosted Sophie, she was dressed expensively: a mink stole tossed easily over a silk blouse, a fashionable hat over her pinned-up hair, and enough gold around her neck to make a jeweler jealous.

"Wait . . . wait just a moment, Cole," Sophie said, coming to a sudden stop.

"Is something the matter?"

"No, I just . . . wanted to check my makeup," she stammered.

"Would it make any difference if I said that you were already beautiful?"

Sophie smiled weakly in answer but began to frantically dig in her purse just the same. So far, she remained beyond the other woman's notice. Thankfully, she had stopped just as soon as she had seen Carolyn; if she and Cole had kept going, they would have walked right past where the woman stood. Still, she certainly was not out of danger of being seen. Over the top of her purse, she watched as Augustus continued to prattle on with no sign of falling silent; Sophie hoped he would run out of things to say and take his young bride home!

Without warning, Carolyn looked in Sophie's direction, a glimmer of recognition dancing across her face. In the split second that followed, Carolyn's eyes filled with equal parts disdain and disgust, narrowing until they were little more than slits. Slowly, she turned her noticeably pregnant body until she was pointed directly at Sophie, looking for all of the world as if she was going to walk over and continue the tongue-lashing she had begun at the newspaper office. She was clearly the hunter; Sophie would be her prey. But just as she was about to take her first step, Sophie already recoiling slightly in fear, her husband took her firmly by the hand.

"Come along, dear," Augustus said softly. "It's time you got some rest."

For a moment, it looked as if Carolyn was going to argue, but instead allowed herself to be led from the theater and out into the night. But before she left the lobby, she managed to give Sophie a wicked smile riddled through with bad intentions, a thin-lipped grin that chilled her to the core.

What did I ever do to that woman to make her hate me so?

Sophie waited a few moments longer, absently digging in her purse for the mirror she knew was not there, before following Carolyn Glass out of the same double doors.

Outside, the summer night air had grown surprisingly cooler; Sophie pulled her thin coat tightly around her shoulders, trying to gain some meager warmth to chase away her chill. Above, the earlier clouds had drifted away and the moon filled the sky. As they walked, their footsteps echoed off the closed storefronts, giving Sophie the worry that they were being followed.

"Now, I'm not one to swoon over any male movie stars," Cole explained, his voice rising with excitement as he recalled the film, "but you'd have to be one spectacular fool not to recognize that Cary Grant sure can take over a picture screen. Boy, he can act! That man is smooth in ways I didn't know existed!"

Sophie could only nod absently in answer.

"Heck, if I were to suddenly wake up and find myself in Jean Arthur's shoes, heaven forbid," he said with a wink, "I can't imagine it would have been all that difficult to make up my mind."

Still, Sophie couldn't bring herself to speak.

"What about you, Sophie? Which one would you have picked?"

Walking along the barren street, Sophie found it impossible to understand all that Cole was saying. Even as he spoke, her mind raced from the burning of the barn, to the encounter at the diner, then on to her confrontation with Carolyn at the newspaper office, and finally to the sight of Riley Mason waiting for her outside of work. No matter how much she wished for her life to get better, no matter how much she enjoyed Cole Ambrose's company, she could not escape the fear and worry that hounded her at every step. She felt an unseen danger around every corner.

"Sophie?" Cole asked. "Are you all right?"

"I just . . . I don't . . ." she mumbled.

Without Sophie realizing it, they had managed to walk back to the truck. She stood before it, droplets of rainwater glistening on the hood, and turned to look into Cole's worried eyes. The sad truth was that she didn't have the slightest idea how to answer his question; much of her life was indeed just fine, but there was no denying the worry and fear that waited at the edges. She had spent so much time bottling up her emotions, erecting a dam through which they could not escape, that in the face of this latest trouble she felt as if she had taken on one problem too many and her already shaky barrier were about to burst.

"Why are you crying?" Cole asked.

Until he spoke, Sophie wasn't aware that she had been. Gently, she raised a hand to her cheek and her fingers came back wet. As she looked back into Cole's eyes, her vision became clouded. Tears began to fall heavily, racing rapidly down her cheeks.

"Whatever's the matter, Sophie?" he prodded again.

"It's nothing . . ."

"Don't tell me it was that bad a date," Cole asked anxiously.

Sophie wanted to reassure him, but her emotions had finally become too great, overwhelming her as easily as a teacup in a tempest.

"Oh, Cole!"

The words had scarcely left Sophie's lips before she rushed across the short distance between them and buried her face into his chest. Her arms laced around his waist as deep sobs began to rack her body. She clung to him tightly, his touch and smell filling her, the beating of his heart powerful enough to be heard over the rending of her own happiness.

Cole never said a word as she cried,

never asked the reason for her outburst, but instead held her close, his hands running gently through her dark hair. Occasionally, he whispered something sweet into her ear, the words lost to her but the sentiment every bit as clear as the stars above.

Calm began to slowly settle over Sophie as she stood in Cole's embrace. She could only marvel at how safe she felt in his presence, protected from the danger that assailed her, secure in the knowledge that he would protect her. When her breathing had righted itself, she pushed herself away from him and, after further composing herself, looked up into his eyes.

"I'm sorry, Cole," she finally said, her voice still heavy with emotion.

"You don't have any reason to apologize," he answered softly.

"It's just that sometimes I get overwhelmed. Sometimes . . ."

"Shhh," he whispered, quieting her explanation. His deep eyes were as luminous as the multitude of stars in the sky, even of the moon that looked back at her over his shoulder. "You don't have to explain yourself to me. Whatever is bothering you . . . you can share it with me when you're ready. All that matters to me is that you stop crying and smile again."

Words failed Sophie. As she looked up into Cole's eyes, a different emotion than fear filled her, a longing for something she couldn't put into words. The sudden urge to give in to those feelings was so overpowering that she surrendered to them.

She rose to meet him swiftly, her lips rushing to his as if they had their own urgent need that had to be answered. His body flinched in surprise for only an instant, but then his strong hands pulled her quickly back to him as he strove to meet her passion. The wet warmth of his searching mouth sent waves of sensation crashing over her; it was as if time were standing still, that they were the only two people the moon was watching over. The more that she kissed him, the more she wished that it would go on forever. Her own boldness had given her a reward greater than she could have imagined, and in that instant she knew that what she shared with Cole Ambrose was far more than any dream. When their lips finally broke apart, his deep eyes continued to hold her tenderly, refusing to completely let her go.

"I guess it wasn't that bad a date after all," he said, smiling.

"No, it wasn't. Even better than a date with Cary Grant!"

"Now, don't that beat any goddamn picture show!"

Graham Grier frowned angrily as he struggled to resist the urge to slug Riley Mason right in his filthy, no-good mouth. Instead, he continued to silently stare across the quiet, blackened street, the sight that greeted him souring his stomach. It was there, standing in front of that worthless, crippled teacher's truck, that he saw the girl of his dreams.

Kissing another man!

When Riley had called him and said that he had just seen Sophie Heller walking into the Majestic Theater, his first instinct had been to hang up the phone. But when the man had kept on, had explained that he had seen her in the company of another man, Graham had felt the need to act. He'd hurried out the door without a word to his father, and had been waiting in the darkened alley across the street for nearly an hour for the film to let out. All the while, he'd been hoping that Riley hadn't seen it correctly, had drunk a bit too much booze and imagined the whole thing. But in that he had been sorely disappointed.

His first surprise upon arriving at the Majestic had been in seeing Carolyn Glass leaving the theater with her husband. Gazing upon her pregnant belly, growing steadily larger since the fateful night he had spent in her bed, erased any lingering hope he might have had that his personal nightmare was simply that, a dream.

She's carrying my child!

Riley had leered and nudged Graham at the sight of Carolyn, clearly reminding him of the rock and a hard place he stood between. While he had no idea how Ellis had found out about him and Carolyn, the threat of revealing their affair was all that was needed to keep him in line.

Graham had wanted to walk away then and there, but the need to know if Riley was telling the truth about Sophie kept him rooted in place. Now that he had seen her kissing another man, he wished he had left.

"You reckon she's gonna head back to his place?"

"Shut your mouth," Graham warned.

"Don't go gettin' in a huff." Riley smirked mischievously. "You're the one that's sweet on her, so I done figured you'd be the one to ask just how easy she is. Besides, if there's anyone that should wanna beat on that there crippled fella, it'd be me. Put a goddamn bruise on my wrist when he snatched it! If it weren't for Ellis, why I woulda . . ."

Graham let the man continue ranting as he kept his gaze trained intently on Sophie. It was hard for him to be so near to a degenerate like Riley without retching. Though Ellis was every bit the scum that Riley was, at least he looked somewhat presentable. If Riley hadn't called about Sophie, Graham doubted he would have come, even if it had meant the other man's life.

"Just think, the two of 'em was in that dark picture show. Bet that sets you off."

"I told you to shut up."

Graham sneered into the darkness. He knew just which two people Riley was talking about, and it made him hate the squirrelly bastard all the more. Being reminded of it caused him to feel weak, utterly powerless. He had agreed to be a part of this madness because he believed that he could protect Sophie and her family. Now it seemed as if she had found a new protector and had forgotten all about Graham Grier.

Since that fateful day in front of the newspaper office, Graham had wondered why Sophie had appeared to be so happy. Now he knew the answer: she had found someone else. He had every reason to blame himself for this turn of events, but his growing rage was making him blind to that particular truth. Surprisingly, he found himself growing angry with Sophie. He was still distraught by the way she had looked in the diner, by how she had spoken to him, but now a new kind of disgust filled him.

"You figure if they were to have a kid, it'd pop out just as much a cripple as that fella is?" the scruffy thug asked.

The thought of what Riley Mason was suggesting was far more than Graham could bear. Grabbing the man by two fistfuls of his filthy shirt, he hefted him off his feet and slammed him into the brick wall of the alleyway. His arms taut, he held Riley in place as easily as he would a child.

All of the pent-up anger and rage seemed to explode from him in an instant, and as he stared into the murky depths of the other man's face, he struggled to suppress the desire to wring the son of a bitch's neck.

"Don't you ever so much as suggest that again," Graham growled.

"You best remember your place, rich boy," Riley threatened. Though he was pinned tightly to the wall, his eyes held the restrained fury of a caged animal; murder and mayhem were only a moment away. "Don't tell me you done forgot what all you stand to lose."

"Keep your mouth shut about her, Riley."

"Or what?" The man smiled.

Without answer, Graham let him go and turned back to Sophie.

"Don't *you* dare forget," Riley hissed through clenched teeth. In that instant, Graham knew that this was another transgression that would not be forgotten, but rather filed away for later.

Chapter Seventeen

THE EARLY MORNING air was filled with a wide variety of sounds: the back-and-forth sawing of wood, the relentless pounding of nails, the deep rumble of trucks, and, quite faintly, the chirping of birds. The sun had barely peeked over the eastern horizon, dappling the treetops with a golden liquid color, and already the day appeared to be in full swing.

Sophie stood on the front porch of the farmhouse, the light of the oncoming day warming her face. She had been awake for hours, since long before dawn, helping her mother cook, for those who would soon arrive. And arrive they had! All around her, dozens of men hurried to and fro, diligently working to raise her family's new barn. Their good-natured shouts broke the stillness of the morning.

"Someone go get another sack of nails."

"Once we get the trusses, it ain't gonna be long until . . ."

"Here you go, Hermann! Hold on to that ladder."

The many noises created a strange symphony. Some men hammered the trusses that would support the barn's new roof; others prepared the sturdy struts that would form the building's base; a few even busied themselves rolling out great lengths of rope that would be slipped through pulleys to raise the framework and hold it in place as it was nailed together. It was quite an impressive sight. With everyone appearing to move at once, it resembled the frenzied work of an anthill.

Cole and his father had been among the first to arrive; the sun had been little more than a smear of blue and orange in the sky when their truck had bounced up the drive. Others had followed closely behind them; the Hellers' nearest neighbors, the Sanderses and the Moores, had shown up in their entirety before the first nail had been pounded. Sophie recognized the face of every man, woman, and child who had come to help.

"My big ol' round belly's already lookin' forward to lunch!" Charley Tatum bellowed as he rose from sawing support planks with a jiggle of his ample midsection. "If Maria Heller don't make the finest corn beef and cabbage this side of the Mississippi, I sure ain't eat from the table of the woman who does! I do believe I might have been dreamin' about it last night!"

"Then why'd you have that big breakfast, Pa?" his son, Will, asked.

"'Cause a man can't work on a empty stomach, neither!"

Loud laughter rose up all around.

Sophie smiled cheerfully at the Tatums' good humor. She wasn't the least bit surprised that Charley and Will had followed through on their pledge to help her father rebuild their barn. Though it had only been a short couple of weeks since she'd last seen them in Ambrose Hardware, the burning of the barn then still as fresh to her as the moment it happened, absolutely scared out of her wits and more than ready to jump at any passing shadow, those moments now seemed as if they had been a lifetime ago.

I'm not the same as I was back then!

This change in Sophie's life was the result of meeting Cole. She easily found him among the working men; he stood beside his father, driving nails into the long boards that would make up the framework of each end of the barn. He stopped for a moment, wiping the sweat from his forehead with the back of his hammer-laden hand, and then his eyes were upon her. Though he was far away from her, she could see his face brighten, giving her a smile that she warmly returned.

Over and over in her mind, Sophie had replayed their trip to the movies; the excitement she had felt when picking out what she would wear, the passion of their first kiss, and everything in between, even including her near-confrontation with Carolyn Glass. Still, it was the memory of the kiss upon which she lingered. She'd lain in bed that night, treasuring her recollections of his lips upon hers, the feel of his hands upon her back. Just thinking about it was enough to make her heart race. She'd had her share of childhood crushes and flirts, but this was developing into something . . . more.

"We could use another saw over here!"

Pulled from the blissful reverie of her relationship with Cole, Sophie again smiled warmly at the scene unfolding before her. Coming to the aid of one's neighbor was a tradition in Victory that was every bit as rich as the black soil of the farming countryside. When she thought of the selflessness of those who had risen with the dawn to help her and her family, she knew that they were simply being true to their sense of community. That Cole Ambrose was among them only reaffirmed her faith in him.

"You best keep your mind on what you're doing."

Cole tore his eyes from Sophie and turned them toward his father. His face was already flushed and wet with sweat but he worried that he'd turned a shade redder at having been caught staring. He expected his father's face to be full of rebuke, a further sign of the man's reproach, but Robert only gave him a nod before turning back to his work.

"Sorry," Cole mumbled. "My mind must have wandered for a bit."

"Just bring it on back, then."

Cole and his father had been working side by side since shortly before sunrise. When they had arrived at the Hellers' farm, they'd first made certain they had everything they needed and then set to work. Thereafter, they'd been joined by a new hand with seemingly every passing minute, but still they had worked together. For the most part, the only sounds they'd made were from the tasks of their labor, but the silence between them had not been cold.

Ever since Jason's train had disappeared into the rainy distance, carrying him off to war and leaving Cole alone with his father, there had been a subtle difference in their relationship. Cole had expected his father to remain as cold and distant as he had been since his own homecoming, but there had been a slight thaw in the older man's icy exterior: he had begun to converse in full sentences instead of his usual grunts; he sat at the kitchen table for the duration of most meals, even those he had finished eating; he even asked Cole a question or two about teaching. While Cole certainly didn't expect the man to completely change his tune, he couldn't help but recognize that it was a start . . . a start that he rather liked.

"Do you think we'll finish today?" Cole asked.

"We'll be close enough."

"We'll have to hurry. The hours are flying past."

"There's no shortage of help," Robert said, nodding toward the men bustling about the yard. "With this many hands, we'll get most of the hard work done, the frame built and up, at the very least. From there, Hermann and Karl will be able to handle the rest."

Cole followed his father's gaze out over the men who were working alongside them. Most of the faces he recognized easily; those that he struggled with often proved to be boys who had grown into men during his years of absence. To have so many hands come together on a Saturday to help out a neighbor warmed his heart. Though he himself had changed, he was relieved to find that Victory was still the community it had always been.

"You have enough nails?" his father asked.

"I think so."

"Then I'm going to see if I can help with the roof," Robert said, rising to his feet, his knees cracking in protest, before he ambled off, leaving Cole to his task.

Though his leg prevented him from doing many tasks, Cole took some small measure of pride from working with his hands. Since he wasn't able to haul lumber or move other heavy objects, he instead hammered away on the heavy beams that would make up each end of the new barn, driving many dozens of nails as easily as if he were pushing them through cotton. He might not be able to march off to war with other men his age, but in this instance, he could more than hold his own. His hard work had not gone unnoticed by the other men.

"Not bad for a teacher!" Charley Tatum roared.

"And a math teacher, at that!" another had added.

Still, worry gnawed at Cole's gut as determinedly as a mangy dog working on a soup bone. Other than the Hellers, he alone knew the truth of what had happened to the family's barn. Only he knew that it had not been an accident that had razed the building, but a premeditated act of ignorant hatred masterminded by a despicable bastard and his patsies. Once the barn had been built, reared up in the ashes of its predecessor, there was nothing that would prevent Ellis Watts from simply destroying it again.

For not the first time since Sophie told him her story, Cole wondered if he shouldn't take the matter to the police. Surely the law would recognize that Ellis was capable of such an act as arson and lock him up behind bars until it could be concretely proven! It would be just another crime among the long litany he had already committed, but enough was enough! Many times, Cole had thought of mentioning the matter to his father, of simply saying the horrible truth in front of him, but . . .

If I did, how would I ever be able to look Sophie in the eyes?

Ultimately, Cole knew that he couldn't

go against Sophie's wishes. When she had told him the shocking truth of what had happened, she'd extended a trust to him that was to be treasured, held with the utmost care. If he were to tell what he knew, if he were to break that trust, it could bring about the end of their relationship, and that was a risk that he was not willing to take. He would have to continue to watch over her in his own way, and make sure that bastard Ellis Watts stayed far, far away.

Cole's relationship with Sophie filled him with a happiness that he had never believed possible. When they were together, all of his worries, all of his insecurities about his leg, no longer seemed to matter. Memories of their night at the movies, of their passionate kiss under the watchful gaze of the summer moon, made him long to hold her against his chest again. Every time they parted, he counted the hours until he could next see her. To be so close to her now, to simply look up and see her smiling face, and not be able to speak with her or to hold her hand was like an itch he couldn't scratch.

"You're doing it again."

Cole looked back over his shoulder to

see his father standing behind him, his handkerchief swabbing over his wrinkled face, his small glasses held gently in the other hand. Robert had come upon him quietly, although it was far more likely that Cole had been so lost in his thoughts about Sophie that he hadn't heard him approach.

"Doing what?" Cole asked.

In answer, Robert nodded across the lawn to where Sophie stood.

"I guess I am," Cole admitted.

"There will be plenty of time for watching Sophie Heller later," Robert said, his voice patient. "For now, you're needed to help Franklin Moore with the roof crossbeams. I'm afraid he might not have it measured right, on account of those bad eyes of his."

As Cole rose to his feet, he knew that his father was wrong about one thing.

There would never be enough time to watch Sophie Heller!

Sophie stood beside Cole as they admired the work that had been done on the barn. From the front steps of the farmhouse, the sight was nothing short of miraculous. Most of the framework had already been completed; working with the pulleys, it had taken over ten men to pull each of the large side frames up off the ground and into place. The building began to resemble a skeleton waiting for its outer skin. Squinting her eyes, Sophie could practically see the finished product; a barn just like the one that had been destroyed.

Glancing at Cole, Sophie marveled at the way the early evening sun shone on his handsome face. Though they had spent much of the day within eyesight of each other, nearly all of it had been in the company of neighbors and friends; the closest that they had come to any intimacy had been when Sophie had brought Cole the water bucket and their fingers had touched as she had passed him the ladle. Even now, after most of the men had left for the day and those who remained were carrying their tools back to their trucks, Sophie felt as if all eyes were upon them and didn't dare to show much affection.

"I can't believe this was all done in one day," she said.

"Me, either," Cole admitted. "I never thought we'd get this far."

"My family can't give thanks enough for

everything you and your father have done for us. If it wasn't for all of your hard work, I wonder if the barn would have ever been rebuilt."

"Thanks aren't necessary."

"They're given all the same."

Though Sophie was aware that Cole had only a few short moments before his father returned from loading the last of their tools into the truck, she was struck by the strong desire to reach out and touch him. To brazenly kiss the young teacher would have been especially foolhardy, setting every tongue wagging, but she wished she could take his hand in her own, to feel the heat of his skin, if only for a moment.

"That looks much better."

Sophie and Cole turned to find Gitta slowly making her way out the front door to join them. With her wrinkled face turned up to the setting sun, she struck Sophie as being smaller than she remembered, so frail that she could be blown away by a strong gust of wind. Gitta settled herself on the top step to rejoice in the remaining light of the day. When she looked down at them, she smiled with a warmth every bit as genuine as that of the sun in which she basked.

"Much better than burned-up remains," she said, nodding.

Sophie introduced her grandmother to Cole. Suddenly she was a bit nervous about the two of them meeting; each was so important to her that she hoped and prayed they would like each other.

"I have heard very much about you," Gitta explained. "My granddaughter's told me many things, but since you have caught her eye, I thought that I might finally take look for myself."

"I hope I can live up to your expectations," Cole said, his voice earnest.

"You are hardworking young man who wishes to take no credit, even when that credit is due. This is not way of most. Being humble, doing for others simply because it is right . . . this was also way of my husband, Sophie's grandfather."

"Then he was a good man."

"He was." Gitta smiled. "He was at that."

Sophie could only watch as Cole and her grandmother talked like old friends who had been suddenly reacquainted after years apart. They spoke of the construction of the barn, Cole's position as a teacher, and even the weather. She marveled at how Cole's eyes held the older woman kindly, patiently waiting until he was certain she had finished speaking before adding to their conversation. When they laughed, the sound of their voices carried over the yard as if it were a summer breeze.

"Cole!" Robert called from the truck, interrupting them. "Time to head home."

"I'll be right there!" Turning to Gitta, Cole gently took her hand in his own and said, "It was a real pleasure to meet you. I hope I haven't said anything that might prevent me from seeing your granddaughter again."

"You will not have me standing in the way."

"I'm glad."

"Don't I get some say in this?" Sophie asked, grinning.

"We have already decided for you," Gitta said with an even bigger grin.

After Cole had made plans with Sophie for lunch the next day, he slowly crossed the yard to join his father. The truck sprang to life with a coughing sound and was soon bouncing down the lane and out into the road, heading west as it melted into the last golden rays of the sun.

"Did you really like Cole?" Sophie asked after the truck was finally out of sight.

"Do you believe I would lie to you, child?"

"No, I don't, *Oma*," she answered. Sophie had known the answer to her question before she had even asked it; simply looking in the older woman's face as she spoke to Cole had told her all she had needed to know. How Gitta Heller felt was often as easy to read as the pages of a book. This moment was no different.

"You will be happy with that man," Gitta said with a broad smile that said the same. "Just as I was, you will be happy."

Chapter Eighteen

COLE WALKED SLOWLY down the dark, rain-slicked streets, his hands stuffed deeply into his pockets. After yet another week of unbearable heat, the afternoon had brought thunderclouds that had bathed the town in a cool rain before finally moving on. In the east, where the storm was headed, thunder continued to rumble. Now, with the clock having not yet struck nine, Cole had the streets all to himself, save for the crickets that had resumed their steady buzz and, in the distance, the occasional barking of a lone dog.

Some of the crisp chill of the departed

storm lingered in the evening air, but Cole could already feel the humidity rising. Too soon, the heat would descend upon the town, smothering it as if it were a wool blanket. But for now, the coolness remained; he would have to enjoy the brief change in temperature for however long it lasted.

The dark of night was a welcome respite. Cole had needed to get outside for a breath of fresh air and to cool his head. Life in the Ambrose home had once again proven difficult; in the days since he and his father had spoken at the Hellers' barn-raising, Robert had once again grown moody. Inside the well-manicured house, silence reigned in every corner; the sound of a clock's striking of the hour was more than enough to startle. Sophie had already made plans with her family, so he'd had no choice but to head out on his own.

Even with his bad leg, Cole liked to walk. Long ago, he'd decided that he wouldn't just lie around and feel sorry for himself, wallowing in self-pity and content to look out the window at the world going by without him. At Jason's side, he'd tried to join in games, run down to the creek, or tramp off to the movies. He'd wanted nothing more than to just be a kid. Still, the going had been hard and failure had come nearly as often as success.

And he was sure there were more of both to come.

Walking down Main Street, Cole paused in front of the tavern. The few cars that were parked along the street glistened with raindrops that shone in the light that spilled out of the tavern's windows. The sound of drunken voices wafted out of the cracked door. He found that he couldn't help but think of Ellis Watts; it had only been a couple of weeks since he'd confronted the man inside that very building, but the stink of whiskey on Ellis's breath seemed as real as if the no-good bastard were standing right before him. With the man's predilection for trouble and drink, he imagined that Ellis was more than likely inside.

A beat-up car drove past the tavern and honked; Cole figured that it must've been a greeting for someone already inside. One drunk hailing another! Before he could chuckle, the faint sound of footsteps rose from behind him, but when he turned, the sidewalk was empty. Shaking his head and silently chastising himself for being so jumpy, he continued on.

At his father's hardware store, he turned off Main Street and headed for the northern edge of town. All around him, houses lay shrouded in the gloomy aftermath of the rainstorm and the darkness of the late hour. A slight breeze rustled the tall elms and oaks, occasionally sending sheets of rain-water cascading down to the earth. Cole raised his arms to protect himself but was drenched just the same. Another rumble of distant thunder rolled across the sky.

Soon, Cole's strides brought him to Victory High School. Two stories tall and constructed of a deep red brick that shone nearly black in the rain, the school was one of the most cared-for buildings in town. The grass was immaculately kept, trimmed flush along the walk that led to the double front doors. Deep hedgerows ran beneath the lower-floor windows. The clasp on the rope of the flagpole clanged against the metal post in the light breeze, naked of its usual charge, the red, white, and blue of the American flag. Cole wasn't certain that the school had been his intended final destination, but it didn't surprise him that it was where his walk ended.

After the death of his mother, the school had been the place where Cole felt the most at home. The click-clacking of chalk against the slate board, the scrape of pencil against paper, and the musty odor of books had all been welcome to his life. The wonders of this building had changed him; the solace he had found in mathematics was the engine that had given him the strength to leave Victory behind.

Cole headed to the second window on the left of the front doors and pressed his face against the rain-streaked glass, peering inside. Soon, the murky gloom of the classroom gave way to the familiar sights he had expected to find; four rows of students' desks sat facing the teacher's at the front of the room, a dusty photograph of Sir Isaac Newton hanging next to the chalkboard, and piles of textbooks waiting to be taken up by the incoming students.

This had been the room in which Clarence Collins had first instructed him in the wonders of math, where he had become enthralled by the order of numbers in his otherwise unordered world. How many other students had sat in these desks, just as he had? Now this room was to be his. In a few short weeks, he would take his place behind that very desk and begin to instruct the children of Victory. Maybe he would be fortunate enough to find a student as passionate about the subject as he had been.

Thinking of the future sent shivers racing up Cole's arms. Before he had met Sophie Heller, he had always imagined his would be a solitary life, that he would be content to submerge himself in his work and to become the best teacher that he could be. Now, things had undeniably changed. When he thought of what lay before him, only one word could describe how he felt . . .

Hope.

The possibility of sharing his life with a wonderful woman had become real. From the first moment that he had met Sophie, he had felt at ease, unashamed of his deformed leg, even when that very leg had initially proven unsettling to her. Seeing her smile, hearing her laugh, and sharing her company had become every bit as necessary to his life as food and water. He couldn't predict where their relationship was headed, but he hoped that it would lead to a courtship, marriage, and then to a family. That he could someday be teaching his own children in that classroom was almost more than he could dream.

Cole was ready to begin the long trek home when he again heard the sounds of footsteps somewhere behind him. Spinning on his heel, he turned as swiftly as he could to again find no one, but this time he was unwilling to attribute the noise to his imagination.

He was being followed!

From the moment he'd confronted Ellis Watts in the tavern, Cole had been waiting for this encounter. Men such as Ellis wouldn't take a threat lying down, certainly not from a crippled teacher, but would instead act to quiet any and all who challenged them. Who knew how long they had been watching him . . . waiting . . . If it was a fight they wanted, then, for Sophie's sake as well as his own, it was a fight they would get.

With his fists tightly balled, Cole strode

back along the front of the school, his eyes darting from shadow to shadow.

"You might as well show yourself," he called angrily. "I heard you."

Stepping across the walk that led to the front doors of the school, Cole could feel the anger rising in his chest. Ellis and his two companions had attempted to force Sophie and her family into doing what they wanted, to threaten them into leaving Victory, but he would have none of their games. They would find that he wasn't so easily scared.

Cole stood completely still and waited, peering into the shadows for any signs of movement, but he couldn't see anything in the inky darkness. The whispering sound of rustling leaves was the only noise he heard. Still, he was certain that he wasn't alone.

"Don't be a coward," Cole mocked. "I'm only one man."

As if his words were the match used to light a stick of dynamite, a shadowy form burst from between the hedgerows to his left and slammed into him. He tried to defend himself, but his attacker had been so silent, so capable of keeping his location a secret, that he immediately found himself a step behind. A hard fist crashed into his jaw with the strength of a hammer, abruptly snapping his head to the side and clouding his thoughts.

"You son of a bitch!" a man's voice hissed.

The first blow had been enough to stagger Cole, his bad leg searching for the ground as urgently as a blind man's cane. Raising his hands up to his swimming head, he attempted to fend off the punches that rained down on him. He managed to block a few, but more found their mark than missed; one to his chest, another to his ear, and then another back on his jaw, so painful that he saw stars.

At first, Cole had worried that he would have to hold off several attackers. Now he knew that he faced only one man, although that lone aggressor fought with the intensity of a wild animal. Strangely, he was convinced that it was not Ellis Watts who assaulted him; this was different, personal, an emotional battering that showed no signs of letting up. Each punch felt harder than the last.

"Fall, damn you!"

With all of the strength that he could muster, Cole tried his best to fight back against his unknown assailant. Blindly, he threw punches, but even those that managed to land did so ineffectually; it was as if he were striking the trunk of a tree for all the good it did him. His attacker seemed possessed, refusing to slow. Still, he would not allow himself to quit.

Finally, a widely arcing punch struck his belly and drove the air from his lungs in a whoosh. His already wobbly knees gave out and Cole fell hard onto his back in the wet grass, gasping. Reflexively, his hand went to his lip and came back stained with crimson blood, the bitter taste filling his mouth. His sight swam between darkness and a murky light. As much as it pained him to admit it, he had been beaten.

He lay woozily on the soppy ground, his head spinning painfully as he tried in vain to find his bearings. Disappointment arced through him, not at his having been physically bested, but because he felt as if he had let Sophie down; how could he expect to protect her when it seemed that he was incapable of taking care of himself?

Powerful hands grabbed two fistfuls of his shirt and pulled his upper body from the ground. Peering through eyes that were little more than slits, he searched the growing darkness for a clear look at the man before him, but there was only the hazy light that had settled upon the edges of his vision; it was as if he had been enveloped by a heavy fog.

"Now you listen and you listen good, you goddamn cripple!" the man snarled, the heat of his words washing over Cole's face. "Stay the hell away from Sophie Heller!"

Shock and surprise raced wildly across Cole's battered face at his attacker's words. He had believed that interfering with Sophie's confrontation with Ellis Watts and his two companions at the diner was undoubtedly why he had been followed and beaten, but now that belief wavered. The stranger's tone was threatening yet different, strange, almost protective . . .

"You . . . bastard . . ." Cole spat, his jaw already aching.

"You'd better watch your tongue if you don't want it cut out," the man kept on. "You aren't going to talk to her again, do you hear me? You're not good enough for her and you never will be!"

"Go . . . to hell . . ." Cole struggled to say.

The last word had barely escaped Cole's lips when another thudding fist hit his jaw and drove him back down to the ground with a thud. Darkness swelled at the corners of his eyes, threatening to overturn him and pull him under, but he fought against the insistent tide and somehow managed to stay conscious.

"Do you think me a fool?" the man asked through clenched teeth.

"Only . . . only if you think . . . that I'll stay away . . . from Sophie," Cole managed to say through a mouth full of blood. "You'll . . . have to do much . . . much more than . . . this."

"Don't tempt me."

Though he was having a hard time struggling through the blinding pain of his beating, Cole still hoped to learn the identity of his attacker. He was certain that it was not Ellis Watts; not only did he not recognize the man's voice, but he felt certain that Ellis would have been even more violent, more willing to inflict injury. He was also fairly sure that it was not the man who had grabbed Sophie by the wrist; though that man was undeniably dangerous, Cole had looked into his eyes and discovered that there wasn't a shred of decency to be found, which he couldn't reconcile with the man's words. That left only one other person.

Was this the third man in the diner booth?

Without any warning or the fanfare of thunder or lightning, the summer rain once again began to fall, a steady drizzle that stung Cole's tender face, pounding him as relentlessly as the stranger had. He wanted to raise a hand, to shade his eyes from the wet downfall, but he found that he didn't have the strength.

"Just look at you," the man said scornfully, his words full of disdain. "What could you possibly have to offer a woman like Sophie? You can barely walk, let alone fight! I won't sit by and let her ruin her life by getting mixed up with the likes of you!"

Cole suddenly understood that his attacker was indeed the third man from the diner. His words were not those of a man intent on warning someone away from his devious plans but of a rival for a woman's affections. They were selfish, petty words tinged with jealousy.

Though he was soaked all the way to the bone by the rain, his wet shirt coldly plastered to his chest, Cole's blood began to heat up. Angry at both his perceived weakness as well as the ridiculous demands the man was placing upon him, he struggled to rise from the ground, his entire body shaking from the effort.

"You'll . . . not have her . . ." he yelled.

Cole had scarcely moved before he saw the man step toward him through the steady rain. Raising a booted foot, he drove the heel down into Cole's temple, the crack of the blow louder than the thunder that arrived from the distant horizon.

This time, Cole knew that no amount of struggling would keep him from slipping beneath the darkness that surrounded him. But just before he could be claimed, just before he finally fell into unconsciousness, the sound of the man's voice reached him.

"If I see you with her again, I'll kill you."

Graham Grier hurried away from the school with his shoulders hunched against the sudden squall. The patter of the raindrops mixed with the whispered rustling of leaves pushed by the rising wind, yet his footfalls still sounded loud in his ears. The knuckles of his right hand throbbed numb and angry, and he shook them to try to regain feeling. As he moved, his eyes never stopped scanning the street, fearful that someone might see him.

"That crippled son of a bitch had it coming," he muttered.

Try as he might, Graham hadn't been able to get out of his head the horrible sight of Sophie kissing Cole Ambrose. No amount of restless pacing, no matter how many fitful hours he spent trying to fall asleep, nothing would make the image go away. Every time he closed his eyes, there it was: he and Riley Mason lurking in the dark shadows across the street as Sophie rose on her tiptoes, closed her eyes, and . . .

What does she see in him?!

Graham hadn't intended to beat the crippled man that night. He'd spent the bulk of the day cooped up in his father's home, taking refuge from the stormy weather, but once the gale had broken, he'd headed out for some fresh air, to clear his equally stormy thoughts. He'd been aimlessly wandering when he'd first seen Cole Ambrose limping along.

In that moment, he'd been content to simply follow, to try to make some sense out of why Sophie would be attracted to such a man, but it seemed that with every step, the furnace that was his fury had grown hotter. He found that he despised the young teacher, not solely because he was the object of Sophie's affections, but because he was much that Graham was not and might never be; honorable enough to stand up for her at the diner, smart enough to have gone to college.

When Cole had arrived at the school, Graham had hidden in the bushes and watched as the young teacher had peered into the windows. While Graham had been itching for a fight, to try to sooth his damaged ego, he'd remained reluctant to do anything; getting caught attacking a crippled man would be nearly as bad as being discovered to have aided Ellis and Riley. Even stepping on a twig and giving his hiding place away wasn't enough to draw him out. For that, it had required Cole's words.

"Don't be a coward."

His anger at those words had been so great that he hadn't been able to resist his impulses. He had attacked without thought, hurling punch after punch at Cole, intent on causing the crippled man as much pain as had been visited upon him. Though Cole had been hardier than he had expected, in the end, he had fallen. It was only then that the bloodlust had left Graham.

He had meant what he said; the next time he met Cole he would kill him.

Graham knew that Sophie was not without blame. She had been the one that had spurned his initial advances, only to fall straight into the arms of another man, a cripple at that. While he would never put his hands on her in a violent way, he knew that he would have to speak with her; she clearly needed his help to overcome her attraction to that man! No matter what it took, no matter how long he had to struggle, they would be together.

Fleetingly, he thought of Carolyn Glass. He knew that none of this would be happening if he hadn't allowed himself to be seduced. If she weren't pregnant with his child, if Ellis hadn't found out about their affair, then Sophie would never have been driven to the cripple's side. With effort, Graham drove such thoughts from his head. Even if he shared some responsibility, he would make sure that Sophie wasn't involved with Cole Ambrose.

Rounding the corner, Graham found himself back at his father's home, a two-story Victorian that was regarded as the nicest home in Victory; beveled glass paned every window, gabled trimmings underlined every eave. In short, the home was a testament to everything that Graham had to lose. Bounding up the steps, he tried to put such thoughts out of his mind. Today was a new beginning for him. Starting today, he would begin to reclaim his life.

And nothing and no one will stop me!

Chapter Nineteen

RILEY MASON FLICKED his cigarette butt into the darkness that surrounded Ellis Watts's shack and cursed under his breath. He'd been standing out in the damp night for over half an hour, rubbing his arms for warmth, his patience burning up just as steadily as his cigarettes. Though cool, the night air was again thickening with insects. Even as the moon peeked out from between a pair of dirty clouds, he wondered just when he would be let inside.

He had shown up when he had been told to, only to find that Ellis was otherwise disposed, busy entertaining himself with a woman in his bed. Riley had been forced to listen to their moans and groans through the open window, the sound of their passion nearly making him sick. It wasn't that he was a prude; he'd had his share of time spent between a woman's legs. His problem was who Ellis was with. For the life of him, he'd never been able to figure what Ellis saw in that bitch . . . especially now.

"We ain't got no time for this shit," he growled to himself.

Frustration rolled around Riley's gut at the thought of those damn Nazis still living out at their farm as if nothing had happened. He supposed he'd been a fool to believe Ellis when he'd said that they'd hightail it out of town just as soon as they saw them in their hoods. But that sure as shit hadn't happened! Riley had driven by the farm a couple of nights earlier to find that the barn had been rebuilt just as good as new. That certainly wasn't the act of a family living in fear; it was an act of outright defiance.

What the hell was Ellis waitin' for?

After they'd been found out by that German bitch in the diner, he'd wanted to shut her up. The thought of being caught and going to jail petrified him. It would've been just as easy as pie to fall upon her in her bed, to catch her unawares and simply snuff her out without a sound. But Ellis had had other ideas.

"'Get 'em good and scared,'" Riley snarled, mimicking the other man. "Bullshit!"

Ellis's instructions had been to remind Sophie Heller of their presence, for her to be aware that they could take her at any time. At first, Riley had gotten a small measure of satisfaction from waiting outside the newspaper office just so the bitch could get a look at him. That first afternoon, the look of fright on her face had nearly given him an erection! But then, something had changed. Now she rarely even glanced at him, and when she did, the look on her face sure as hell wasn't one of fear.

She needed to be put in her place!

Riley was quite certain that what had changed the Kraut was Cole Ambrose. He hadn't the slightest idea what a comely young thing like her would see in a good-for-nothing cripple, but whatever it was, it had gotten her back up. Still, if she believed that a teacher would keep her out of danger, she'd find out that she was sorely mistaken.

A woman's voice floated out the window. "Oh, Ellis!"

"Give it to me, baby," Ellis groaned.

"Goddamn! Ain't they through yet?" Riley grunted.

Ellis Watts was another matter entirely. Although he claimed to have a plan and that they should stick to it, sometimes Riley had to wonder . . . Ellis had taken him under his wing, had given him a direction, a purpose toward which he could direct his energy; there was a time he would have sworn that he would follow the man to hell and back. Sure, Ellis yelled at him and told him that he was worthless from time to time, but Riley could tell that he didn't really mean it. But he still couldn't begin to understand why Ellis sat idly by, content to simply watch. Riley wanted more. They needed to act soon, otherwise he might just have to do something on his own.

Lighting another cigarette, Riley returned to his pacing.

Sweating and spent, Ellis Watts rolled roughly off the woman who lay beneath him and collapsed on the dingy mattress, panting deeply. Even with the windows open and a gentle breezing blowing, the thick smell of sex hung heavily in the close air of his cramped bedroom. No light shone in the tiny room, but there was enough of a glow from the half-hidden moon to show him that his partner was already gathering her clothes and preparing to leave. Blindly, he reached for the pack of cigarettes that lay on the table beside the bed.

"What's the matter?" he asked, scratching a match to life against his fingernail and lighting his cigarette. "You're in such a hurry to get on out of here, it makes me think you've got another date."

"You knew my visit was going to be a short one."

"Just a slam, bam, and you'd be on your way, huh?"

"That's all this will ever be, Ellis. Don't tell me you have a problem with that."

"Nope," he said with a chuckle between drags. "Can't say that I do, Mrs. Glass."

Carolyn Glass spun toward Ellis with a look that would have turned a lesser man into stone. Though he undoubtedly found her beautiful, he'd always known that there was a vicious coldness that lay just below the surface, a darkness of her spirit that was only one perceived slight or ill-advised word from being released. Her brow furrowed tightly, the veins on her neck rose and flushed her face, but it was the unfiltered malice in her eyes that he found the most disturbing. Still, Ellis could not prevent a chuckle.

"Relax, Carolyn," he said. "Ain't no point in ruinin' our night, is there?"

"You need to watch how you choose to speak to me," she answered coldly, an untoward frown creasing her pursed lips; it was as if she were carved from ice. "I will walk out that door and never look back."

"What would I ever do then?" Ellis asked sarcastically.

"Find some other woman to lie with, I suppose. I can't imagine that you don't have a couple of tramps stashed around town as it is. Besides, isn't that what I already am to you, Ellis? Some tramp that you can have your way with just so long as I cooperate?"

Much of what Carolyn was saying to him was already true, particularly the part about other women. With his good looks,

Ellis had never had a problem attracting the fairer sex. From the time before he could even shave, he'd been slipping his fingers between the folds of blouses, under the hems of skirts, all sorts of places that they didn't necessarily belong. As he had gotten older, nothing had changed. He was a cad, a fornicator, a womanizer, or any other name folks wanted to pin on him.

"Don't worry," he said. "You're my favorite whore."

"What an honor," she sneered and set back to gathering her things as he continued to watch her intently.

Ellis had long ago determined that only a fool wouldn't have been attracted to a woman like Carolyn Glass. The first time he'd set eyes upon her, so many years back that he'd lost count of them, he'd instantly known that he would have done anything to ensure that he lay between her legs. Even then, she'd seemed so damn haughty, so completely out of his class that he might have well been pining for the Queen of England. Still, he'd occasionally catch her looking his way with a look on her face that he read as much more than disgust; he'd seen the hint of interest. He knew that his looks were prone to turning a head or two, but to attract the eye of a woman like her was something that surprised him.

But then one night, she had shown up at his door . . .

Ellis Watts was no fool. He knew exactly what he was to Carolyn; nothing more than a plaything who would remain at her side only as long as she was interested in him and not a moment more. He was dangerous, a fling, a temporary walk on the wilder side of life, and certainly nothing like her husband. He was everything she wanted but could never claim.

But Ellis was also one more thing to her; discreet. He understood that what they had together could be taken from him just as easily as snuffing out a candle. Even if he were to try to expose their relationship, to suddenly show up at the newspaper office and give Augustus all of the sordid details, who would possibly believe a scoundrel like him? All it would take was for Carolyn to turn on the waterworks and there wasn't a soul in Victory who wouldn't judge that he was trying to extort money from her husband. In that way, he was at her mercy. So instead, he just enjoyed what they had.

But then she'd gotten pregnant.

Regarding her in the scant moonlight, Ellis could see Carolyn's slightly extended stomach. She wasn't far enough along in her pregnancy to show much, but this was a condition that would rapidly change. When she'd first told him that she was with child, a spasm of fear had coursed through him, a fear that she was about to tell him the responsibility was his, but she'd never mentioned such a possibility. On the contrary, she'd seemed utterly sure that the true identity of her child's father was Graham Grier. She didn't care; it cemented her ties to Augustus Glass and his money.

But there had been possibilities for him in her pregnancy, as well. Listening to Carolyn talk of her life, Ellis had been struck by how easily exploitable parts of it were. Many of his previously hatched ideas, at first facing insurmountable obstacles, suddenly seemed possible at second glance. Carolyn had been easy to persuade; after all, she was with him because of a tendency toward mischief. From there, it had been a simple matter of getting the ball rolling, consequences be damned.

In the end, they were simply using each other, nothing more or less. There was no regret on Ellis's part; his parents had long ago taught him that there was nothing to be gained from developing attachments to others. He would take what he needed from Carolyn and then she would be discarded and he would never think of her again.

"I saw her again the other night," Carolyn suddenly said.

"Who?" Ellis asked, taking a heavy drag on his cigarette.

"Who do you think? The Kraut girl."

"Really?"

"Augustus had dragged me off to the movies again, completely ignoring the fact that I didn't want to go." She sighed as she buttoned the front of her silky blouse. "When it was finally over, when we were standing in the lobby, she and that cripple came out."

"She was with Ambrose?" he asked, even more interested in her answer.

"Is that who he is?" she asked offhandedly. "Someone said he was going to teach in the school this fall, but I hadn't put a face with the name. He wasn't bad-looking, really. That is, if you don't mind the crippled part. Your girl mustn't care."

"What did she do when she saw you?"

"Well, that was the best part of my evening." Carolyn smiled cruelly. "She took one look at me and I would have sworn that her eyes were about to fall out of her pretty little head. I was just about to march over and give her more of a tongue-lashing than I did at the goddamn paper, but then Augustus decided that he'd had enough gabbing for one night and we headed out the door. Either way, she was definitely frightened."

Ellis nodded. "Good."

"Sure looked as if they were on a date. I wonder how it all ended."

"Who cares? Ain't nothin' but a Nazi and a gimp."

"Ever the romantic, aren't you, Ellis?" she teased him. "No wonder it was so easy for you to get me into your bed."

Ellis held his tongue, refusing to be baited into arguing with her, knowing all along that that was exactly what she wanted. Carolyn Glass thrived on conflict, whether real or imagined. Men like her husband spent all of their time trying to soothe her moods, which only made her contempt for them greater. Ellis was usually more than willing to give as good as he got; some of their best sex had come after nearly hysterical arguments. But tonight he wasn't in the mood. Tonight, his mind was elsewhere.

He could have easily answered her question; Ellis knew exactly what had happened to the lovebirds after they left the theater. He'd gotten the story from Riley, about how he and Graham had stood in the shadows across the street and watched as Cole Ambrose had kissed the German as if they had been Hollywood stars on the set of their latest picture. He hadn't been surprised by this turn of events, only slightly disappointed; obviously, the young teacher had paid no mind to Ellis's warning in the bar.

"You aren't going to have trouble with a cripple, now are you, Ellis?"

"You can't know me very well if you're worried."

Carolyn shrugged. "He seemed quite strong to me."

"What do you know?" he spat, his temper rising from her needling.

"It just seems to me that getting rid of the Germans is proving to be a more difficult task than you'd thought, that's all," she kept on, her singsong voice jabbing him with every word. "Here you are with your big plans and it's all being done in by a crippled teacher and his Kraut lover."

"Why don't you just shut your mouth!" he barked.

"What kind of a man would you look like if you were done in by a teacher with a bum leg!" she cackled, the humor in her words overpowering any restraint she might have. "Here you are, trying to protect your beloved town from the threat of a handful of Germans, and you're going to find yourself bested by a man who didn't even put on the uniform of a United States soldier!"

Ellis flicked his still smoldering cigarette butt into the far corner of the room; at that moment he didn't give a damn if the whole shack burned to the ground, even if he were still inside. He was up from the bed in a flash, his nakedness kissed by the cooling breeze of the storm's aftermath, but inside he raged like a furnace. Carolyn had no more than risen from the bed before his hand clamped down around her throat and drove her back onto the mattress in a tangle of blonde curls and bedclothes. She gasped once but her hands never flew to his, never tried to scratch him or pry his flesh from her own. Instead, her eyes bounced wildly and a yearning smile spread across her features.

"That's it," she cooed, licking her lips. "That's my Ellis."

"You're out of your head," he answered, his revulsion growing with every passing second. He began to let go of her, to back away, only to find that she had entwined her legs around his torso.

"Where are you going, lover?" She smiled. "Don't you want me anymore?"

It sickened Ellis to know that he had been played for a fool. Letting his anger get the best of him had been just what she had wanted, just what she had needed him to do, and he had been more than happy to oblige. It was in this way that she wrapped men around her little finger, lonely, tortured souls like Augustus Glass; in the end, Ellis was proving little different.

Carolyn sighed. "If you want, you can burn my house to the ground."

Just as he had several times before,

Ellis wished that he had never spoken to her of what he, Riley, and Graham had done to the Hellers. But he'd wanted to share his glories, he supposed that he'd wanted to impress Carolyn, and had told her of his plans. She'd listened intently, absorbing every word. Since that day, whenever she had needed them, she'd wielded his secrets as deftly and as painfully as daggers.

"That ain't somethin' to joke about," he warned.

"Who's joking? Augustus would just build another anyway."

"Everythin' is just a game to you."

"And I aim to win," she agreed as she ran her fingers up his forearm.

Forcefully, Ellis pulled himself free of her grasp and retreated to the open window, staring out into the night beyond. The wind had risen again, swaying branches and rustling leaves, carrying with it the distant smell of rain. He peered intently into the darkness, as if he was searching for something, but nothing looked back.

"What are you so afraid of?" she asked, rising to stand behind him.

"I ain't afraid of anythin'," he answered,

though his voice sounded small to his own ears.

"You're frightened of going too far," she suggested as she slid one hand up the length of his bare back and onto his shoulder. "You're still thinking about what it means to play by the rules when you should be making your own. Followers wait until everything is just right before they act, but leaders wait for no one. You're a leader, Ellis. It's time to start acting like it."

"It ain't as easy as all that."

"Yes, it is," she disagreed as she turned him back from the window to face her. "My whole life, I've had only one goal, and that was to get everything that I felt was coming to me. By hook or by crook, that's what I have done. If anyone gets in my way, I don't so much as bat an eye as I run them down and I eliminate them. That's just the way you need to live. If you don't want those Germans living in this town, it's up to you to drive them out, no matter the means."

Looking down into Carolyn's face, Ellis couldn't help but believe some of what she was telling him. *Why shouldn't I get what I want? How far is too far to go in ridding this town of such trash?* Her words were intoxicating to him and he found himself nodding his head.

"Maybe you're right," he said.

Carolyn's hands reached between his legs and caressed beneath his manhood with a touch that sent his knees to quivering. "You were born with these," she murmured, "so it's to be expected that you would use them."

"I'm thinkin' about usin' 'em right now."

"Augustus will be waiting for me."

"Then let him wait," Ellis growled, his throat thick with desire.

Pushing Carolyn back down on the bed, he reached for her blouse, only to find her fingers already unbuttoning it. If Riley were pacing around outside, he'd just have to be impatient a bit longer.

It was time for Ellis Watts to take what he wanted.

Chapter Twenty

SOPHIE MOVED QUICKLY along Main Street, her short heels clicking against the pavement of the sidewalk, her purse clutched tightly against her side. On this particular Saturday morning, the shops and streets were filled with people eager to be out on such a gloriously beautiful day, the summer heat having retreated in the wake of the previous night's storm. Sophie paid no attention to the activity. She'd come to town with her father and brother, leaving them at the grocery store to tend to her own plans.

Today I have a lunch date with Cole!

Like her family's barn, Sophie felt her life was slowly being rebuilt, bit by bit and day by day. Though she wasn't so completely devoid of worry that she didn't look around for an unwanted face, she marveled at how much of her fear had simply fallen away. Only weeks earlier, she'd been too petrified even to leave the newspaper office for lunch, fearful that she would encounter Ellis, Riley, or Graham. Now she marched on with a smile every bit as bright as the sun.

Meeting Cole Ambrose had changed her life. Now she rose to greet each day with a confidence that she hadn't previously known. Once she had wondered where her life was headed as she lay in her secret place and dreamed about a future that seemed impossible. Now she had begun to believe that a life at Cole's side was one not only worth living, but cherishing. At his side, nothing seemed out of reach.

Rounding the corner, Sophie hurried up the steps of Ambrose Hardware and went inside. Even in the midst of such a gorgeous day, the inside of the store was gloomy; scant light penetrated through the front windows, leaving the interior masked in shadows. Still, her eyes immediately found Cole. While Robert Ambrose was busy tending to a pair of middle-aged women who were eyeing the latest-model iceboxes, Cole was helping a young couple decide between a pair of washtubs. His back was to her, but she would have recognized his sandy blond hair and broad shoulders anywhere.

Since the day of their first picnic, Cole had slowly opened up to Sophie about his strained relationship with his father. He had spoken to her of a difficult childhood spent painfully missing his mother and of the divide that loss had created between himself and Robert. She'd said little during their talks, content to simply listen, but it had become clear to her that the barrier between the two men still existed. With Jason shipped off to the war, Cole had begun to work more at the hardware store; the closeness of their contact only made the tension between them more obvious.

"Thank you, Mr. Gordon," she heard Cole say.

Returning her attention back to the man who had taken full hold of her heart and dreams, Sophie watched as Cole slowly turned toward her, but instead of brightening at the first sight of his face, Sophie found herself spiraling down into the depths of despair.

The side of Cole's face was a ravaged mess of bruises and bumps all stained a motley kaleidoscope of colors; the corner of his mouth heavily marked with an upsetting brown, his cheekbone soiled an ugly purple, and his temple dirtied with two raspberries of crimson red. Sophie couldn't help but let out an audible gasp at the sight.

Instantly, she knew what had happened: Cole had been true to his own word, but in attempting to defend her honor, had instead paid the price of a savage beating. Furious anger rose in her heart at Ellis Watts, Riley Mason, and even Graham. Seeing Cole in such a state was every bit as painful as when she had watched her father being struck with Ellis's rifle butt. Just as at that moment, her first instinct was to act.

"What happened to you?" Sophie asked as she hurried toward him.

"It's nothing," Cole answered, his eyes avoiding hers.

Gently yet insistently, her trembling fingers touched his chin and forced his gaze back to her own, her eyes sweeping over the damage. "You must think me some kind of fool if you expect me to believe that this is nothing," she said forcefully, her voice rising. "Tell me who did this to you, Cole. Tell me the truth and tell me right now!"

"Not here," he said, locking his gaze upon hers.

"But—" she started, but he hushed her with a raised hand.

Sophie suddenly became aware of the other people in the hardware store; the two women's attention had wandered from their prospective iceboxes to the scene unfolding beside them. Though she couldn't see him, she was certain that Cole's father was also watching them closely.

Shame colored Sophie's face at making a scene, but she pushed her embarrassment down, choosing instead to focus upon the anger rising in her breast. Just as she told herself when walking to meet Cole only moments earlier, she was rebuilding her life as surely as the once destroyed barn; no longer would she retreat from the life she wanted.

"Don't hush me," she demanded of him. "Tell me!"

Instead of giving her an answer, Cole grabbed Sophie by the arm and pulled her toward the rear of the store. She stumbled along behind him, struggling to maintain her balance, her arm hurting from the rough way his fingers dug into her flesh as they passed through the short hallway that led to the rear door and out onto the landing.

Closing the door behind them, Cole turned to face her, his eyes full of as many emotions as she could imagine: anger mixed with worry and even a touch of sadness.

"What happened to your face?" Sophie asked again, the worry seeping into her voice.

"Tell me who the other man was," Cole said in answer.

"What other man?"

"The third man at the diner," he pressed. "Not Ellis Watts and not the one that grabbed your wrist, but the man who sat with his back to the front of the diner, the man who didn't move or say a word. I want to know who he is."

Sophie's heart pounded, skipping beat after beat as the realization struck her as to what Cole was asking.

It was Graham . . . it was Graham who had attacked Cole!

Cole stared solemnly at Sophie's face, reading the way in which she avoided his eyes, her gaze sweeping down to the wooden planks beneath their feet. He'd seen the glimmer of recognition that had crossed her face at the mention of the third man and was convinced that she knew exactly who he was talking about. That she was reluctant to give his name pained him.

"Who is he, Sophie?" he kept on.

"I don't know . . . don't know who . . ." she unconvincingly muttered.

"Don't know or don't want to tell me?"

"Cole, I just can't . . ."

"Yes, you can, Sophie," Cole argued. "You just choose not to."

"It's not that easy," she pleaded, tears rising in her eyes.

"Just a few moments ago you were the one insisting that I tell you about what happened to my face," he said, his growing anger and frustration beginning to get the better of him. "But now, when I'm the one asking you to tell me the truth, you're the one holding your tongue!"

"I just can't . . . believe that he'd do . . . such a thing," she stammered.

"Look at my face!" Cole barked. "He can do exactly such a thing!"

The countless bruises and welts on Cole's face throbbed angrily, a painful reminder of the vicious beating he had received only the night before. Somehow, he had managed to limp his way back home, finally collapsing on his bed with the scant comfort offered by a wet washcloth pressed gingerly to his aching face. He'd been unable to sleep a wink, tossing fitfully from both the soreness of his wounds and the beating that had been inflicted on his pride. All night and early into the dawn, he'd wondered about Sophie's reaction, not only to the condition of his face but also to the questions he knew he would have to ask. Now he had the answer and it was proving just as painful.

Still, Cole knew that he was being too hard on Sophie; with the way his voice was rising, it was as if he were blaming her for what had happened to him. It undeniably rattled him that even after she had gotten a good look at his bruises, she still was reluctant to disclose his attacker's identity.

"Just tell me his name, Sophie," Cole said softly, his hand reaching tenderly to her own. "He's one of the hooded men that attacked your family. There's no reason for you to protect him."

Slowly, Sophie's eyes rose to meet his and, in that moment, Cole knew that his words had reached her. She nodded as tears streaked down her cheeks. "You're right. If he's responsible for what happened to you, if he's in league with a man like Ellis Watts, then there's nothing that I can do for him."

Sophie told Cole all about Graham Grier; about how they had been close for a long time, friends from nearly their first meeting. She spoke of how that friendship had changed in Graham's eyes and blossomed into something more, of how he had come to her and laid his heart bare, professing feelings that she wasn't able to return. With pain in her eyes, she explained how hurt she had been at the revelation that Graham had been involved in the burning of her family's barn, of how she had incredulously asked him about it in the diner and of how he had refused to answer.

"Why would he be involved with a man like Ellis Watts?" Cole asked.

"I just don't know!" Sophie exclaimed. "I can't understand what would cause Graham to follow along with men like that! When we were children, he was never cruel, never hurtful. He never showed anything, any sign that would lead me to believe that he would end up this way!"

"Do you think it has something to do with you rejecting his advances?"

"No . . . no, it can't be the reason," Sophie answered, but Cole could clearly see from the way she hesitated that she wasn't convinced of the truth of her words. Based on how Graham had lashed into him with his fists and the words that he had spoken when doing so, Cole was certain that her rejection had played a large part.

"Tell me what happened," Sophie urged yet again.

Though he knew that his words would pain her, Cole recounted the details of the attack outside the school. He told her about how he had felt he was being followed, first outside the tavern and finally in front of his soon-to-be classroom. He spoke of how he had called out his pursuer, only to find himself on the receiving end of a furious attack, replete with nearly as many hurtful slurs as bone-rattling punches.

"Are you sure that it was Graham who attacked you?" Sophie asked.

"It was him," he answered simply.

"And he was by himself?"

"I thought at first that there might have been more than one man following me," Cole admitted. "But in the end, it was only Graham."

Though it pained him to admit to having been outdone by one man, Cole knew he had simply been caught off guard. When Graham Grier had exploded from the bushes and lit into him, it had taken only a split second for the man to gain the upper hand. If they were to meet again, Cole swore he would never let his guard down.

"Did Graham say anything to you?" she asked. "Did he give you any idea why he was doing such a thing?"

Cole was reluctant to answer Sophie's questions truthfully; it was quite clear to him that she was having difficulty digesting what Graham had done. The murderous words that he had spoken while unleashing his furious assault would undoubtedly upset her further. To withhold Graham's brutal words could only spare her that pain.

"If I see you with her again, I'll kill you."

"All he said was that I should stay away from you."

Sophie gasped. "There was a threat, too, wasn't there? It wasn't just advice."

"There was, but that doesn't matter," Cole explained. "Since I've already gone against his advice, it doesn't leave us with much time to act."

"So what do you suppose we should do?" Sophie wondered.

"What choice do we have? We need to go to the police."

"No! We can't! My father—"

"Do you think that this is just going to go away?" Cole asked, cutting Sophie off mid-sentence. "Do you think that after attacking me these men are just going to stop? The next time it's going to be your father who is beaten, or maybe they'll choose to go after your brother. Either way, unless we do something, it will happen again! Is it going to take someone being killed before you realize that this has to stop?"

"You gave me your word," she sobbed, her tears falling freely.

"I wasn't lying to you, Sophie," he explained, his voice grave. "But we would be fools to think that these men aren't going to strike again. After what they've already done to your family, you couldn't have believed that they were just going to stand aside and let you go on with your lives, could you?"

Sophie remained silent, her gaze evasive. Over their last few weeks together, Cole had noticed that she had let her guard down a bit, that she had convinced herself that the worst was over. She'd allowed herself to become comfortable and complacent.

But from the first moment that Cole had looked into Ellis Watts's face, his green eyes filled with a deep malice, the precariousness of their situation had been obvious to him. They were not safe! The threat that faced them all was still there, but had simply gone into hiding, biding its time, waiting for the opportunity to rear its ugly head. That time appeared to be now.

"We need to go to the police," Cole repeated.

"Cole, I—" she started but quickly fell silent, her moist eyes searching his own as if she were weighing whether to expose her words. When she finally spoke, her voice was nearly as soft as a whisper. "I know you believe what you're saying, and, quite frankly, I find it hard to argue, especially after what happened to you," she said. "But I still want to talk to Graham first, to try to make some sense of just why he's behaving this way. Please, Cole, let me at least try."

He was about to argue his point further, to try to explain to Sophie that there was no way he was going to allow her to speak with the very man who had attacked him just hours earlier, when a muffled scream reached him. The sound momentarily startled Cole.

"What in the devil was that?"

"Where did—" Sophie stammered in confusion.

"The store," he answered simply, already making his way in the door, Sophie following on his heels.

Back inside the hardware store, Cole found the two middle-aged women who had been looking at iceboxes standing frozen in place. One raised a shaky arm and pointed. Cole followed their direction but could see nothing save the open door to the storeroom below.

"What happened?" he asked. "Where's my father?"

"He . . . he . . . just collapsed . . ." one of the women managed to stammer.

"Your father," the other woman said, her gloved hand rising to flutter before her face. "He was going . . . to show us some new pans . . . he said that they'd just arrived, but . . ."

"He had only made it to the door," the first woman continued, picking up the story where her companion had left off. "He seemed . . . to stumble . . . like he was dizzy, and then . . . he just fell . . ."

"Oh, Cole," Sophie whispered behind him.

Suddenly, the horrible truth of what the women were telling him sank in.

As quickly as he could manage, he went over to the open door and looked down the stairs. There, lying in a heap, was his father. Robert Ambrose had previously looked to be the vision of good health, but he now appeared small and frail. His body was awkwardly draped over the last couple of steps, a pool of dark blood spreading from the spot where his head had struck the floor.

Chapter Twenty-one

BLOOD POUNDED FURIOUSLY in Cole's ears at the sight of his father lying motionless at the foot of the stairs.

"Get the doctor, Sophie. Run to Dr. Palmer's office," he urged, his voice trembling. "It's just around the corner. Bring him back as fast as you can! Hurry!"

Sophie followed his directions, whipping open the front door and hurrying out into the sunlight. Fixated on his father and unaware whether the two middle-aged women had stayed in the store or if they had left, Cole faced the nightmares that had been plaguing him for most of his days.

Even though it had been more than ten years since the fateful day that his mother had fallen down the tall staircase of their home, the memory of discovering her broken body still haunted him. The image of her, lying just as his father lay now, badly hurt and seemingly beyond his reach, was one that he could not erase. When he allowed himself to remember that moment, he was forced to recall his own impotence, his failure to reach her in time, and the pain of his loss. Now he found himself faced with the same dilemma once again.

Taking a tentative step onto the stairs, he steadied himself before forcing his handicapped leg to move forward.

"Dad? Are you all right?" he called, but his father did not stir.

Cole struggled to keep from toppling headlong down the stairs. He would be no good to anyone if he were to take a fall of his own. Patience was a virtue he didn't seem to have enough of; twice his twisted foot slipped off a step and he only maintained his balance by gripping the rickety railing.

"One step at a time, Cole," he warned himself.

Finally he arrived at the bottom of the stairs, kneeling at his father's side and gently pulling the man's bleeding head into his lap. A deep pair of cuts had been opened up at the top of the man's scalp, crimson blood pouring forth with little sign of stopping. Cole did his best to staunch it with his own shirt. Robert was still breathing, his chest rhythmically rising and falling, albeit shallowly, but he had been knocked unconscious by the fall. In his current state, his father seemed so frail, so old. The evidence of his vulnerability was frightening.

"Dad, can you hear me?" Cole asked, but received no answer.

The reality of the situation was grim; there was no way he could carry his father back up the steps. Cole cursed his leg's deformity. If only he were a healthy man, if only he weren't a crippled failure, then things might be different . . .

All that he could do was wait and hope that help would arrive in time. Unlike when he had managed to reach his mother's side and been unable to go for help, he now had Sophie racing toward the doctor's office.

"Hurry, Sophie," he whispered. "Please hurry!"

Sophie raced out the hardware store's front door, leaped down the steps in one treacherous bound, and dashed down the street just as fast as her legs could carry her. Panic held a tight grip on her heart, urging her forward. The sight of Cole's father lying in a growing pool of his own blood had chilled her and she found she couldn't help but fear the worst.

"Faster," she willed herself. "Run faster!"

Rounding the corner next to the post office and running the short distance to the doctor's office, Sophie burst through the door gulping large gasps of air. It hadn't been a long distance to run, but the burden of her fear and apprehension had been exhausting to carry. She imagined that she was the one who looked to be in dire need of medical attention.

Philip Palmer stepped out of his examining room and regarded her curiously. Victory's lone doctor, middle-aged, with a thick paunch circling his midsection, charcoal gray hair swept casually over a round face, Dr. Palmer's ever-watery eyes carried an air of sympathy that was equally evident in the gentle way in which he cared for his patients; given the current emergency, Sophie was thankful that he didn't appear to have anyone else requiring his assistance.

"Sophie?" he asked, concern written large on his round face. "Whatever is the matter, dear?"

"You need . . . you need to come . . ." she gasped, the words caught in her throat so tightly that she couldn't dislodge the ones that she needed. "You need . . . to come . . . with me . . . There's been a . . ."

"What happened?" Dr. Palmer pressed, his expression suddenly anxious. He stepped toward her, placing his hands upon her shoulders, steadying her. "Is someone hurt?"

Sophie furiously nodded her head, hoping that gestures would succeed where words failed. "It's . . . it's Robert Ambrose . . ." she finally managed. "He's had a . . . fall and is . . . hurt . . ."

"Where is he? Where did it happen?"

"At the . . . at the hard . . ."

"Is he at his store?"

"Yes . . ."

Without any further hesitation, the doctor snatched up his small medical bag and rushed for the door. Though emotionally and physically spent, Sophie did her best to hurry along behind him.

She could only silently pray that they would arrive in time.

Cole did his best to wait patiently, his father's damaged head cradled in his arms, but his eyes kept darting back to the top of the stairs, ever hopeful that Sophie would suddenly appear with the doctor in tow. Every passing second seemed as painfully slow as if it were an hour. He kept the hem of his shirt pressed tightly to his father's bleeding scalp as his fingers smoothed the man's thinning hair away from the syrupy blood.

"Dad?" Cole asked over and over. "Dad, can you hear me?"

As if he were trying to see in a burning room choked tight with stinging smoke, Robert blinked slowly, his eyes languidly searching about until they lit on Cole's face. Recognition took a moment to follow, but when it did, the injured man gave the faintest hint of a smile.

"Cole . . . what . . . what hap—?" Robert whispered.

"Don't try to talk, Dad," Cole soothed. "You took a fall down the stairs and hit your head. Sophie's gone to fetch the doctor so everything's going to be all right."

Robert's hand rose as if he wanted to bring his fingers to his aching head and check for blood, but he could only raise it partway before it collapsed back down against his chest. His breathing was ragged from the effort, his eyes swimming dizzily.

"Don't move, Dad. Just lie still until the doctor gets here."

"I'm . . . I'm sorry . . . son . . ." Robert managed to say.

"There's nothing for you to be sorry about," Cole corrected him. "You just fell down the stairs is all. It could have happened to anyone. Heck, it probably should have been me."

"That's not . . . that's not what . . . I'm sorry for . . ." With great effort, Robert once again raised his hand, this time placing it on Cole's and giving it a gentle squeeze. "What I . . . have to be sorry . . . about," Robert continued, "is . . . far more than just . . . a tumble down . . . the stairs."

"You don't have to apologize to me," Cole protested.

"Yes . . . yes, I do . . . and we both . . . know it."

"This isn't the time."

"It most . . . certainly is . . ." Robert insisted. "I've known that it was . . . wrong to blame you . . . for what happened . . . to your mother . . . but I guess it was . . . easier to blame . . . you than myself."

"Neither of us is to blame for what happened to her," Cole explained, recalling Jason's words to him the night before he left for the navy. "What happened to her was an accident."

"An accident . . . that might have . . . been prevented if . . . I'd been . . . home more often . . ." his father argued. "You did . . . all that you . . . could, Cole. You have . . . always done all . . . that you could."

"But it wasn't enough to save her."

"There was . . . nothing that either . . . of us could have done," Robert said. "But the greatest . . . tragedy of all . . . has been how I've pushed . . . you away for something . . . that you could . . . not have changed. For that . . . my son . . . I'm as sorry as I . . . can be."

For years, Cole had struggled to obtain his father's forgiveness, but when it hadn't been attained, he'd rebelled against the man as many sons eventually did. But now that he had what he had so desperately wanted, he felt no sense of triumph, no gloating happiness, but rather a calming, soothing sense that everything was as it should have been. It was as if he had found redemption for what had happened when he was a child; he'd managed to reach his father and somehow find him at the same time.

Cole knew that, in the end, Jason had been right all along; all that had been needed between him and his father was a little time and patience. A breakthrough had been developing between them, a few cordial words spoken over breakfast and their time together rebuilding the Hellers' barn. All were signs of a gradual thawing of the silence. While it was unfortunate that it took a vicious tumble down the stairs to finally break through the ice of their distance, Cole was glad that it had happened just the same.

Everything is going to be all right . . .

"I've always been proud to be your son," Cole said, meaning every word.

"Not as proud . . . as I have been . . . to be your father."

Before Cole could say another word, there was a commotion at the top of the stairs and he looked up to find Sophie and Dr. Palmer staring down at them. Happiness flooded his heart at the sight and his spirits soared with the renewed hope that his father was going to be all right.

"What happened, Robert?" the doctor asked just as soon as he had hurried down the stairs to join them.

"Took a . . . spill . . . is all . . ." the man said in answer. "Must have been . . . the heat that . . . got to me . . ."

While Dr. Palmer began to look over his father, Cole's eyes found Sophie and he held her gaze for what felt like forever. The harsh words that he had spoken to her only a few short minutes earlier seemed as if they had been uttered years before, but that did little to staunch the regret that suddenly overcame him. Forcing her to tell him about Graham Grier seemed a selfish act, a trifling thing compared to what had just happened. He'd been able to depend upon her to help save his father's life, and that was all that mattered.

"Thank you," he said to her. Her only answer was an understanding smile.

Emotions that Cole had only ever been able to imagine rushed over him as he stared into Sophie's eyes. He was struck by how beautiful she was, both on the inside and out, and the sudden realization struck him that he had fallen in love with her. Whatever their future together might hold, he knew that his feelings for Sophie Heller would burn on until his dying day.

"We'll need to move him, Cole," Dr. Palmer said.

"Will he be all right?"

"He doesn't appear to have any broken bones," the doctor explained. "There really isn't much to do for him other than stitch up that cut in his head and make sure he gets plenty of rest."

"Oh, thank goodness!" Sophie exclaimed.

"For now, we need to get him back to my office so I can tend to him."

"I don't know if I'll be able to help," Cole worried. "I had a hard time getting down these steps. Even without carrying my father's weight, it won't be easy."

"I can help . . . son," Robert said.

He and the doctor managed to raise the wounded man to his feet, each of them slinging one of Robert's arms over his shoulder. Cole had to steady himself, straining to keep his bad leg still, but he managed to hold the man's weight.

Together, he and his father took the first step.

Chapter Twenty-two

NIGHT HAD LONG since darkened the sky by the time Cole was able to drive Sophie back out to her family's farm. They rode with the windows down; the sticky warmth of the day clung long after the sun had slid out of sight. A restless wind did little more than stir the heat. Crickets chirped noisily from the darkness. Sophie stared out the window and into the sky, the crescent moon looking back silently.

"He'll be all right," she said, breaking the quiet of the truck's cab.

Cole grunted in answer.

"The doctor assured us that all he needed

was to be observed for a few days if we made sure that he got plenty of rest," she continued. "The next thing you know, he'll be back on his feet and as good as new."

When Robert Ambrose was taken from the hardware store to the doctor's office, his wound was stitched, but there was little else that could be done. Dr. Palmer had been confident that he would make a full recovery, but Sophie could clearly see that his cheery prognosis had given Cole little comfort.

"I just felt so damned helpless," Cole muttered.

"But why?" Sophie exclaimed. "If you hadn't been there, who knows what would have happened!"

"It's . . . because of my mother."

It was then that Cole finally told Sophie about the fateful day when he had lost his mother, the day that had changed his life forever. He told her about the awful sound that first alerted him that something was wrong and the trepidation that filled his heart as he walked out onto the landing, finding her lying at the base of the stairs. With his fists clenched tightly around the truck's steering wheel, he recounted his failure to reach her, of his inability to get his leg to do his bidding, all the while screaming for her to wake up. When he'd finally managed to reach her, he'd been overcome by fear, retreating to a corner while her life slipped away. His brow furrowed as he explained how this failure, *his failure*, had impacted his relationship with his father ever since.

"Oh, Cole," Sophie whispered, her chest tightening with emotion.

"I always believed that he blamed me for her death."

"What happened to your mother wasn't your fault," she disagreed. "You were a child! No matter how great his loss, your father couldn't possibly blame you."

"I think that I can finally believe that," Cole explained. "But when I saw him this afternoon, lying at the bottom of the stairs just like my mother had been, I couldn't bring myself to move. It was like I was a child again, just as scared and helpless as ever."

"But you did move," she argued. "You did reach him, Cole."

"Yeah," he admitted with the faintest hint of a smile. "I did."

"Whatever problem your father's had because of the death of your mother, I have no doubt that he cares for you. No matter what, you will always be his son. Emotions sometimes get the better of us all, but family is a bond that can't be broken. Nothing can change that."

Cole nodded. "You're right. And even though we've had our problems by the bucketful, to see him lying there, wondering if he was dead, was almost impossible to bear."

Sophie found herself struck mute. She knew just how Cole had felt; the night that her family's barn had been burned, she'd been forced to stand face-to-face with the same nightmare. Just as Cole had done, she had cradled her father's bleeding head in her lap, all the while wondering if he was going to die. His was a fear that she knew all too well.

"Thank you," he said, his hand leaving the wheel to find hers.

"Why would you need to thank me?" she asked, suddenly self-conscious but glad to feel his touch.

"Because even though I found the

strength to make it down those stairs, none of it would have mattered if you hadn't been there," Cole explained.

"There's no need to thank me," Sophie said, flushing slightly.

"I'm grateful just the same."

When her family's farm finally came into view in the sparse light of the moon, Sophie couldn't help but feel a twinge of disappointment. Though her day with Cole had gone nothing like what they had planned, she'd still taken joy at spending it at his side. That it was about to come to an end was regrettable.

After they had bounced around the inside of the truck's cab during the drive up to the house, Cole said, "Do you think your father would get offended if I showed up one day and fixed all of these holes?"

"You'd ruin all of his fun if you did," she said with a laugh.

"If he's not careful, one of these days he's going to hit his head so hard that he'll get a visit of his own from Dr. Palmer."

Cole brought the truck to a halt but didn't shut off the engine. While Sophie would have liked for him to join her for a bit, maybe for a talk out on the back porch, she understood his desire to look back in on his father.

Save for the never-ending calling of insects, the farm sounded quiet through the open windows of the truck. Even if Bing Crosby were to step out of the recently finished barn and start crooning, Sophie doubted that she could have heard him over the pounding of her heart.

"Cole, I—" she began before his lips found hers.

Though they had kissed several times since that first night outside the theater and under the moon, Sophie still felt as if she were floating on air every time their lips touched. An intense passion raced through her, a magical feeling that she never wanted to end.

"Oh, Cole," she moaned into his mouth.

Sophie met his advances tenderly at first, even a bit tentatively, but the flame of her desire quickly grew. Pushing herself closer to him, her body pressing up against his, she found her fingers traveling up the length of his arm, crossing his shoulder, and playing with the soft hair at the nape of his neck. When he finally broke their kiss and buried his face in her hair, she was happy, even if she wished he hadn't stopped.

"My darling Sophie," he whispered into her ear.

When she finally broke from him and got out of the pickup, Sophie stared back at Cole through the open window. "I'll come to town tomorrow and check in on your father."

He smiled. "He'd like that. And so would I."

This time, instead of rushing to the house in tears, she watched as he reversed the pickup truck to back down the hazardous drive. Before he headed back toward Victory, she stood on her tiptoes and waved, hoping that he would see her in the inky darkness. Then he was lost from sight, leaving her alone.

Sophie headed to the farmhouse with a spring in her step and joy in her heart; she wondered if she'd be able to sleep a wink! She'd just given thought to how lucky she was to have found a man like Cole Ambrose when the sound of a stick snapping froze her in place. She knew, beyond a shadow of a doubt, that it had not been an animal—and that she was not alone.

In that instant, all of her familiar fears came rushing back with the speed of a locomotive. *Who is waiting for me? Ellis Watts? Riley Mason? Can I possibly make it to the house in time?* Sophie was just about to throw caution to the winds and make a break for the house when a shadowy form stepped out from the deep darkness at the side of the barn and stood directly in the moonlight. Though the moon was nowhere near half full, she could clearly see who it was.

It's Graham!

"Sophie," he said. "I think it's time we talked."

For a moment, fear grabbed hold of Sophie's heart and would not let go, but when it finally did, anger took its place. She couldn't believe the utter contempt that Graham must have for her and her family to show his face under the shadow of the very building that had replaced the one he had helped burn. But after everything that had been done to her, after all the laughing and slurs, she found that she was tired of running.

Striding determinedly across the yard, Sophie came to a stop right in front of Graham, reared back, and slapped him across the face with all the strength she could muster. The crack of the blow seemed to hang in the air, trapped in a moonbeam or caught in a light breeze.

"Why, Graham?" she demanded of him. "Tell me why!"

"Sophie, I—"

"How could you become involved with such men?" she barked, refusing to let him give an answer until after she had said her piece. "How could you do the things you've done?"

Graham Grier could only stand silently, not answering Sophie's frenzy of questions. His hand never once rose to touch the red cheek that Sophie had slapped, his eyes turned away and pointed toward the ground. He seemed willing to take the abuse she was heaping upon him.

Never in Sophie's wildest dreams would she have imagined that she would strike Graham, or even speak to him so harshly. But then she also never would have thought that he could do the things that he had done to her and her family. She would get the answers she was seeking, though she hoped it meant that she wouldn't have to strike him again.

"How could you just stand there, doing nothing, while a man like Ellis Watts used his rifle to strike down my father?" she asked accusingly, her voice cracking with emotion. "You let them burn down my family's barn! And then you just sat there with your head in your plate while Riley Mason put his hands on me! How could you do all of these things? How can I begin to understand this, Graham?"

"You can't," he agreed. "Not when I can't understand it myself."

"Just tell me the truth!"

"I'm telling you that I can't!"

"Then I've got nothing more to say to you!"

Exasperated, Sophie turned on her heel and began to march toward the farm without a second glance. Though it frustrated her to not learn the reasons for Graham's bizarre behavior, she was through being played for a fool. *Why did he come if he didn't want to explain himself?* But she had only gone a few steps before he grabbed her by the shoulder and spun her around; even in the near-dark of night, she could see his eyes glittering.

“Can’t you understand how hard it is for me to even be here?” Graham tried to argue. “The guilt over what’s been done to you and your family is tearing my insides apart! I can’t sleep! I can’t eat! I can’t do anything without seeing that night replayed before my eyes!”

“You were here!” Sophie shot back. “You could have stopped it!”

“No, I couldn’t have.”

“You’re a grown man, Graham,” she declared, her voice shot through with anger. “We aren’t children anymore! You made a choice to accompany those bastards here, so you have to share in the consequences. There’s no one for you to pass blame to besides yourself.”

“There are . . . things that you can’t begin to understand, Sophie,” Graham said, turning his back to her and throwing his hands up toward the night sky in frustration. “Something happened . . . something that I hadn’t expected and that I now regret. I wish that it hadn’t occurred, but it’s far too late for that. Try as I might, I can't take it back."

"I don't care."

"But you have to," he pleaded. "It's the only thing that matters."

"Then tell me what it is."

Briefly, it seemed as if Graham was going to do as she asked, but just as he opened his mouth to speak, it closed shut yet again. "I just . . . I just can't do that, Sophie."

"Then we've got nothing to say to each other."

For the flicker of an instant, the thought of another awkward night between the two of them passed across Sophie's memory; the moment when Graham professed his feelings for her. She could still see the hurt ripple across his face when she had told him she didn't return his affection. Then, just as now, he had also been unable to meet her eyes. After she'd left the diner in tears, she had wondered if his reasons for joining in the terrorizing of her family weren't linked to her refusal. It was a question to which she needed the answer.

"Is this because of what happened between us?" she prodded.

"What . . . what do you mean?"

"Is this because I refused your advances?" Sophie asked further, the words surprisingly hard to say. "Did you decide to go along with Ellis and commit these crimes because I told you that I couldn't be with you, that I didn't see us as anything more than friends?"

Graham scarcely moved, didn't flinch at her accusations, but his hooded eyes rose from the ground to find hers, holding them steadily. Sophie's vision had adjusted to the darkness, allowing her to see that, regardless of his true reasons for joining Ellis Watts's plan, her rejection had hurt him deeply. There was a time when she would have done anything to take that hurt away. But now, after all that Graham had done, after meeting Cole Ambrose, she knew that whatever pain this man held, it was for him and him alone.

"No, Sophie," he said solemnly. "I give you my word that's not the reason."

Though she could see that he wasn't about to tell her the whole truth, Sophie allowed him his pride. Still, doing so did nothing to bring her closer to the truth. "Then why, Graham? You at least owe me that."

"Doesn't it mean something that I came to see you?"

"Should it?" she asked in amazement. "Not after what you've done." Sophie couldn't believe how evasive Graham was; if he would just be honest with her, tell her why he had been with the other men, then maybe, *just maybe*, they could go forward.

"I'm trying to talk to you about what's happening," Graham said.

"Then tell me what you're doing with a man like Ellis Watts. Your father is the town mayor, Graham! What can you be thinking?"

"I'm not with them . . . out of choice."

With his hesitance, Sophie suddenly understood that Graham had done some terrible thing, something so horrible that he was in Ellis Watts's thrall. But what could it be? "Is this the thing that you can't talk about?" she asked. "Does Ellis know what you've done?"

Graham paused, as if his mouth had suddenly filled with glue. "Yes," he finally mumbled.

"What is it that he knows?" she pressed. "Is it something illegal?"

"Yes . . . no . . . I don't know anymore," Graham answered in exasperation. He suddenly crossed the distance between them, so quickly that Sophie could do little more than flinch, his hands grabbing her fiercely by the shoulders. His eyes looked wet and pleading. "Don't you see that this is precisely the problem? If I tell you what I've done, you'll never want to speak to me again! It will never be the same between us!"

Gently but firmly, Sophie pulled Graham's hands free. "What you've done cannot be wished away, Graham," she explained, her voice calm yet strong. "Refusing to tell me what motivated you won't make it any less real. What's done is done. You know that."

"Then I've already lost you," he concluded gravely.

Sophie knew that, in a way, Graham's words were the truth: Cole Ambrose had stolen her heart. While there had undoubtedly been a time when she'd been confused about her feelings for Graham, there had never been any doubt regarding the emotions she held for Cole. She had never been Graham's to lose, but now any hopes he'd had were lost to him forever.

Thinking of Cole dislodged another of Sophie's memories; that of the bruises and bumps that had colored his face, the result of a beating at Graham's hands. There had been so many other things for her to be angry about, so many reasons for her to be disappointed in her old friend, that she'd forgotten one of the most important. No longer . . .

"Why did you attack Cole Ambrose?" she asked, her anger rising.

"Sophie, I—" Graham stumbled, surprised.

"Don't even think of telling me that you had nothing to do with it," she said, her voice threatening. "Cole told me you were responsible, that you were acting alone. Tell me why you would do such a thing."

"Because he's not good enough for you!" Graham replied harshly.

"That's not for you to decide."

"I can't just stand by while you throw your life away on a . . . on a cripple!"

The force of Graham's words struck Sophie just as if he had returned her slap. She recoiled from him, unable to believe that he would say such a thing, knowing full well that whatever bond had existed between them was now irrevocably broken. Part of her wanted to cry, but another struggled to maintain her composure. She thought of what her grandmother had told her, about how the true measure of a man was what was on the inside, and it strengthened her resolve.

"You've no right to stand in judgment of me!" she barked.

"What am I to do, Sophie?" Graham asked, incredulous. "How is a man like him, half a man at best, to take care of you? He can't truly provide for you, support you, protect you as you deserve. What good is he going to be the next time Ellis and Riley come for you? He couldn't even fend me off, what hope does he have against hard men like them!"

A sickening feeling filled the pit of Sophie's stomach at Graham's words, bile rising in her throat. Standing before her, rationalizing what he had done to the wonderful man who had entered her life, Graham was nothing but a shadow of the man she'd known. With horror, she realized that he was just as dangerous to her and her family as the others, an insight that chilled her. He'd left her with no other choice.

"Don't ever speak to me again, Graham," she said calmly.

"What—?" he started. "What are—?"

"Stay away from Cole and my family or I'll take what I know to the police."

"You can't . . . you can't do this, Sophie," he exclaimed, fear rising in his face as his eyes darted nervously about. "If Ellis Watts were to be exposed, then he'd have no reason not to take me along with him. If my father were to find out, it would kill him."

"Yet you let those two bastards nearly be the death of mine."

Just as Graham's words had been nearly as powerful as a physical blow, now her words struck him hard enough to blunt his anger and his arms dropped to his sides in defeat.

"Don't make me regret giving you this last chance," she said simply as she turned and walked away from him, leaving him at the site where his actions had destroyed the bond between them forever.

This time, he did nothing to stop her.

Chapter Twenty-three

SONG AND LAUGHTER burst out of the open doors of the Hellers' barn as if it were floodwaters set free from the gates of a dam. The dancing light of a blazing bonfire carried skyward toward the moon and sea of stars, while setting shadows dancing across the buildings and far tree line. Children scurried about underfoot, chasing each other from the darkness to the light and back again, their squeals of joy mixing with the other sounds in a glorious song.

Sophie walked from the farmhouse to the barn carrying a tray of apple pies still hot and steaming from the oven. She and her mother had been cooking for hours in anticipation of the festivities; a dance to give thanks to those who had toiled in re-building the destroyed barn. Though the celebration had been going on for hours, there was no telling when it would end. More than likely, it would continue on through dawn.

As she walked, voices called to her from all around.

"Best save a slice for me, Sophie!"

"Tell your mother to get out of that there kitchen and join in the fun!"

"Here's to the Hellers!"

Sophie smiled and nodded to each passing call, happy that her family could bring such joy to their neighbors and friends. Still, her heart remained heavy because of her talk with Graham. Although nearly a week had passed since he'd startled her in the shadow of the barn, she found herself thinking about it often, replaying the things he had said over and over in her mind. Even now, she was no closer to understanding.

Get it out of your head, girl! There's a party to enjoy!

The inside of the barn was even more festive than the exterior. The center of the barn had been cleared and a haphazard array of chairs and benches lined up around the walls. People milled about, some dancing, some talking, but everyone smiling. A band had set up in the far corner, consisting of a pair of violins, an accordion, a harmonica, and even someone clinking spoons. One of the violinists struggled to carry a tune, his deep voice warbling so badly that it was hard to pick out the words, but no one seemed to mind.

"You just keep it comin', Chester!" Charley Tatum bellowed from in front of the stage. The heavyset farmer swung and swayed, occasionally pounding his booted foot on the ground in an odd form of dance, a half-eaten chicken leg clutched in his greasy hand.

"Right back at you, Charley!" someone yelled back.

Sophie brought the tray of pies over to a long table set near the door and placed it down among the other dishes. All kinds of food had been brought in great abundance: baked chickens, steaming pots of beans, fresh vegetables and fruits, and pies and cakes of all shapes and sizes took up nearly every square inch of the table. It was truly a feast.

Still receiving thanks for all that she and her family had done to throw such a magnificent barn dance, Sophie searched the room for sign of Cole. She found him leaning casually against one of the barn's support beams, tapping his foot rhythmically to the music.

Moving toward him, Sophie couldn't help but smile. Cole looked dapper this evening, his blond hair perfectly combed, his shirt starched and shoes shined, handsome not beginning to describe him. He'd come early, helping to set up the party against her father's protestations that he didn't need to lift a finger, but it had been more than an hour since she'd last seen him.

An hour too long!

Cole looked up as she neared and a bright smile lit his face. Sophie was glad to see him escape his worries, if only for a little while. It had been more than a week since Robert Ambrose's mishap at the hardware store. Though he was still confined to bed with occasional bouts of dizziness, he continued to show marked improvement, both physically and in his relationship with his son; it appeared that near-tragedy had brought them closer together. It had been his father who had encouraged Cole to go and enjoy the dance.

"I expected to find you lurking over by the food table," she said when she got near him, sliding up close enough to be heard over the noise of the band. "There are an awful lot of good things to eat."

He smiled. "It's dangerous over there. If a fellow's not careful, he could lose a finger or two."

"I think one of my mother's pies was gone before I even set the tray down."

The band chose that moment to wind down their song and the inside of the barn erupted in applause. Over a dozen people took that opportunity to head toward the food table, Charley Tatum in the lead.

"You look beautiful tonight," Cole said into the relative quiet. "I like your blouse."

Sophie blushed at the compliment but was pleased that he had noticed her attempt to dress up for him; she'd bought the new white blouse only a few days earlier, admiring the way that the neckline dipped slightly, hoping beyond hope that Cole would feel the same.

"You don't look half bad yourself," she offered in return.

"If there's one thing I've always been good at, it's cleaning up."

They talked easily with each other, as if they were the only two people in the barn. Sophie spoke of how much work her mother had done in the kitchen, while Cole told of a letter he had just received from Jason in California, reciting it nearly word for word. He'd just finished when the band started playing again.

"Would you like to dance?" Cole asked.

Sophie was so surprised that she couldn't respond with words; instead, she grabbed him by the arm and led him out to the center of the barn, her smile brighter than the bonfire.

"Take it easy with me," he cautioned, so she did.

The melody of the song was quick, a furious scratching of the violins with the wheezing and bellowing of the accordion, the other instruments pitching in for good measure. Nearly a dozen people joined them, exulting in the music and the company of friends.

Cole made certain to find his balance, his good leg planted firmly on the dirt floor, and began to clap his hands to the tune. His dancing skills were minimal, a hesitant bobbing of his shoulders and bending of his good knee, but he seemed genuinely glad to be there. For her part, Sophie danced in front of him, her body a whirling dervish of dark hair, slightly raised skirt, and no small amount of happiness.

On and on they danced, the music seeming to stretch into the night. The way that Sophie was feeling pushed her ever on, until she finally began to spin, and everything around her dissolved into a mess of colors and sound. Still, with every twirl, she always returned to Cole's eyes.

They danced until they were spent, both of them breathing heavily, Sophie's black hair wet with sweat. This time, when the music ended, they were both clapping, their heart pounding in their chests but their mood light and ebullient. Cole took her by the hand and led her off the makeshift dance floor.

"Would you like something to drink?" she asked.

"It's either that or I have to dunk my head in the horse trough."

"Whatever am I going to do with you?" Sophie laughed before heading off into the throng.

Graham Grier walked the last half mile to the Hellers' farm. From the moment that Sophie had left him standing in the dark night shadows of her family's barn a week earlier, he had done nothing but stew in his own frustration, plotting how he would regain his honor, how he would regain Sophie's hand. Kicking at the dry brush that lined the road, he heard the first sounds of the barn dance drifting along the evening air, a shout here and a snippet of laughter there, but the joyous noises only served to enrage him further. Graham was very angry.

He was also quite drunk.

Tipping back the whiskey flask that he had stolen from his father's office, he took a deep slug of the liquor, savoring the way that it burned down his gullet, giving him more courage to do what he knew was needed. He'd already had plenty of the booze, more than he'd ever drunk before, but that wasn't about to stop him. Sloshing the whiskey around in the flask, he was happy to hear that there was at least a bit more left.

"And I'm gonna drink it too," he vowed.

Weaving tipsily, Graham struggled to stay upright as the farmhouse entered his view. He'd come out to the farm often when he'd been younger on visits to Sophie, but it seemed that all of his recent trips were now rife with bad intentions: burning the barn in the company of Ellis and Riley, confronting Sophie a week earlier, and for what he was about to do.

Especially for what I'm about to do . . .

Graham held no doubt that Cole Ambrose would be in attendance at the barn dance; there wasn't any part of him that could imagine Sophie not inviting the man. He had given the crippled bastard a chance, warning him to stay far away, but he hadn't paid attention. Now he would have to reap what he sowed.

Drowning himself in liquor served another purpose: easing away all thoughts of

Carolyn Glass and the bastard child that grew in her belly. That unborn baby and the night it had been conceived was Graham's cross to bear, his burden. Sophie had wanted him to tell her the truth, but he knew that if he were to be honest, she would never speak to him again.

Cresting a low rise at the edge of the Hellers' property, Graham finished off the last of the whiskey, some of it dribbling down his shirt. Angrily wiping his mouth, he nearly tipped over, his head suddenly lurching, but he kept his balance and looked out over the grounds.

The rebuilt barn was the spitting image of the one he had helped to destroy, right down to the red and white paint that covered it. He was surprised to see a blazing bonfire so close to the building; he would have thought that Hermann would have had enough bad associations with his buildings and fire to allow such a thing. He was too far away to make out any individual faces, but he knew that his quarry was there . . . he was certain of it. Stumbling forward on unsteady legs, he headed toward the bonfire and the barn beyond.

"Hey, Graham!" someone shouted, but he never turned his head.

Somehow, he managed to make his way to the open barn, dropping the flask and grabbing on to one of the doors, holding on for dear life. Loud music poured over him, disorienting him further. The whiskey had a hold on him and his vision swam; the sight that looked back at him from inside the barn was one of swirling movement.

Fighting back the urge to vomit, Graham began looking for Cole Ambrose in the depths of the barn. The going was harder than he had anticipated; stumbling along, bumping into someone, then a chair, then another person, all the while the effects of the whiskey grew stronger and stronger on his addled head. The way things were going, running into the crippled son of a bitch was bound to happen by dumb luck.

"Goddamn it all," he muttered to himself.

Suddenly, the music came to a halt, the dancers stopped moving, and a round of applause broke out. As couples moved off the dance floor, Graham searched the room for some sign of the teacher. He had just managed to avoid being run down by a man making a beeline for a table overloaded with food when, through a part in the crowd, he saw Sophie. She had her back to him, pulling a loose strand of her black hair behind her ear, Cole Ambrose smiling at her over her shoulder.

Looking at the man who he'd already beaten down like a rabid dog, Graham could not help but sneer; that this cripple was usurping his rightful place at Sophie's side was an insult that he could not stomach. He'd meant what he'd said to Sophie a week earlier; this was a man who could no more provide for her than he could run a mile! But what would Sophie say about what he was about to do? Would she attempt to interfere? Would she understand that he was doing it for her own good?

But can I go through with it?

The truth was Graham wasn't entirely certain why he had come to the farm. If Ellis knew what he was doing, he would be furious with him for having jeopardized their future plans. He had some hopes that he could repair what he had broken with Sophie, but somewhere inside him he knew it was all an illusion, a broken mirror that could never be put back together; simply trying to pick up the shards would get his hands cut and bloodied. All that remained to him, the only option he could see, was to hurt the cripple, to show Cole Ambrose what a real man looked like.

Then Sophie walked away, leaving Cole alone.

Cole saw Graham coming. Sophie had moved only a few feet away when the man came stumbling toward him, swaying and wobbling like a farmer who suddenly found himself out to sea in the midst of a raging storm. For a moment, it looked as if he would fall, but he somehow stayed upright, finally coming to a halt just in front of Cole. Graham's eyes were bloodshot red, his lips wet with spittle, and he reeked of liquor.

This was a confrontation that Cole had been expecting. Sophie had told him all about Graham's late-night visit of a week earlier, of his failure to give her a clear explanation as to why he had joined with Ellis Watts to terrorize her family, saying only that it had something to do with a mistake he had made.

"I told you . . . to stay away from her," he mumbled.

"I remember."

The memory of the vicious beating Graham had given him outside the school remained fresh in Cole's head; most of his bruises had only just faded, though a cluster of mottled brown still marked his cheekbone. His first thought was to return the favor, to ball up his fists and pummel the man senseless, but he couldn't find the anger in his heart. Surprisingly, the only emotion that Cole could find for Graham was pity.

"You had best leave, Graham," he said. "There isn't any . . ."

"Don't give me that shit, goddammit!"

Heads turned at Graham's outburst, the pleasant air of the barn dance upset by his drunken words and tone. Out of the corner of his eye, Cole saw Sophie abruptly turn, her eyes growing wide at the man responsible for the commotion; he could only hope she would stay away.

"Why did you come here?" Cole asked.

"Because you didn't listen to a word I said!" Graham shouted. "You were supposed to stay away from her! You're not good enough for Sophie, and you never will be! She should be with me!"

"What Sophie wants isn't for either of us to decide," Cole answered solemnly and carefully; Graham was clearly a powder keg that was ready to explode. "Neither one of us has the right to tell her what's best for her."

"You worthless cripple! I told you what would happen if you didn't stay away from her!"

"There hasn't been a threat uttered that would make me do that."

Without warning, Graham lurched toward Cole, looping a punch that clearly had little chance to reach its mark; the alcohol the man had consumed had deteriorated both his judgment and his body. Cole easily blocked the punch with his forearm and reared back to throw a right hand of his own. His fist struck Graham square in the jaw, snapping his head abruptly to the side, and the man's knees instantaneously left him. He fell to the ground as if he were a limp doll, his arms and legs splaying in the dirt, unconscious.

Looking down at Graham's still body, Cole found no pleasure in what he had done. There was no joy to be had in defeating such an impaired man, regardless of the irony, even one that had only days before felt no such reluctance in attacking him.

"Cole, are you all right?" Sophie worried as she rushed to his side.

"I'm fine. He didn't hurt me."

"Someone best go and call the police," Charley Tatum said. "This boy needs a night in jail to cool his head."

Cole watched as Sophie's eyes found her father's where he stood among the group of people looking down at Graham. Hermann Heller seemed deep in thought, his brow furrowed and his face a mask of concentration, but when he looked up, his eyes seemed clear.

"Go on up to the house," he said to Karl, "and call the sheriff."

Sophie's hands stiffened around Cole's arm, but he knew that the right decision had been made. It had been a mistake to allow the three men who attacked Sophie and her family to get away with their crimes. Now, finally, it appeared that justice would be served.

Chapter Twenty-four

IT WAS WELL after midnight when Sophie took Cole by the hand and began to pull him toward the woods behind her family's barn. Many of the barn dance's revelers remained, the sound of their voices carrying in the night air, but the gathering was clearly winding down. Though several hours had passed since Graham Grier had confronted him inside the barn, hours since the drunken man had been hauled away by the sheriff, Cole's heart thundered like a jackrabbit's.

"Where are we going?" he asked.

"You'll just have to trust me," Sophie answered mysteriously.

"With everything that's happened, I don't know if it's such a good—"

"There's nothing to fear out here."

Stepping into a rut of a path that cut among the tall grass, they plunged into the tree line and were swallowed by the darkness. Tall elms and oaks towered over their heads, their branches swaying slightly in the breeze. Sounds assaulted them from all around; the rustling of branches and the occasional creak or groan seemed to come from every direction at once, setting Cole's nerves on edge.

"Sophie, I just don't—"

"Hush," she silenced him. "I know what I'm doing."

Picking his way slowly along the darkened path, Cole held tightly to Sophie's hand as she led him farther into the woods. He couldn't help but stumble occasionally, tripping over a rock or errant tree branch, but every time she was there to steady him, patiently waiting until he had balanced himself before moving on. Wherever she was taking him, he knew that it was a place with which she was intimately familiar.

Still, Cole couldn't help but to think about what had happened earlier. When Graham had collapsed onto the floor in a heap, he'd instinctively known that the beginning of the end was coming. Ellis Watts was not the type of man who would sit idly by for long. While Graham's drunken arrival wasn't likely to have been planned, it signaled that things were changing quickly. It wouldn't be long before Ellis and his flunky showed up to finish what they had started.

Sophie led him down a shallow embankment and along a gurgling creek little wider than two hands. The sound of the water was comforting, a steady, constant noise far different from the random emanations of the inky dark woods around them.

"We're almost there," Sophie said.

Before them, an outcropping of rock rose toward the sky; set in the middle of a clearing, its mottled surface shone in the moonlight. There were three boulders haphazardly laid one upon another, rising up until the one on top nearly touched the branches of a nearby elm.

"This is it."

"Here?" Cole asked.

"This is where I wanted to take you. It's my special place."

Finding a foothold, Sophie quickly climbed up the first rock before stopping to offer her hand to Cole. "The going can be kind of difficult," she explained. "We'll have to take it slow with your leg, but I don't have any doubt that you can make it to the top."

Cole stared at Sophie as her confidence in him caused his heart to swell with happiness and a smile brightened his features. Taking her hand, he planted his crippled leg and stepped onto the rock. *Even if it takes me all night, I will manage to climb to the top!*

With equal parts sweat and determination, Cole followed Sophie as she rose toward the top of the rocks. Inch by inch, foot by foot, his fingers scrabbling among the edges and crevices for a handhold, he carefully pulled himself upward, determined not to fail. All around him, the sounds of the night seemed to soften, to disperse as if they had been blown away by the wind, until all that remained was the sound of his breathing and the steady thumping in his chest. As he climbed, Cole knew that he had been changed; where once he had been petrified of a flight of stairs, he knew that there was now nothing he would not attempt so long as Sophie was at his side.

Finally, they reached the top. Stepping onto the flat surface of the highest of the rocks, Cole found Sophie waiting for him, a smile on her face and a blanket spread out at her feet.

"You planned this, didn't you?" Cole asked.

"I did," Sophie admitted.

"What's the occasion?"

Stepping toward him, Sophie placed one hand gently upon his chest and fixed her gaze upon him with such intensity that he was momentarily taken aback. "I brought you here, to my special place, because I love you."

The words had no sooner than left her mouth than Sophie could see in Cole's face that he returned her feelings. She felt short of breath, nearly overwhelmed with emotion, and joyful tears filled her eyes. All that she had wanted was for this night to be special, and now, even after the scene that Graham had caused, her wishes looked to be coming true.

"You love me?" he asked.

"I do."

Without another sound, Cole reached out and pulled Sophie to his chest. In his powerful arms, she could hear his heart beating as intensely as her own and, reveling in his touch, she hoped that this moment would never end. Breathing in his scent, she returned his passionate embrace.

The last several weeks of her life had been a never-ending succession of conflicts and frights, each more horrible than the last. With every passing day, Sophie had gotten further and further away from the joy that had previously defined her life, but now, in Cole Ambrose's arms, under the stars, in her special place, she felt that happiness returning.

"What is this place?" Cole asked.

"It's where I come to be alone," she explained, her voice as soft a whisper as the breeze gently rocking the branches above their heads. "I found it just after arriving in Victory and it's been my sanctuary ever since."

"If it's the place that you come to be alone, why did you bring me?"

"Because I want to share everything with you," she answered, moving her gaze from his chest to stare up into his eyes. Though the darkness of the night obscured most of Cole's face, she still felt that she could see into the depths of his gaze; it was as if she were seeing through him and into the multitudes of stars shining above.

"I'm glad that you brought me here."

"From the moment that I first met you in the diner, even before everything that happened, I've known that you were special," she said, giving voice to the many thoughts that had been racing through her head since that very day. "Every moment since then has given me more reason to believe that my judgment was true. I know that in you, I've found the man with whom I want to share my life. I can only hope that you return these feelings as intensely as I give them."

"I do," he answered.

Rising up onto the balls of her feet, Sophie placed her lips against Cole's and kissed him deeply. Just as the moon continued to rise above them, so too did her passion, an ardor that was as relentless as an ocean's wave, wearing her down until she gave in to its thrall. Her lips parted, her tongue darting forward and finding his, waiting and willing, only complete when they were together.

When their lips finally parted, Sophie stepped confidently back, allowing her fingers to begin unfastening the buttons of Cole's shirt. She had only managed to undo one when he gently grabbed her by the wrist.

"Are you sure this is what you want?" he asked.

"I am."

"You feel that strongly about us?"

"Without question," she answered assuredly. "Don't you?"

"From the moment I first met you."

With her fingers once again prying apart the buttons of his shirt, Sophie soon had it undone, pushing it back on his shoulders where it soon dropped to the boulder below. Gently, she ran her hands through the thick, soft hair of Cole's chest, an audible inhalation of air through clenched teeth rewarding her for her efforts.

No sooner had Cole's skin been bared

to the night than his fingers began to smooth the fabric of her blouse, tracing the curvature of her breasts, then unfastening the buttons. In what seemed no longer than the blink of an eye, her own bare skin was first revealed, her brassiere undone and discarded, and her nipples kissed erect by the warm yet insistent wind.

Neither of their hands stopped there. Hastily, he unbuttoned her skirt with the same fervor as he unbuckled his belt. Passionately, he removed every bit of clothing until both stood revealed to the other, standing bare and unashamed.

Deftly, Sophie lowered herself onto the blanket she had spread out earlier in the day for that very purpose, and helped Cole to join her, one of his muscular biceps taut as he positioned his awkward leg beneath him. She lay flat on her back, one leg scissored between his, his rigid sex pressing against the soft flesh of her thigh. For the longest moment, she was content to simply gaze into his face, one hand gently brushing the hair against his temple.

"I've never . . . never . . ." he fumbled, his meaning every bit as clear as if he had spoken the words.

"Nor I," Sophie admitted. "But we'll learn together."

As if the floodgates to their passion had been flung open, Cole's hands began to roam across her body, sending waves of pleasure racing across her. Delighting in the soft, kneading pressure on her breasts, the faint, almost tickling glide across her stomach, and a finally inquisitive yet tender touch between her legs, Sophie rose to meet every new sensation, desperately craving what was still to come.

In turn, she allowed her hands to roam across his body, the flesh that shone silver in the moonlight. Tracing the contours of his muscular shoulders, she allowed herself to explore his chest, the indentation of every rib down his side, and alighted upon his manhood, the heat of his flesh surprising her. As she traced her thumb over the length of his sex, she felt him tremble, a sharp gasp that rose from his throat, escaping from his mouth into the soft contour at the base of her neck.

"Oh, Cole," she whimpered, her voice quaking. "I want you!"

"I love you, Sophie!" he deeply moaned into her ear, setting off an entirely new cascade of passion. Her fingers dug into the flesh of his forearms, willing him to come to her at that moment, to consummate the love that had grown between them.

"Now!" she exclaimed. "I need you now!"

Cole could wait no more than she and rose up above her, positioning himself between her legs, his weight borne on his powerful arms. He hung there, the moment drawing itself out with a breathless anticipation that both frustrated and excited her. Sophie found herself nodding, embracing his face between her hands, hardly able to believe that the moment was at hand.

"Come to me," she urged him.

When Cole moved forward, arching his hips and sliding inside of her, there was a momentary sharp pain, an ache that signaled another of the many steps taken into womanhood. Biting down on her lip, she quieted the whimper that rose in her throat, burying her head into the flesh of his arm. He proceeded slowly, as if he were measuring how badly he was hurting her, until finally, they were joined completely, one inside the other.

"Are you all right?" he asked softly, tenderly.

"It hurts no more than I expected," she said truthfully.

"Do you want me to stop?"

"Not now, not ever."

Slowly at the outset but getting faster, Cole began to slide inside of her. He moved awkwardly at first, unsure of what he was supposed to do, but he soon found a rhythm that satisfied them both. Sophie's body rolled with the movement as her pain began to become pleasure, as if she were melting into the blanket, the boulders, the night sky, and even into Cole himself.

Sweat beaded on her forehead and upper lip, her pulse raced. Cole's body lowered until his chest was pressed against hers, his breath hot against her neck. His movements became shorter, more direct, but the physical reward seemed only to grow.

"Oh, darling," she moaned as his hand caressed the back of her thigh, crossed the bone that jutted from her hip, and hurried up her ribcage until it held her breast.

"My Sophie," he whispered in return.

Though the physical act between them brought intense joy of its own, Sophie knew that it was made all the more powerful because of their intense emotional connection. Meeting him had undeniably changed her life, bringing her a pleasure and happiness that had been missing. From the day he had shown up at the *Gazette*'s office with a picnic basket in hand, she had been smitten, though a bit unsure of how to proceed. To her surprise, the pathway had been easy to find. She had given him her heart, but now, giving him all of her, she knew that it was a decision she would never regret.

Cole's body moved faster and faster, his breathing growing ragged as sweat dripped from his brow. Though Sophie was hardly experienced in the art of lovemaking, she knew that he would not be able to last much longer.

While the pain of losing her virginity still ached, Sophie had little difficulty in matching Cole's amorous advances. She rose to him, meeting each of his thrusts with one of her own, wanting and willing them both toward a greater ecstasy, joined together as one.

Daring to open her eyes, Sophie stared into the mass of stars littering the sky above them. The moon, most of its luminous body obscured by the branches of the elm directly above her head, seemed to be stealing a glance at them. But instead of being self-conscious, instead of feeling the crimson sting of embarrassment, she felt as if the moon were somehow giving her its blessing; after all, it had witnessed all of the maladies that had been visited upon her family since the burning of their barn . . . it had to be there for the joy, as well. They made love to each other beneath the sea of the night.

"Oh, my darlin'," Cole said breathlessly, "I can't . . . I can't . . ."

"Don't . . . don't hold . . . yourself . . . back . . ."

The muscles in Cole's body tensed, his frame shuddered, and in that instant, searing warmth filled Sophie as all of his passion was let loose inside of her. When he collapsed upon her, she wrapped her arms around his quivering body, holding him as tightly as she could.

"I love you, Sophie," he said in the instant before his lips found hers.

And I love you . . .

As they kissed, Sophie knew that the bond between them was cemented for the rest of their lives. From this moment forward, they would face together whatever challenges arose. Though there was much about her past that darkened her days, now, with Cole, her future seemed to loom as brightly as the coming dawn.

Chapter Twenty-five

GRAHAM GRIER SAT on the meager cot in one of the two cells in Victory's jail, his fists balled in anger. He'd largely managed to sober up, the effects of the whiskey slowly dwindling with each passing hour, but he had a throbbing headache to go along with the dull pain of his already swollen jaw. On this night, far more than his pride had been bruised.

Through the iron bars of his cell, he could see the moon rising, a sign that this terrible day was indeed coming to a close. His poor decision to go out to the Hellers' had been made all the worse because he'd been beaten by Cole Ambrose. He'd jeopardized everything, his good name, any chance that he might have with Sophie, and even his precarious standing with Ellis over a jealousy that sought to devour him. But as bad as this day was, he knew the morning would be worse.

"You're nothing but a stupid son of a bitch," he muttered to himself.

Through the use of whatever little persuasion he could muster, Graham had managed to persuade the sheriff not to tell his father what had happened until morning; he supposed he had been helped by the fact that the lawman was dreading the confrontation as much as Graham was. Still, he knew he was only postponing the inevitable tongue-lashing he was sure to receive.

Why must you be such a disappointment?

The words Graham imagined his father speaking were so clear to his ear that he would have sworn that the old man was sitting right beside him in the cell. All that he had wanted, all that he had ever striven to achieve, was to be seen as a success in his father's eyes. But try as he might, he had always seemed to come up short. What had happened tonight would do nothing to change that perception.

Down at the far end of the room, a key was fitted into the lock of the iron door that led from the cells into the sheriff's office beyond. After the door had swung open on well-oiled hinges, one of the sheriff's deputies, a fat lump of a man named Terry Lambert, waddled into the room. Holding the door open, he said, "He's right in here."

For a moment, Graham feared that the sheriff had gone back on his previous word and informed his father, but the man that followed the deputy through the door chilled him far worse than Calvin Grier ever would.

Ellis Watts walked into the cell room with the air of a man who had spent too much time in its confines; his nose rose as if he had smelled a strong, putrefying odor even as a look crossed his face that resembled that of the cat that had eaten the canary. Reaching into his pocket, he pulled out a roll of bills, peeled off a couple, and handed them to Terry Lambert.

"Much obliged," the lawman said.

"I'll knock on the door when I'm ready to leave," Ellis told the deputy.

"Don't take too long, you know that—"

"Quit your worryin' and get the hell out."

When Deputy Lambert had left, locking up behind him with an audible click of his key, Ellis turned his attention back to Graham, striding down the narrow space until he stood before the man's cell, his boots clicking on the concrete floor.

"What are you doing here?" Graham asked, suddenly concerned.

"I'd reckon that the better question is what are *you* doing here." Ellis smiled in a manner that carried little friendliness. "It's a question that I've been askin' myself ever since Deputy Lambert was kind enough to call and tell me you'd been brought in. So what do you say, Graham? You wanna tell me just what was goin' through that so-called head of yours?"

"I made a mistake," he answered simply.

"Damn right you did," Ellis snarled. "And here I thought you knew better'n that. What kind of damned fool goes traipsin' right back to the place where he committed a crime? It ain't as if that whore don't know you was in on it. I told you and Riley to be careful. My mistake was thinkin' you was smarter than that. All it'll take is one bad flap of her gums and the whole thing will be shot to hell!"

"The only thing that happened was I had too much to drink and made a fool out of myself," Graham said defensively. "Nothing more, nothing less. There's no reason for you to get all worked up."

"You can imagine that it don't seem so cut and dried to me."

As much as Graham had dreaded his father discovering what he had done at the Hellers' farm, he'd been just as worried about what Ellis would say. His notorious temper was known to flare as rapidly as a windswept prairie fire, burning everything that got in its way. From the moment he had first confronted Graham with the knowledge of the mayor's son's secret, Ellis had always appeared to be an errant spark away from burning Graham, his father, the whole damn town right to the ground.

"Was the cripple there?" Ellis asked.

"Yeah, he was," Graham answered, the shame rising to color his face.

"He do that to your face?"

"I had too much to drink, otherwise—"

"Ain't no use in makin' excuses," Ellis cut him off. "I done told this to Riley and I reckon I should've made it plain to you, but that Ambrose fellow's a lot tougher than he looks. The biggest mistake you made was in under-estimatin' him. That's what put your sorry ass in that cell."

Anger rose in Graham's chest. The worst part of being chided was that the man was right; he'd failed to take the crippled schoolteacher seriously, and it had cost him his pride as well as Sophie Heller's hand.

"He's not worth you worrying about," Graham said.

"Ain't him that concerns me," Ellis replied. "More likely to be you."

"Me? What are you talking about?" Graham asked incredulously. He tried to hold Ellis's gaze, to give the man some sign beyond mere words, but the raw harshness of his stare was too much and he looked away.

"You gettin' thrown in here gives me plenty of reason to worry."

"I told you I didn't say anything to the sheriff!"

"And why should I believe you?"

"Ellis," Graham pleaded. "I'm giving you my word!"

"I suppose you think that's supposed to have some sort of value to me," Ellis sneered, his face full of disdain. "You and yours might spend an awful lot of time thinkin' you're better than us common folks, but the truth is that your word ain't worth a damn."

Fear began to creep in at the edges of Graham's mind. In all of his time with Ellis and Riley, he'd been worried about just such a moment; somehow he would displease them and then they would no longer have a reason to keep his secret quiet. *If I don't convince him otherwise . . .*

"I haven't talked, Ellis," he said. "I swear."

"Best keep it that way, not unless you're lookin' to be ruined."

"It's far too late for that."

"This little scrape you got yourself in don't amount to nothin'," Ellis explained, waving a hand around the jail cells as confidently as a teacher in a classroom. "Why, I wouldn't expect more than a slap on the wrist in addition to a shitty night's sleep. So you got drunk and popped off a bit, so what? The real trouble would be if you opened your mouth and started talkin' about what you know. That'd get you ruined in a hurry."

Graham felt no need to correct Ellis's error. Though he surely wasn't looking forward to his father's disappointed reaction to his spending the night in jail, his ruin had come long before he'd helped in the burning of the Hellers' barn; the moment when he had given into Carolyn Glass's passionate words, when he had lain with her in her bed, he had signed away all that he held dear. His despair was so great that he couldn't help but wonder why he continued to fight against it any longer.

Besides, it will only be a matter of months before the future will be there for all to see!

"Do you want the whole damn town to know what you've done?" Ellis asked.

"No," Graham sighed, "I don't."

"'Bout the only thing worse would be if that Kraut you're so damn sweet on knew the truth," Ellis continued. "What do you reckon she'd say if she knew you done knocked up some other woman?"

"No!" Graham pleaded. "I told you that

I'd go along with whatever you wanted so long as you didn't tell anyone!"

"Then you'd best keep your mouth shut."

"How many times do I have to tell you that I won't talk?!"

"All I'm doin' is remindin' you of the danger in changin' your mind," Ellis replied. Leaning forward, he rested his arms against the cross section in the cell's bars; even though he was safely separated from the other man, Graham couldn't help but feel uncomfortable with the additional closeness.

Before Graham's discomfort could grow any worse, the door to the cell room opened and Terry Lambert stuck his head back in; from where he sat, Graham could see beads of sweat lining the deputy's forehead, his hat twitching nervously in his hand.

"Ellis," he said hesitantly, "you just can't be in there too—"

"I could finish my business a hell of a lot faster if you'd keep your fat ass out of here, you stupid son of a bitch," Ellis bellowed. "Now git before I forget our agreement!"

The door banged shut with a loud clang.

"That man's as worthless as tits on a boar," Ellis snarled under his breath.

"Why did he let you in here to see me, anyway?" Graham asked, thankful for the deputy's interruption of their earlier conversation.

"You think you're the only one in town whose secrets I know?" Ellis laughed. "Hell, you'd be downright amazed at how much a fella can learn just by keepin' his ear to the ground and his eyes open. Discoverin' the secrets of a man like Deputy Lambert don't amount to much, although I reckon that it must be somethin' to him. I can't say it hasn't proved useful, but it weren't nothin' like what I found out about you."

"Aren't you worried about the sheriff walking through that door?"

"Should I be?"

Graham watched as Ellis measured him; from the first moment that he'd met the man, he'd been discomforted by Ellis's eyes, sizing him up, constantly appraising him. "If I were in your shoes, I suppose that it's something that I'd be concerned about."

"Other than that goddamn deputy, there

ain't no one gonna keep us from our business."

"And what business is that?" Graham asked cautiously.

"Huntin' Krauts."

At Ellis's words, Graham's chest tightened. Worry about Sophie's safety caused him to rise to his feet; he'd joined in Ellis Watts's ridiculous scheme not because of some misguided hatred toward Nazis, but because of a desire to keep the woman that he loved safe. Now, standing behind bars, he knew that was a task he could no longer perform.

"What are you going to do?" he asked harshly, nearly demanding an answer.

"I'm going to finish it," Ellis answered matter-of-factly.

Having spent time with both Ellis and Riley Mason, Graham knew exactly what the man was talking about; he meant to rid Victory of its perceived menace violently.

"You can't, Ellis," Graham warned.

"Why the hell not? We've done tried everything else, but from the burnin' of that barn to givin' that bitch a fright, ain't nothin's worked. The only thing they're gonna listen to is deeds."

"You'll end up right here in this cell beside me."

Ellis shrugged. "The folks of this here town might not appreciate what it is we done, at least not right away. But give 'em enough time and they'll come to understand that it was for the better good, for the sake of the country. They'll know that we done it to protect 'em and then we'll get the parade in our honor we done deserve."

Listening to Ellis Watts speak, Graham knew with certainty that he was insane; no man in charge of his faculties would believe the Hellers to be Nazi agents, let alone buy into it strongly enough to act on his fears. He had to keep Ellis talking, had to give himself time to come up with a plan, some way in which he could prevent any blood from being spilled.

"What about Ambrose?" Graham asked. "What if he's there?"

"Then it'll go just like I told you before," Ellis explained, recalling their meeting in his shanty just after the encounter in the diner. "If he chooses to get in the way, to not do his duty as a true American, he'll share their fate, if not the same hole in the ground."

"That's murder you're talking about."

"No, it ain't," Ellis corrected. "It's defendin' my country and doin' what's right."

"You can't . . . you just can't . . ." Graham stammered, as unsure of what to say as if he were still drunk. He knew that he couldn't allow Ellis to go ahead with his despicable schemes, but he had been struck mute with indecision.

Think! Sophie will die if you don't act!

"Don't go gettin' any ideas that you're gonna be able to stop us," Ellis spat, his words dripping with venom. "Not unless you want the whole damn town to know who it was you stuck—"

"Stop!" Graham shouted. "Don't say another word! I won't talk!"

"Best keep repeatin' that to yourself," Ellis said as he pulled a revolver from his waistband. Cocking the hammer, he leveled the weapon at Graham, the barrel centered squarely on the center of his chest. "Otherwise, you might find yourself on the receivin' end of this."

Pure terror struck Graham as hard as if Ellis had pulled the trigger. Falling to the concrete floor, he scrambled backward on his heels, desperately trying to escape the range of the gun, but knowing that he could never truly get away. As he waited for the gun-clap that would signal the end of his life, Graham could only plead to be spared.

"Please, Ellis! I won't talk! I won't tell a soul! I promise!"

Ellis stood stoically for a moment, before an amused smirk spread across his features as he returned the gun to its hiding place. "Don't forget, Graham," he said coldly. "You've got much more to lose than your reputation."

Graham was still sniveling when Ellis walked to the door, shouted for the deputy to let him out, and set off to finish the job he'd started.

Ellis Watts crossed the dark shadows that covered the space between the sheriff's office and where Riley had parked his car. The rangy man was sprawled across the beat-up Ford's hood, his muscular arms laced behind his head. When he saw Ellis approaching, he swung off the automobile, his boots crunching on the gravel beneath his feet.

"That son of a bitch talk?" he asked.

"Not as far as I can tell," Ellis answered, pulling a pack of smokes from his breast pocket and offering one to Riley. "Graham seems a mite too worked up about what his daddy's gonna think come mornin' to do much talkin'." Patting the pistol in his waistband, he added, "And don't think I didn't remind him of all he's got to lose."

"We should never have involved him in the first place."

"You know damn well why we did."

"Now that he ain't no good to us no more, what's the plan?"

Taking a draw on his cigarette, Ellis held the smoke in his lungs until it began to burn before blowing it toward the moon above. Until recently, his intentions had been to be patient, to keep a close eye on the Nazi saboteurs so that they couldn't commit any mischief, but things seemed to be spiraling out of his control.

From the confrontation with Cole Ambrose and the Kraut bitch in the diner, to receiving his draft notice, and now to

Graham being tossed in jail for being goddamn stupid enough to show up drunk on the Nazis' land, it was as if he were being told to act, to take care of this threat to his nation and community before it was too late.

And then there was Carolyn . . .

With her whispering into his ear and playing with what hung between his legs, Ellis felt entranced, prodded into acting so that he could please her. Being manipulated was infuriating. Hell, if there was anyone who should be the one pulling the strings, it was him. Still, he found it next to impossible to resist Carolyn Glass; the more excited she got about what he was trying to do, the more worked up it made him, a vicious cycle that showed no sign of ending until the problem was taken care of. In the end, he didn't give a damn whose child she was carrying. Fighting against her charms was something he didn't want to do, leaving him with but one option.

"We do what we set out to do," he answered simply.

"Right now?" Riley asked with more than a hint of excitement in his eye.

"Yeah, now," Ellis said with a nod, pulling the gun from his waistband and holding it up to the faint light. "Now's the time to show them Krauts what disobeyin' us gets them. Now's the time to end this. *Once and for all.*"

Chapter Twenty-six

COLE DROVE his father's truck from the Hellers' farm back toward Victory with one elbow slung easily out the window, whistling a happy tune. Thousands of stars lit the night sky, all witnesses to the epic change in his life that the night had brought. He wasn't aware of any of the bumps, shakes, and skids of the gravel road; it was as if he were floating on air, racing across the heavens like a comet.

The memory of Sophie's touch, the feel of her skin beneath him as they made love to each other, remained fresh in Cole's mind. Every sensation, every passing second of their time atop the rocks had been burned into his brain with such an intensity that he knew he would be able to recall it all even on his deathbed; the sound of the wind in the trees, the smell of her hair, the pounding of his own heart would all be treasured as if they were precious jewels. The pleasure of her company, sharing an experience that could never be undone, would link the two of them forever.

I am in love with Sophie Heller!

The truth of that thought was as undeniable to Cole as the sight of the moon hanging in the western sky. From the first moment they had met, he'd known he was on a slippery slope. With every meeting, every smile, and even every tear, feelings had grown between them until they became a passion impossible to contain. When she'd led him into the woods, he'd known that they were about to cross a threshold from which they could never return. To that end, he'd gone along willingly.

Though Cole could not help but dwell on the past, his thoughts were also exploring the future. When Jason had first spoken to him about his relationship with Mary

Ellen, Cole had hoped that he and Sophie could someday share the same. Now it seemed as if that dream had come true. Once he was settled in at the school, once he had moved out of his father's home into lodgings of his own, he would go to Hermann Heller and ask for his daughter's hand in marriage. When the time was right, he had little doubt that Sophie would accept his proposal.

Still, Cole wasn't naïve enough to believe that the future did not hold menace, as well; Graham Grier's sudden drunken appearance at the barn dance was a reminder of what challenges they faced. Ellis Watts was still out there somewhere, plotting his misguided plans to rid Victory of a threat that didn't exist. Until Ellis was sharing a cell with Graham, Cole knew that his relationship with Sophie would never truly be secure.

Not for the first time, Cole wondered if he should have confided in his father or Jason, anyone who could have helped him pursue the right course of action. Come morning, he'd once again speak to Sophie about the matter; she'd be upset, but now with all that had been shared between them, maybe she would allow him to persuade her to finally tell the police.

Stifling a swelling yawn, Cole crossed the edge of town; Victory was sleeping peacefully, only a random light or two behind closed drapes indicated any activity. Ahead of him, an automobile turned a corner and began heading in his direction, gathering speed. The two vehicles passed each other underneath one of the few streetlights in town, illuminating the interior of the car for only an instant, but it was more than enough time for Cole to see who was inside and to set his heart to pounding.

Ellis Watts and Riley Mason, the squirrelly man who had grabbed Sophie in the diner, both stared ahead grimly, their car quickly crossing underneath the streetlight before being swallowed by the darkness and heading away from town. Cole had no doubt as to whom he had seen; Ellis's was a face he could not forget no matter how much he tried. Encountering them now, so soon after his confrontation with Graham, made Cole's nerves stand on end. For them to be out at this late hour surely meant that they were up to no good. Looking into the truck's rearview mirror, he could only watch as the men drove out of town.

"What the hell?" he muttered into the night.

Pressing down firmly on the truck's brakes, Cole stuck his head out the window and peered intently into the inky darkness into which Ellis had gone.

Why were those two out at this hour?

Why were they headed toward the Hellers' farm?

In his gut, Cole already knew the answers to both his questions; the threat he and Sophie had faced from these men had not disappeared, but had instead been lying in wait, biding for time until the opportune moment to strike. Watching Ellis Watts and his crony drive past him, their faces masks of bad intentions, he knew that their moment appeared to have come.

The only thing left to was to decide what to do about it.

While Riley drove toward the Heller farm, Ellis's attention was fixed on the pistol he held in his hands. He snapped open the weapon's chamber, spinning the bullets quickly as he watched the ends of their casings shine in the moonlight, before he flipped it shut with a flick of his wrist.

"You reckon you're gonna need to use that?" Riley asked, watching him.

"More likely than not," Ellis answered plainly.

"What about them hoods?" The burlap sacks they had worn when they had burned the Krauts' barn to ashes lay strewn haphazardly on the backseat.

"It's too damn late for us to go hidin' our faces," Ellis explained as he repeated his examination of the gun. "Besides, ain't like there's gonna be one of 'em left to point us out when this night is over."

"Goddamn right there ain't gonna be!"

Outside, the Illinois countryside sped past the open window, a cool breeze the temperature of a summer pond washing over Ellis's hot skin. Countless insects called from the night, a thousand droning voices that were at once earsplitting and calming.

Ellis paid it all little heed. He felt at ease, almost relieved that all of his plans were coming to an end. Once the moon had set, the sun rising to take its place, he would know that he could head off to war secure in the knowledge that he'd already served his country.

"You suppose she's gonna put up much of a fight?" Riley asked.

"Which one?" Ellis answered indifferently.

"The one from the diner. The daughter."

"I don't think any of them is gonna just let us have our way."

"I sure wouldn't mind gettin' me a taste of that one before we're done havin' our fun," Riley cackled as he ran his tongue over his lips. "Can't be no harm in screwin' a Nazi if'n you finish her off after, is there?"

"I suppose not."

"Then she's gonna be screamin' my name before this here night's out!"

Smoke from the cigarette in Riley's mouth curled off into the night with each word he spoke, wisps that disappeared in the blink of an eye out the open window. Ellis had decided to give the man a few indulgences before they acted, but both Riley's cigarette and his less than amorous intentions toward Sophie Heller would have to be extinguished before they reached the farm. On this night, he would allow for no mistakes.

"Graham's gonna be missin' out," Riley said.

"It was his choice to go on a bender and get his ass tossed in—"

Suddenly, the coal black dark of night was lit up as brightly as the noon hour of a July day, blinding Riley so badly that he struggled to keep his beat-up car straight on the road. Though the light clearly came from behind them, it was so glaring that Ellis had no alternative but to shade his eyes. Unpleasant as the light was, it was soon followed by the incessant blaring of a horn; itself such an obnoxious sound that Ellis believed it could have wakened the dead. The noise sounded over and over again.

"What in the hell's goin' on?" he shouted.

"Beats the shit out of me!" Riley replied.

Turning around in his seat, Ellis's confusion dissipated at the realization that the origin of the light and sound was a vehicle right on their tail. He could only stand to look at it for the briefest of moments, the beams seemingly piercing him, before he had to turn away.

"How in the hell did another car get on our ass?" Ellis bellowed.

"I don't know!" Riley answered defensively. "I've been watchin' in the rearview mirror but I ain't seen nothin' comin' up on us! It's like it appeared out of thin air!"

Jarringly, the vehicle behind them rammed the back of the Ford, the force of the blow sending both men bouncing from their seats, the pistol skittering from Ellis's hand down into the footwell. By some miracle, Riley managed to right the car after a dangerous drift to the left, but he was clearly unnerved. "What the hell am I supposed to do, Ellis?" he shouted.

Searching blindly for his missing pistol, Ellis didn't answer. The truth struck him as solidly as the vehicle that collided with their bumper.

The driver of the car behind them was Cole Ambrose.

Planting his foot on the accelerator, Cole once again drove the front of the truck into the back of Ellis Watts's car. The force of the impact was violent, a blow that sent him reeling backward in his seat before rebounding hard enough for his chest to strike the steering wheel. Through it all, his eyes never left the rear of the car in front of him, fixed intently on the men who meant to hurt his beloved Sophie.

After passing Ellis's car on his way back to town, Cole had turned around and followed. He knew that he would have to hurry, pushing the truck until its frame shook. Dousing the lights in order to maintain the element of surprise, he'd driven by what scant light was offered by the moon and stars above, ready at any moment to slam on the brakes. Sure enough, he had come up behind them a little more than two miles from the Hellers' farm. Flipping on the lights, he'd put his plan into action.

All I can do is drive them off the road!

In the blinding glare of the pickup truck's headlights, Ellis's face once again became visible through the Ford's small rear window. Though the man was shielding his eyes with his hand, Cole could see that his face was contorted in rage and confusion.

"How do you like it, you son of a bitch," Cole muttered.

Pounding on the truck's horn, Cole

hoped that if he were unsuccessful in his plan to drive the other vehicle from the road, he would at least be able to draw attention to what was happening. If someone were to hear him, to notice two cars speeding dangerously down Colvin Road, then it might not be too much to hope that they would contact the police. That way, even if he were to fail, Sophie's family might be protected.

Before him, the country road began to dip as it ran south toward the river, to descend into the low valley in which the Hellers' farm lay. Cole knew that little opportunity remained for him to prevent the men from reaching their intended destination.

If I'm going to act, I'm going to have to do it soon!

With Ellis in the passenger seat, it was Riley Mason behind the wheel; somehow, he had so far managed to avoid a crash, surviving two collisions with the truck and still hurtling forward. There was no guarantee that the scruffy bastard couldn't keep up the driving until it was too late for Cole to stop them.

"Think, damn it all, think!" he exhorted himself.

Cole was well aware that one if not both of the men might be armed; the idea that a thug the likes of Ellis Watts wouldn't be carrying a weapon seemed ridiculous to him. Drawing closer to the Ford, giving the men a moment to steady themselves might get him a lead slug for his troubles. If he were going to make a move, he would need to be fairly certain that it would have a chance to succeed.

Once again, Cole stomped on the gas and brought the two vehicles together in a sickening collision. But this time, instead of falling back and allowing the Ford's driver to steady himself, he waited until the car swung awkwardly to its left before zipping into the space that it had vacated. The truck's engine growled angrily but Cole turned a deaf ear to its protests, pulling alongside the car's passenger side.

"Goddammit, Ambrose!" Ellis snarled into the night.

"Go to hell, Ellis!" Cole shouted in answer.

So close to the Ford that he could see the worry and anger in the other men's eyes, Cole kept a steel grip on the truck's wheel. When Riley compensated for being pushed left by swerving back to his right, Cole was ready; the screech of metal when the two vehicles collided was deafening, but he refused to budge, holding his line as he raced down the dirt road.

Time and again the two vehicles banged together, each contact more bone-rattling than the last as each driver tried to drive the other off the road. Cole had an advantage; since the pickup truck was both wider and heavier than the automobile, it had more traction. Still, he was worried; the Hellers' farm couldn't be much more than a mile away.

He was running out of time.

Glancing over at the speeding car, Cole was surprised to see Ellis hunched over on his side, his face turned away from the window. For a moment, Cole hoped that the bastard had been flung against the car door and been knocked unconscious, but that thought proved fleeting.

Ellis suddenly sat upright, a pistol clutched in his hands. Even as the vehicles continued to slam against each other, the man's eyes found Cole's and an unchecked glee seemed to light his face. When Cole had confronted Ellis in the tavern after his first picnic with Sophie, he had been warned what would happen if he chose to interfere. Now it seemed as if Ellis Watts were about to make good on his word.

"Shoot that cripple!" Riley bellowed. "Shoot the son of a bitch!"

Cole knew that he had only a few short seconds in which to act. There was always the option of slamming on the truck's brakes, but that would allow the two of them to reach the Hellers unscathed.

Instead, Cole grabbed the wheel and yanked it to his left with all of the might he could muster. The truck leaped toward the smaller car with such ferocity it resembled a wild animal pouncing on its prey. Plowing into the front end of the car, Cole heard the unmistakable explosion of tires and the rending of metal, before the truck began to shudder, the wheel jerking so uncontrollably that he could no longer hold it. As if he were caught in the teeth of a tornado, Cole was swept along by forces he could not control.

It was over in seconds. Both vehicles hurtled to the left, driving clear of the road and down into the ditch, passing from the raging sounds of revving engines, exploding glass, and twisted metal into a silence broken only by the calling of thousands of insects and the intermittent moaning of men.

Chapter Twenty-seven

SOPHIE LAY BACK in her bed and stared up at the ceiling. It had only been minutes since she had stolen quietly into the house, tip-toed up the staircase to her room, slipped into her nightgown, and eased herself into bed. Still, from the moment she had led Cole back to her secret place in the woods, her heart had sung a joyful song.

Cole Ambrose is the man I am going to marry!

From the afternoon in which she had first met Cole inside Marge's Diner, she had known that there was something special about the young teacher. When he defended her against Ellis and the others, she'd known him to be honorable, someone who would protect her and keep her safe. Now, through their lovemaking, he had become so much more to her . . . and she had finally become a woman.

Sophie knew that it would only be a matter of time before he would approach her and ask for her hand in marriage. *Cole Ambrose as my husband!* Closing her eyes, she imagined him nervously asking the fated question, a smile crossing her face even though she knew that she could only give him one answer. It was then that their life would truly begin . . . a life together.

Though happiness coursed through her, the matter of Graham showing up at the barn dance and causing a drunken scene was worrisome. When she had left Graham standing in the night shadow of the barn a week earlier, she'd held the fleeting hope that he would abide by her wishes and stay away. Apparently, he had decided differently. Seeing him being taken to jail in the back of a police car had been difficult to watch, but she knew that he had no one to blame but himself. If only he had told her the reasons he had aided Ellis Watts. If only he—

In the distance, the sound of a car's horn reached her ears.

Sophie lay still, listening to the insistent, repeated bleat as it was carried over the late summer breezes. What at first had been merely strange quickly became disquieting as the sound grew louder with each passing second. Rising from her bed, she moved to the window and looked back toward Victory and soon found the source of the noise; there, still more than a mile distant but closing in a hurry, were two pairs of headlights.

"Cole!" she whispered instinctively.

Horrified, Sophie watched as the two vehicles drove erratically down the dirt road, weaving together and then apart as if they were doing a bizarre dance. Nearer and nearer they came, the sounds of banging and scraping metal joining the strange symphony of horn blasts. Finally, little more than a half mile from the farmhouse, there was a terrific collision, one car swerving in front of the other before they both flew from the road toward her father's cornfield.

"Oh, no!" she gasped, her hand rising to her throat.

All of the earlier sounds fell eerily silent as Sophie searched the night for some sign of movement. She hoped to see Cole, but she was too far away and there was too much darkness and gloom.

Stepping away from the window, Sophie knew that she had to do something. In her heart, she knew what was happening; Ellis Watts and Riley Mason had returned to finish what they'd started. If she were to protect her family and herself, as well as Cole, she'd need to move quickly.

Grim and determined, she ran from her bedroom.

Riley lay flat on his back in the dew-wet grass, his eyes dancing dizzily as he tried to focus on the stars floating high in the sky above his head. Slowly, swimming through the black edges of his vision, the world around him started to settle. He lay near the open door to his car, the vehicle tilted at an unnatural angle after it had pitched down into the shallow ditch that lined the road. The air smelled ripe with burning oil and other engine fluids, the ruptured radiator spilling scalding water onto the ground below.

"Goddamn, my head!" he moaned.

Raising himself up onto one elbow, Riley touched his forehead, wincing as he drew back fingers stained with blood. Throbbing pain laced his joints; his shoulder felt as if it had been struck by a hammer. He didn't remember much from the crash, but it was clear that he had been thrown free from the car, landed on his back, and had been briefly knocked unconscious.

"Ellis!" he called. "You there?"

There was no answer.

Struggling to get to his feet, Riley surveyed the carnage around him. Both of the vehicles had plowed off the road, crashing headlong into the low ditch; Ambrose's truck was still stuck up against his own ruined car. In the smoke-choked night, it was hard to tell where one vehicle ended and the other began. He wondered if the cripple were still inside his busted-up truck but he couldn't see anything past the heavily laced spiderweb cracks that covered the windshield.

"Ellis! Where are you?"

This time, Riley was answered by a rustling in the dense cornfield that lay on the other side of the ditch. While both headlights on the pickup had been extinguished, one of the Ford's still managed to shine, casting a strange glow through the smoke. Wincing painfully as he pulled a large knife free from the leather scabbard above his boot, Riley readied himself to settle matters with Cole Ambrose once and for all.

Instead, Ellis Watts burst from between the cornstalks, his pistol held at the ready in front of him. There was a vicious cut running down the side of his face, a matching smear of crimson bleeding through the fabric of his shirt at the bicep. Angrier still was the expression on his face.

"Where's the goddamn cripple?" Riley asked.

"He must've managed to wrangle his way out of the truck before either of us could come to," Ellis explained, his lip curled in a snarl. "Made his way through them fields right about there," he added, pointing to a section of cornstalks that had been bent down or snapped.

"Then let's go get him!"

"Not us," Ellis disagreed. "You."

"Just me? What are you gonna do?"

"What we came here for," he said with a nod up the road to where the Heller farmhouse sat in stillness. "I can make it up there a hell of a lot faster than Ambrose can through them fields, so I can set about our work without him bein' able to do a damn thing about it. Besides, with you right behind him, he's gonna have his hands full."

A wicked grin crossed Riley's lips at the thought of having Cole Ambrose all to himself; he still owed that son of a bitch for grabbing his arm in the diner and showing him up in front of Ellis. Even after being dinged up in the crash, he was more than capable of taking care of a no-account crippled teacher.

I'm going to enjoy this . . .

"Do what you need to do, then get your ass on up to the house," Ellis ordered.

"Ain't gonna take long."

"Hurry just the same," Ellis said and then was gone, staying close to the cornstalks as he rushed up toward the Hellers' farm. In a matter of seconds, he was swallowed by the night.

Riley moved over to the spot in the cornfield that Ellis had indicated, looking into the rows of crops, but he could see no sign of Cole Ambrose. Gripping the knife's handle tightly, he began to relish the opportunity to slide the blade between the man's ribs.

"I'm a comin' for you, cripple," he sneered.

Sliding into the cornstalks, Riley began his hunt.

Cole moved as quickly as he could manage between the tightly bunched rows of corn, growing ever wetter from the dew that clung to the husks in the still humid night. The tall stalks rose far higher than a man, far taller than he, blotting out the stars and moon above. Sounds were swallowed inside the rows, muted save for the wispy brush of the stalk leaves scraping together and the frantic rasps of his own breathing.

Pain throbbed on the left of Cole's chest, right in the spot where the steering wheel had slammed into his ribs. Every breath sent flares of agony racing across his body. Simply getting out of the truck had been an exercise in endurance and patience; since the truck had crashed against the other vehicle, he'd needed to slide across the front seat and exit by the passenger door. All the while he made his way down the ditch and up into the cornfield, he'd expected to hear the crack of Ellis's pistol, driving a lead slug into his back and ending any hope he had of rescuing Sophie. But nothing had come . . .

"Move, you damn worthless leg!" he exhorted himself. "Move!"

You've got to get to Sophie!

Every step Cole took was agonizingly slow. Trying to move his lame leg was difficult enough when the ground was smooth and level; in a cornfield, where the churned-up earth was raised in furrows and rocks and corncobs littered the ground, the conditions were far from ideal. Trying to navigate such obstacles in the dark was doubly difficult. He stumbled once, crashing to the hard ground on one knee, but he quickly scrambled back to his feet and hurried forward, his legs as unsteady as a man at sea.

Cole had no idea how far behind him the other men might be or even if they were following him at all, although given how dangerous Ellis Watts was, he dared not assume he was in the clear. His fear was that he would get turned around in the cornfield, moving away from Sophie's house instead of toward it, and that he would find himself circling right back into the two men. To that end, he occasionally stopped, wincing painfully, trying to ensure that he never deviated from his path.

Cole was just about to raise his head to take another look when the noise of a cornstalk snapping from somewhere behind him instead forced him to freeze motionless in place, his heart thundering in his chest. Squatting down, his crippled leg jutting awkwardly into the row next to him, he strained his ears for another sound, wondering if his imagination had gotten the better of him. In seconds, he knew that the threat was real.

"Come on and show yourself, you gimpy son of a bitch," a voice snarled.

The voice hadn't belonged to Ellis; Cole had spent more than enough time in the tavern with that bastard to have become familiar with how he spoke. That meant that it was the other one, the man from the diner, Riley Mason. It sounded as if he were somewhere in front of him, flailing his arms about, rustling the stalks, trying to scare him out of hiding.

Cole peered intently into the inky darkness, but couldn't see more than a few feet in front of his face. If he were to be aware of his hunter's approach, distinguishing the path Riley took, he would have to depend upon his hearing far more than his sight.

"Ain't no one comin' to help you, cripple," Riley kept on. "You might as well come and get what's comin' to you."

Suddenly, the sound of Riley's movement changed direction; earlier he had been crossing directly in front of where Cole crouched; now he seemed to be moving straight toward him. Peering into the inky darkness, Cole still couldn't see the man, but now he felt confident that he knew where he was. If his senses could be trusted in the forest of corn, Riley would soon pass near where he hid, albeit a couple of rows to his right.

With a certainty every bit as piercing as a lightning bolt, Cole knew he had to do something. If he were to allow Riley to get past him, the thug would then be between him and Sophie, and that was not a risk he was willing to take. When Riley got close enough, he would have to spring from his hiding place and put an end to this madness once and for all.

"Ain't no point in hidin'." Riley kept on, coming ever closer.

Suddenly, the realization struck Cole that Riley might not really be acting alone; Ellis could be silently moving along beside him, the two of them working together to trick their intended victim into exposing himself. If that were the case, then the very moment that Cole moved, he would be stepping right into the jaws of their intended trap.

Still, Cole knew that there was no way he could risk staying hidden, even if it meant that in revealing himself he would be facing two men instead of one. Sophie's safety, as well as that of her family, was resting in his hands. If it meant sacrificing himself to ensure that the Hellers had a better chance of escaping, then that was a price he was willing to pay.

"What with the way you stood up at the diner, I didn't expect you to be such a coward," Riley snarled. "Your leg ain't much, but I figured you'd have a parcel of guts."

Anger simmered in Cole's chest at the man's words. The irony was that they were remarkably similar to those he had spoken the night he had been set upon by Graham Grier outside the school. When he had said such things, he had done so in an effort to bait his opponent into showing himself, a tactic that had backfired; he hadn't noticed his attacker until it was far too late. Maybe now was his chance to return the favor.

I will not be beaten again!

Cornstalks rustled nearby and Cole tensed. His body grew ever tighter, coiling to attack at the first sign of the man. To his immediate right, there was a parting among the stalks and the faint glow of the moon gave Cole enough light by which to make out his target.

"Wait until that bitch gets a real man between her legs!"

Before Riley could finish his disgusting thought, Cole leaped from the deep shadows, crashing into Riley's midsection and driving both of them right through several rows of corn. They had no more than touched the ground before Cole planted himself atop the man's chest and began raining down punches on his exposed face. Right hand followed left as he showed no remorse, hoping to end the fight before it had really begun. In a matter of seconds, his blows began to sound wet, slick with blood from cuts gouged into Riley's flesh.

"You no-good, worthless bastard," Cole snarled.

Beneath him, Cole felt Riley grow slack, the fight apparently driven out of him from the relentless beating he had received. Nevertheless, he reared back, hoping to land one last punch to finish the man, anxious to hurry on to Sophie and ensure that she was safe. But just before he let his fist fly, a roaring, sharp pain lanced through his bad leg, a blazing heat that struck him so hard that it felt hard to breathe.

"Goddamn cripple," Riley coughed through a busted mouth.

In the faint light from the heavens above, Cole could see the deep gash sliced into his upper thigh, the wound dark and ugly. Instantly, he saw the knife blade glinting in Riley's hand and slick with blood, raised to strike another blow. Without thinking, Cole's hand flew toward the knife, grasping Riley's wrist, struggling to hold it still, all the while realizing that he'd been overconfident as the man played possum.

"I'll kill you, you no-good son of a bitch!" Riley shouted.

"The hell you will!"

Though he had peppered Riley with stiff punches, Cole felt no ebb in his foe's strength, all of his muscles straining to hold the knife in check. With a sharp rotation of his waist, Riley flung Cole off him, pivoting his weight so that they rolled over each other, each trying to gain the upper hand. Elbows smashed into ribs and knees collided as they continued to wrestle among the cornstalks. Just as it seemed one of them had the advantage, the other would somehow manage to turn the tide.

"I ain't . . . gonna lose to . . . the likes of you!"

Suddenly, Riley freed one of his elbows and drove it fiercely into the bridge of Cole's nose. The pain was tremendous; a kaleidoscope of agony that filled his vision, dazing him as he struggled to maintain the precarious balance between them. But in that moment, the man once again rolled across him, this time ending end up on top, the tables now completely turned to his advantage, the knife's blade poised directly above Cole's throat.

"Ain't no cripple bestin' me," Riley boasted, a sick smile twisting his lips.

"It's not . . . over . . . yet . . ."

Sweat beaded on Cole's forehead, his muscular arms quaking as he struggled to maintain his grip on Riley's powerful wrist. The tip of the blade shook violently, inches from his body, and his heart pounded in step with the still throbbing ache in his leg.

Do something, damn it! Do it now!

Arriving as unbidden as a spring squall, the vision of Sophie standing before him after their date to the movies sprang before Cole's eyes. He saw her gleaming smile, the excitement in her eyes, and even the way the moon made her new white blouse more lustrous. It was as if he could smell her perfume, feel her touch, and revel in simply being with her. The thought of never being able to experience such a moment again infuriated him and made him struggle all the harder.

Do it for Sophie!

With all of the strength left to him, Cole pushed Riley's wrist to the side, while at the same time bucking upward with his hips. The man's menacing look evaporated in an instant and he fell to the side with a face full of both surprise and shock. Cole followed him over, ever mindful of the knife.

Once again they were rolling, a tangle of sweat and struggle, until suddenly, a piercing cry escaped from Riley's lips, howling skyward toward the moon. The sound was brutal, guttural, agonizing in its fury. Instinctively, Cole recoiled from the stricken man, repulsed by the noise, skittering across the destroyed stalks and ears of corn, trying to get as far away as he could.

Bathed in the moonlight, Cole gasped at what he saw. There, the hilt of the knife buried deep between his ribs, Riley Mason lay dying. Crimson blood permeated his shirt, an angry stain that grew with every ragged gasp of breath or strained beat of his heart. He tried to look down at his injury, his hands spread around the knife, unable to actually touch it, but his strength seemed to be ebbing as fast as his life's blood.

"You . . . son of . . . a . . . bitch," he spat, blood trickling from his mouth.

Then, suddenly, Riley was dead, done in by his own weapon and hand. As Cole rose, bruised and battered, he felt no remorse; this man had been intent upon killing him and all that he held dear. From the moment he had joined with Ellis Watts, he had been traveling a path that had been destined to end violently.

The man got what he deserved!

Cole knew that there was no time to linger. Somewhere in the darkness Ellis lurked. Until he was stopped, Sophie and her family would never be safe. Struggling to limp forward despite the gash in his leg, Cole set out to put an end to their nightmare.

Chapter Twenty-eight

DARK, WISPY CLOUDS trailed across the luminous moon as Ellis approached the Heller farmhouse. He'd hurried along the dirt road that fronted the property before darting into the cornfields just short of the drive. Picking his way among the cornstalks, he paused before the lawn, examining the house for any sign of life, but he couldn't see a single light.

Ellis breathed heavily, steeling himself for what was to come. Until that very moment, he had preached discipline, wanting to avoid being impatient in undertaking his plan. But the time for waiting had come to an end. With Graham behind bars and Carolyn whispering in his ear, he'd realized he needed to act, to rid his town of the Nazis in their midst. Besides, the day that he was to be shipped off to the war was soon approaching; he couldn't possibly leave Victory to the mercies of a family of Hitler's willing minions. If he were to be punished for his actions, then so be it.

For a moment, Ellis wondered if he shouldn't wait for Riley. He wasn't a big enough fool to believe that the goddamn Krauts hadn't heard the calamitous smashing of automobiles back down the road. Even if the place was dark, that didn't mean they weren't waiting to give him hell. But in the end, he decided to go on alone; Riley would be along soon enough, just as quickly as he could dispatch Cole Ambrose.

"Time to get what's comin' to you," he muttered into the darkness.

Inching along the edge of the cornfield, Ellis went over his options. He could run up toward the rear of the house, gain entry through a door or window, and hopefully take them all by surprise. Otherwise, he could mill about in the hopes that the Nazis would make a mistake, showing their hand

and playing right into his. He was still mulling over what to do when the hint of a shadow played along the moonlit night at the side of the house.

"Well, I'll be goddamned. They ain't so scared after all."

Moving as quickly and as silently as a fox, Ellis began to stalk his prospective prey, his eyes never leaving the spot where he had seen the shadow move. The thundering of his heart sounded in his ears, his grip tightening on the butt of his pistol. If he could just make it to them without being seen, if he could just maintain his advantage, it wouldn't matter how many of them there were or if they were armed.

There was another ripple of a shadow, followed seconds later by yet another. He knew without a doubt that it wasn't an errant tree branch or some other trick of the deepening night intent on leading him on a fool's errand. His feet began to move as quickly as his heart as he cut sharply toward the house, hoping to keep the angle of sight between him and his target as narrow as possible. Halting in the deep shadows, Ellis waited, his senses alert.

Slowly, a figure emerged from the gloomy

darkness and stood near the edge of the farmhouse. Ellis couldn't be certain, but it looked as if whoever was waiting for him carried a rifle. The mysterious shadow was peering in his direction, but Ellis wasn't the slightest bit worried about being seen; the house blocked him from the moon, leaving him swathed in inky black shadows of his own.

Because his target was standing almost thirty feet away from him, Ellis couldn't be sure which of the goddamn Nazis had been brave enough to come outside and investigate, but in the end it hardly mattered. Calmly, he raised the cold steel of the pistol, patiently sighted down the short barrel, and, with a gentle squeeze, pulled the trigger.

Sophie let loose a startled scream at the sound of the gunshot, the loud crack nearly deafening in the still quiet of night. Before the noise had even begun to fade, she saw her father's body crumple to the ground in a heap. Hermann Heller rolled in agony, a painful moan escaping his lips. Without a moment's thought, Sophie began to run toward him.

"Father!" she shouted fearfully.

Not again! This cannot happen again!

After hearing the sound of the car crash outside her bedroom window, Sophie had gone right to her father's side. He'd already been awakened by the noise and was dressed in his nightclothes, brandishing his hunting rifle. After ordering his wife and mother to remain upstairs with the doors locked, he and Karl had headed outside to investigate. Against his vehement protests, he had finally relented and allowed Sophie to come along.

Outside, Sophie had felt as vulnerable as a newborn calf caught in the middle of a storm. Unlike the night that Ellis, Riley, and Graham had come to burn their barn down, the Hellers now knew the danger they were facing. Still, that danger was hidden; behind every corner or lurking in every darkened shadow could be someone looking to do them harm.

"I'll go look," Hermann had said.

Standing beside Karl, Sophie had wanted to shout to her father, to warn him away from exposing himself, but before she could give voice to her worries, he'd already stepped around the corner of the house. It was then that the gunshot had split the night.

"Father!" she shouted again as she ran. "Father!"

The horrific irony of what she was doing slammed into Sophie with such fury that she felt as if she had been the one shot. *This is happening just as before!* When Ellis Watts had slammed the butt of his rifle into her father's head, her instincts had led her to run to him, to care for him when he could no longer care for himself. This was no different.

Sophie collapsed on the dew-wet ground beside her father. Blood seeped from a small hole in his shoulder, staining his nightshirt a gruesome shade of red. He held tight to the wound, his fingers already wet and sticky. When Hermann had fallen, he'd landed hard upon his own rifle, his body covering most of the weapon; Sophie's fingers instinctively went to the rifle's stock, but her attention remained riveted upon her father. A low moan of pain escaped through his tightly clenched teeth, his breathing ragged.

"Get . . . get away . . . Sophie . . ." Hermann gasped.

"I won't leave you!"

"You have . . . to run . . ." he muttered before finally passing out from the pain.

"She ain't gonna be runnin' anywhere, are you, girlie?"

Ellis Watts emerged from the darkness to stand above Sophie and her father, a vicious smile spreading across his handsome face. The pistol in his hand was pointed directly at the center of Hermann Heller's chest.

"You best get out where I can see you, boy!" Ellis called into the shadows.

Sophie turned around to see Karl step slowly into the moonlight, his hunting rifle trembling in his hands.

"Now you throw that rifle over here," Ellis shouted. "That is 'less you want to be the reason why your old man and sister never get to see the light of another day."

"Don't do it, Karl!" Sophie shouted. "He's going to kill us anyway!"

"Sophie? What should . . . ?" Karl asked hesitantly.

The thunderous eruption of the pistol brought Sophie's hands to her ears as bits of earth rained down on her. Her head swung around in horror, terrified that Ellis had taken her father's life, but instead she saw that he had fired the gun into the ground beside his fallen body.

"Next one goes in the middle of his chest, boy," he barked, his narrow eyes fixed on Karl. "You ain't gonna want to see what happens if'n you give me a goddamn reason to ask twice."

"Don't, Karl!" Sophie implored her brother yet again, but it was already too late; Karl flung the rifle through the blackened night where it crashed in a clatter to the ground near where Ellis stood. Before Sophie could react, the man picked it up. The only weapon that remained at their disposal was the rifle that still lay under her father.

"There now." He smiled. "That weren't so hard, was it?"

Hopelessness and despair relentlessly hammered at Sophie's will, threatening to break her and make her give in to Ellis Watts's twisted reality. Still, anger continued to burn in her chest at the indignities that had been visited upon her and her family. Though heavy tears streamed down her cheeks as freely as rushing water in a spring brook, she refused to surrender, turning to face her enemy with a defiant visage.

"You won't get away with this, Ellis," she snarled.

"Who's gonna stop me, darlin'?"

"Cole will—" Sophie began, but Ellis's laughter cut her short.

"That cripple ain't gonna be botherin' anyone anymore," he explained with a maniacal cackle. "I warned him what was awaitin' him if he stuck his goddamn nose into our business. He had his chance to do what was right but he wasn't smart enough to take it. Now on account of his stupidity, Riley's takin' care of him out in those fields."

Listening to Ellis's words chilled Sophie to the very center of her heart. There was little she could do to stop her mind from imagining the worst; the thought of Cole being at the mercy of a man like Riley Mason was nearly more than she could bear.

"You bastards!" she cursed.

"Watch your mouth, you Nazi whore," Ellis warned, leveling his pistol at her head and cocking the hammer.

In that instant, Sophie felt her fear vanish. As bad as it would be for her to be killed, to leave her family behind, the thought of living in a world without Cole Ambrose was utterly unimaginable. She would have to content herself with the knowledge that someday, somehow, Ellis and those who had aided him would surely get their just rewards for all of the damage they had done. She was at Ellis's mercy; even if she were to yank the trapped rifle free, there was no chance that she could bring it to bear upon Ellis before he finished her off. Closing her eyes, she waited for what she knew was to come.

But unlike the first time that Ellis Watts had pointed a gun at her head, this confrontation did not end with a sudden descent into darkness, but was instead interrupted by the sound of Cole Ambrose's voice, calling from somewhere behind where Ellis stood.

"Get the hell away from her, you son of a bitch!"

Cole burst through the rows of cornstalks at the rear of the Hellers' property to find Sophie and her family once again at the mercy of Ellis Watts. Though he was exhausted from his trek through the field and his leg throbbed ceaselessly from his cut, his anger was more than enough to quell the pain.

The sound of his voice clearly startled Ellis, who turned quickly while raising his pistol; though his face was bathed in shadow, the moon hanging in the sky behind him, Cole had no doubt that surprise was written on his features. Ellis didn't say a word in answer, his head turning about as if he were looking for someone else.

"He's not coming," Cole said simply.

"What did you do to Riley?" Ellis asked, his eyes narrowing in question.

"What I had to do."

Ellis stood silently, taking a long moment to digest what Cole had said to him before turning his attention back to Sophie and her wounded father. When he finally spoke, his voice was empty of emotion. "Ain't none of that shit matters no more," he said. "Even if I'm the last one of us that's drawin' breath, I'm gonna do what needs to be done."

"Are you all right, Sophie?" Cole called. "Is your father badly hurt?"

"He needs help," she answered, her voice full of worry. "We need to—"

"Shut your goddamn mouth, bitch," Ellis snarled. "One more word and I'm gonna shut you up for good."

The blood in Cole's veins froze as solidly as the surface of Potter's Creek in wintertime. Ellis Watts was clearly out of his mind and dangerous, even if he hadn't been armed with a pistol. Cole wondered if he shouldn't have freed the knife from between Riley's ribs, not out of any sympathy for the fallen man but so that he might have been able to use it as a weapon. As it was, Ellis would be able to shoot him down like a dog long before he ever reached Sophie.

The only option that presented itself to Cole was to stall, to somehow distract Ellis from the violent task he had set for himself long enough for something far better to come along.

"You don't have to do this, Ellis," he said. "You have no reason to fear these people. They're good Americans just like—"

"I ain't gonna stand here and listen to no more of your shit," Ellis growled in answer, his voice full of malice. "I done already told you that these Nazis are goddamn dangerous! You're too busy fallin' head over worthless leg for a Nazi whore to see what's really goin' on around here!"

Cole wanted to snap at Ellis, to let him know that he would not stand for Sophie to be spoken about in such a way, but he knew that it would only serve to put his beloved in greater danger. Instead, he had to swallow his pride as well as his tongue and try to find an opening, some way in which he could deliver the Hellers from the threat that hung over their heads.

"Let me guess," Ellis continued. "The whore spread her legs and let you finally become a man, and now you gotta use the pair of balls you found to stand up for her honor or some shit."

Ellis could hardly have known that Cole had consummated his relationship with Sophie only hours earlier, but the hurt of his words fell quite close to the mark. Balling his hands into tight fists, he said, "If you so much as lay a finger on her, I'll kill you where you stand."

"Don't think that you can threaten me, cripple," Ellis answered, rage evident in his voice. "I tried to warn you, to set you straight! I gave you the chance to understand the truth, but you chose to turn your back on what was right, to deny your country! Far as I'm concerned, you ain't no better than them Nazis! You're gonna be treated the same!"

"Ellis, I don't—"

Before Cole could say another word, Ellis raised the gun in his direction and fired, the sound as deafening as a thunderclap. There was no time for him to so much as think, but simply to move, and he dove backward into the relative safety of the cornfield. His hands flew to his body, sure that he had been shot, but they came back without blood. Scurrying out of harm's way, determined not to give Ellis another shot at him, Cole had to stifle the scream that rose in his throat from the agonizing pain of his wounded leg.

"Don't hurt him!" Sophie screamed.

"Shut up, bitch, or the next bullet's for you!"

Fear rose in Cole's chest that he wouldn't be able to rescue Sophie and her family. Time seemed to be moving too fast, the horrific events spiraling out of control before he could ever hope to contain them. *How can I stop Ellis?!*

But at that moment, deep in the wells of his despair, Cole heard the unmistakable sound of automobiles: the hard revving of engines, the recognizable noise of tires racing over gravel, and even the knocks and ticks of a hotly run engine brought to a skidding halt. Peering through the stalks, he could see the bright headlights of several cars. Finally, there was a shouted voice that sounded like music to his ears.

"This is the sheriff! Put down the gun and step away from the girl!"

Oh, no! Oh, my Lord, no!

Though Sophie had clearly heard the sheriff's instruction to Ellis, she did not feel the least bit relieved. While the beams of the car's headlights completely illuminated the ground around her, including the gruesome wound in her father's shoulder, her eyes remained riveted upon the spot in the cornfield where Cole had fled, hoping beyond hope that she would see some sign of him, something that would allow her to believe that he hadn't been hurt.

"Put down the gun!" the sheriff barked yet again.

"Go to hell, lawman!" Ellis answered defiantly, the veins on his neck pulsing with anger, the pistol still pointed at Sophie. "You ain't fit to do the sort of hard work that's needed in these parts! What kind of sheriff lets a nest of Nazi spies just go on livin' in his midst?"

While Ellis ranted on, Sophie's heart leaped as she saw Cole's head poke out from the cornfield. His intentions were as clear as the moon; with Ellis so distracted with the police, he meant to make his way across the yard and disarm the man. Startled by the boldness of Cole's plan, Sophie began to shake her head in an attempt to warn him off, but with the glare of the headlights, she knew that he couldn't see her.

But before she could begin to formulate a plan, Sophie heard a familiar voice that was as startling to Ellis as it was to her. "Leave them alone, Ellis," Graham Grier said as he stepped out in front of the parked vehicles.

Looking up at Ellis, Sophie could see the surprise written across his face; his stubble-covered jaw hung slack and his eyes were as wide as saucers, even with the glare. When he finally found his voice, it was as deep as a growl. “You no-good, backstabbin’ son of a bitch!”

“It’s gone too far,” Graham answered simply. “It has to end.”

Sophie found that she was every bit as shocked by Graham’s appearance as Ellis; maybe even more so. She had last seen him only a few hours earlier, still drunk as he was driven away from the barn in the back of a police car; he was wearing the same clothes and sporting the same bruises from the beating Cole had given him. But there was something in his voice that reminded her of the man she used to know.

“Stupid bastard!” Ellis continued to rant. “How in the hell could you do this to us? You’ve got as much to lose as anyone . . . hell, you’ve got more! Did you convince yourself I wouldn’t follow through on my promise if you went to the police? Did you think I was a fool?”

“It doesn’t matter anymore,” Graham answered.

“What the hell are you talkin’ about?” Ellis asked incredulously.

“The only thing that matters is that I do

right for all the trouble I've caused," Graham explained. "What I've done with you is a mistake . . . a mistake I hope to atone for."

"So that's the way you want it to be, huh? You just want to take back all the things you done and be the good son again?" Ellis said in a voice heavy with sarcasm. "Well, I got news for you! Once I tell what it is you done, ain't no one gonna look at you the same again!"

"I've told the sheriff everything, Ellis," Graham said, his voice as flat and cold as a grave marker. "Everything that I did at your side. There's nothing left for me to hide."

Sophie listened to the conversation between the two men with no small amount of curiosity in her heart. After her confrontation with Graham outside the rebuilt barn, she'd wondered what secret he was intent on keeping from her, what truth he refused to allow to be told. Now, in the face of Ellis's threats, it seemed as if the whole story was finally going to come out.

"You don't mind if this tramp hears it?" Ellis challenged, waving his pistol in Sophie's direction. "You were sweet on her from the start, and I figured you'd do about anything to keep her from learnin' that you ain't what you appear to be."

"She'll find out eventually," Graham said before lowering his gaze.

"Then you can be the one who tells her," Ellis sneered. "'Less you want to see her head blowed off!"

Sophie's eyes rose until she found Graham's, the expression on his face equal parts shame and worry. It seemed as if he wanted to argue, but changed his mind when Ellis cocked the hammer on his pistol.

"You ain't gonna get another warnin'!"

"The truth of the matter is that I didn't take your rejection of my feelings all that well, Sophie," Graham said, his voice little more than a whisper. "Because of my own stupidity, I ended up committing an act that I can't take back no matter how much I wish that I could."

"Get on with it!" Ellis barked.

Graham sighed, resigned to his fate. "The truth is I started sleeping with Carolyn Glass while her husband was at work. There's no reason to doubt that the child she's carrying is mine."

The force of Graham's words struck So-

moment's pause, pulled the trigger, blasting away the night's quiet with another thunderous clap.

The bullet slammed into the center of Ellis's chest; at such a short distance, he flew from his feet as if he had been kicked by a horse, crashing onto his back, his pistol flying out onto the grass unfired. His legs kicked once, and his chest rose in an awkward gasp for his dying breath, before he fell still, staring up into a moon that looked back silently.

Even as the gunshot echoed in Sophie's ears, Cole raced to her, pulling her into his arms and holding her tightly. He kissed her cheeks and forehead gently, consoling her as he whispered softly into her ear.

"It's over, Sophie," he soothed. "It's over."

While tears streamed down her cheeks, Sophie knew that Cole was right.

Epilogue

October 1945

SOPHIE WAITED IMPATIENTLY on the crowded train platform, wringing her gloved hands in excited anticipation. Sweat beaded her forehead as she waved a hand fan feverishly in front of her face; a gentle fall breeze licked at her skin but the heat of Victory's long Indian summer still clung to the air, refusing to let go. Still, her heart was as happy as she could imagine.

It's the perfect day for a homecoming!

Bright WELCOME HOME banners were hung high above the tracks and all around the depot. At the far end of the platform, band members tuned their instruments in anticipation of the train's arrival. The atmosphere was festive, celebratory, a mood that was as perfect a fit as the wedding band on her finger.

"When is it scheduled to arrive?" a man beside her asked.

"Any minute now," Sophie answered.

"Seems like we been waitin' forever!"

Sophie understood the man's sentiment; it felt as if it had been far longer than the nearly four years since America had called for Victory to send her soldiers off to war. With the day-to-day responsibilities of the home front, it had become difficult to imagine things changing. But then the Nazis had surrendered, followed soon after by the Japanese, and the anticipation of their return to normalcy had grown with every passing day.

After the horrible events of three summers past, Sophie's own life had settled back into the relative quiet she had always known. With the deaths of Ellis Watts and Riley Mason, the nightmare that she and her family had endured had come to an end. That Ellis had died at her hand had been more than unsettling; Cole had assured her that the man had perished as a result of his own actions, because of his own prejudices, but the sound of the rifle firing in her hands still troubled her from time to time. In a way, she was glad that it did; it proved that she wasn't immune to conscience.

Graham Grier had come clean about all of his involvements with Ellis and Riley and had accepted his punishment without challenge. He'd been sentenced to prison, but had been let out early in order to enlist in the army; Graham had been killed in the line of duty when his unit had been among the first to enter into Germany. The shame of his son's actions followed so closely by his death had been more than Graham's father could handle; he, too, had died of a broken heart earlier in the spring.

Graham's confession had also managed to ensnare Carolyn Glass. Talk of their scandalous relationship set every tongue in town wagging, although Augustus refused to listen to the sordid gossip, gallantly standing by his wife even if it meant denying an obvious truth. But when one of Ellis Watts's neighbors told him how he had seen her coming and going from the man's shack at all hours of the night, the indignity became too great and he divorced her. Carolyn left town with her still unborn child, never to be heard from again. The secret of her baby's parentage went with her. Was the child Graham's? Or had Graham been blackmailed into crime without deserving the shame he so dreaded? Perhaps the child was the offspring of Ellis's lust—or even of Augustus's misplaced love. Or was the father someone else entirely?

"Just about missed it," Karl said as he breathlessly joined her on the platform.

"You're late," Sophie scolded her brother.

Karl smiled. "As long as I made it before the train, then I'm not late."

Sophie found that she couldn't help but smile at Karl. The ordeal with Ellis, the burning of the barn, and the shooting of their father had been difficult on her brother, but Karl had slowly come around. He'd soon be graduating from high school and heading off to college in Chicago. While her mother and father would be sad to see him go, they wanted the best for their only son. Besides, they had many tasks of their own to tend to; life on the farm went on whether you were ready for it or not.

But life for the Heller family was not all happiness; there was sadness to be had as well. Just before the previous Christmas, Gitta Heller, Sophie's beloved grandmother, had passed away quietly in her sleep. While her body had slowly aged, her mind had remained sharp all the way to the end, and she had regaled them all with story after story. Though she knew that her *Oma* had been happy to see her marry Cole, had been happy to see her rise in standing at the *Victory Gazette*, not a day passed that Sophie didn't miss the older woman. She knew that Gitta was looking down on her even now.

"Where's Cole?" Karl asked.

"He went to get his father," Sophie explained.

"He better hurry if he doesn't want to be late."

"They'll make it," she said confidently. "They wouldn't miss this for the world."

"And we didn't," Cole answered as he came up behind Sophie and gave her a gentle kiss on her cheek. His hand found hers, their fingers lacing together, and

Sophie smiled into her husband's eyes, still ever thankful that their lives had been joined.

Four months after the night when Ellis Watts's evil plan had been brought to a violent end, Cole and Sophie had married. With Robert's help, they'd built a home near to the one in which Cole had grown up and settled into a life that brought them both great joy. Matching Sophie's success at the paper, Cole had happily taken to his life as a teacher. Every day, he brought his enthusiasm for mathematics to the children of Victory, shaping their minds for future careers. Without complaint, he did his job on the home front with as much conviction and energy as he would have if he'd been able to fight on a battlefield.

"How's my son doing today?" he asked as he rubbed Sophie's pregnant stomach.

"Don't you mean daughter?" she answered playfully.

Cole chuckled. "I guess we'll find out in a couple of months."

Nothing gave Sophie greater joy than her impending motherhood. To have a child with Cole Ambrose was the greatest gift she could ever have asked for; she reveled in the prospect. She wished only that she'd been able to tell her grandmother about her baby, but she knew that Gitta would always be a part of her and that she would share in her joy in her own way.

"I think I see the train," Robert said.

Every head on the platform peered down the tracks and saw the first billows of dark smoke rising from the engine's smokestack. A loud cheer rose up from the crowd and the band began to play. Looking around, Sophie saw many an eye grow moist with tears at the sight.

Surprisingly, Robert Ambrose pulled a handkerchief from his back pocket and began to dab at his eyes. In the years that had passed since the ordeal with Ellis Watts, no one had changed quite as much as Robert. He and Cole had finally managed to settle their differences, accepting that what had happened to Cole's mother was an accident for which no one could be blamed. With that breakthrough, the bond between father and son had grown stronger, day by day, month by month, and year by year. Robert's excitement at becoming a grandfather seemed to know no bounds; there had been so much baby furniture built that Sophie had begun to wonder if they would have room for it all.

The train pulled into the depot with a screeching of iron against iron and a sharp blast of its whistle. Servicemen crowded every door, some of them jumping off before the train had even come to a complete stop. Then, his head peeking out an open window, Jason came into view.

"I told you I was coming back!" he shouted at the top of his lungs.

"Didn't doubt you for a second!" Cole answered.

"Get off that train right this second!" Mary Ellen Carter shouted beside Cole, tears of joy streaming down her cheeks. For all of the years Jason had been gone, Mary Ellen had patiently waited. Though fearful that something would happen to the man she loved, she believed him when he told her he was doing everything he could to return to her safely. On this day, he was making good on his word.

Then Jason was among them, hugging them all, clinging to them so tightly it seemed as if he would never let go.

"I can't believe it's over," he said.

"But the best part," Cole said, pulling Sophie close to him and gently laying his hand back upon her stomach, "is still to come."

Sophie smiled and agreed.

About the Author

Dorothy Garlock is one of America's—and the world's—favorite novelists. Her work has appeared on national bestseller lists, including the *New York Times* extended list, and there are over fifteen million copies of her books in print translated into eighteen languages. She has won more than twenty writing awards, including five Silver Pen Awards from *Affaire de Coeur* and three Silver Certificate Awards, and in 1998 she was selected a finalist for the National Writer's Club Best Long Historical Book Award. Her novel *A Week from*

Sunday won a Romantic Times Reviewer's Choice Award for Best Historical Fiction.

After retiring as a news reporter and bookkeeper in 1978, she began her career as a novelist with the publication of *Love and Cherish*. She lives in Clear Lake, Iowa. You can visit her Web site at www.dorothygarlock.com.